A Misanthrope Teaches a Class for Demi-Humans

Mr. Hitoma, Won't You Show Us the Light of Hope...?

2

Kurusu **Natsume**

Illustration by **Sai Izumi**

CHARACTERS

Neneko Kurosawa

Machi Nezu

Rei Hitoma

Karin Ryuzaki

"You want to? I don't mind."
"Score! Wanna cop a feel of mine in return?!"
"I would love to, Isaki!"
"You would?!"

"Have you ever been angry, Mr. Hitoma?"

"...Yes."

"Anything you hate?"

"...Plenty."

"Anything good ever happened to you?"

"...Plenty of that, too."

"Painful things?"

"Truckloads."

"Ever given up on anything?"

"Every single day."

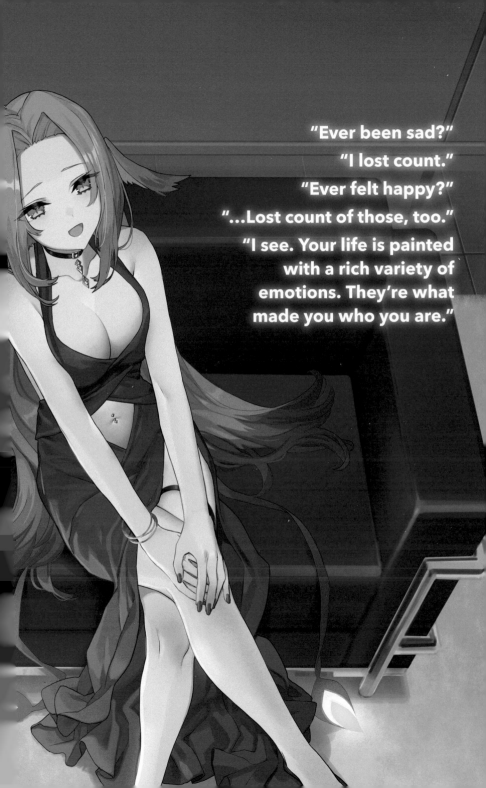

"Ever been sad?"

"I lost count."

"Ever felt happy?"

"...Lost count of those, too."

"I see. Your life is painted
with a rich variety of
emotions. They're what
made you who you are."

KARIN RYUZAKI

REI HITOMA

MACHI NEZU

NENEKO KUROSAWA

A MISANTHROPE TEACH
CLASS FOR DEMI-HUM

A Misanthrope
Teaches a Class for
Demi-Humans

Mr. Hitoma, Won't You Show Us the Light of Hope...?

Kurusu Natsume

Illustration by
Sai Izumi

New York

Misanthrope
Teaches a Class for
Demi-Humans

2

Kurusu Natsume

Illustration by
Sai Izumi

Translation by Linda Liu

JINGAIKYOSHITSU NO NINGENGIRAIKYOSHI Vol. 2
HITOMASENSEI, WATASHITACHI NO KIBO O MITSUKETE KUREMASUKA......?
©Kurusu Natsume 2022 ©2022 ANYCOLOR, Inc.
First published in Japan in 2022 by KADOKAWA CORPORATION, Tokyo.
English translation rights arranged with KADOKAWA CORPORATION,
Tokyo, through TUTTLE-MORI AGENCY, INC., Tokyo.

Yen On
150 West 30th Street, 19th Floor
New York, NY 10001

Visit us at yenpress.com • facebook.com/yenpress • twitter.com/yenpress
yenpress.tumblr.com • instagram.com/yenpress

First Yen On Edition: March 2024
Edited by Yen On Editorial: Rachel Mimms
Designed by Yen Press Design: Eddy Mingki

Library of Congress Cataloging-in-Publication Data
Names: Kurusu, Natsume, 2000– author. | Izumi, Sai, illustrator. |
Liu, Linda (Translator), translator.
Title: A misanthrope teaches a class for demi-humans / Kurusu Natsume ;
illustration by Sai Izumi ; translated by Linda Liu.
Other titles: Jingaikyoshitsu no ningengiraikyoshi. English
Description: New York : Yen On, 2023– |
Contents: v. 1. Mr. Hitoma, won't you teach us about humans...? —
Identifiers: LCCN 2023028672 | ISBN 9781975371050 (v. 1 ; trade paperback) |
ISBN 9781975371074 (v. 2 ; trade paperback)
Subjects: CYAC: Fantasy. | Schools—Fiction. | Identity—Fiction. | LCGFT:
Fantasy fiction. | Light novels.
Classification: LCC PZ7.1.N3735 Mi 2023 | DDC [Fic]—dc23
LC record available at https://lccn.loc.gov/2023028672

ISBNs: 978-1-9753-7107-4 (paperback)
978-1-9753-7108-1 (ebook)

10 9 8 7 6 5 4 3 2 1

LSC-C

Printed in the United States of America

On the top of the mountain, there was a large cedar tree.

From there, I looked down upon the sprawling forest.

Newly built in the expanse of trees was a crow *tengu* shrine in which several *mononoke* and one human toddler were merrily chattering together, calligraphy brushes in hand.

Mononoke spirits desired to become human. Humans taught them how.

This was the school I had established.

I wondered what the students were learning about.

The culture that humans shaped was impossibly strange and fascinating.

"So this is where you have been, Lady Shiranui."

"Shirou," I said.

This young crow *tengu* was the master of the shrine. His long white hair was neatly tied, and he had on a pair of tall wooden sandals.

"The elder called you here with regards to the school," he told me.

"Got it."

The elder, the head of the previous generation, had little love for my school. I followed Shirou to where the elder was waiting.

"Hey, Shirou," I said.

"Yes?"

"Remember how you once told me that the students won't approach you 'cause they think you're scary-looking?"

"I suppose I do, yes."

"How 'bout changing your personality to be more inviting?"

"…What exactly does that entail?"

"First, always smile. That's fundamental. And…why don't you try calling people by a pet name? 'My boy,' or 'my dear,' let's say."

"My dear…is it?"

I stared at him with a smirk. *You can do better than that, right?*

"Ugh… I will try…my dear!"

"Heh-heh. Very well done."

I found it charming that Shirou was being more proactive about getting along with humans.

In the shrine, the *mononoke* and human were writing something on the ground.

A breeze swept through.

I looked toward where the wind was blowing: a single cherry blossom tree.

The flowers were blooming lusciously, as if they were celebrating something.

This is a story about—you guessed it:

Me and my school.

My school, which had only just begun.

CONTENTS

Prologue

My phone's alarm sounded so far away.

It seemed that I had fallen asleep, once again, in the middle of a game.

My laptop was showing the loss screen of a first-person shooter, and the chat box was inundated with profanities.

I exited out of the game and turned off the alarm on my phone lying on the bed.

My life had gone slightly off the rails after I'd moved out of my parents' house and started living on my own. But…it was spring vacation. My schedule would surely sort itself out when I went back to work.

In any case, the previous day had been exhausting.

I had met with the director of Shiranui Private High School, where I'd been teaching for the past year.

The biggest shock was that Director Shiranui turned out to be a student in my advanced class. She spent her days as Tobari Haneda in the classroom alongside other students.

I hadn't noticed this the entire year I'd been working there. *Am I oblivious, or is she a genius for having covered her tracks so thoroughly…?* I wondered as I recalled my conversation with her from the previous day.

* * *

"By the way, Mr. Hitoma, we're leaving the advanced class in your hands next year, too," the director said to me as if it was obvious.

A question rose to the front of my mind. "…Will you—will Tobari Haneda be attending that class as well?"

"Yep, you bet. Treat me like you would any other student, got it? Oh,
and if you spill the beans, you're fired."

"Come again?!"

Don't tack on a crucial stipulation for my employment as an afterthought!

Despite my reproachful gaze, the director merely looked exasperated
and let out a small sigh.

"It goes without saying," she replied. "If you can't keep a secret of this
scale, how can I trust you?"

"You're not wrong, but...do the other teachers know Haneda is the
director?"

"Nope."

"So I'm the only one!"

I guess the director's identity isn't kept secret from just the new teachers...?

"Shirou and Haruka are the only ones who know. Up until a
moment ago."

"Who?"

"Me and the school nurse, my daughter!" the principal said.

"Ah, should I have just said the Karasuma family?" the director wondered aloud.

"That's not the problem...," I replied.

It didn't matter whether she called them by their first names or grouped
them together as a family. It would've been hard for me to make the con-
nection either way. More importantly...

"Why tell me something only the principal and Ms. Karasuma know?"
I asked.

"Hmm, that's a secret!"

"You've got to be kidding me!" I exclaimed. "Hold up—rewind to the
part about me being fired if word gets out. Does that apply to students as
well as the other teachers?"

"Well, yeah. Obviously."

The director's nonchalance made my head spin. If I ran into any
problems involving her, the only person I would be able to turn to for help
woule be the principal...

I peeked over at Principal Karasuma. He must have noticed my gaze, because he flashed me a jolly smile. *Guh... This is giving me anxiety...*

"Why wouldn't you share something this important with Mr. Hoshino and Ms. Saotome...?" I asked the director.

"I have my reasons. You know how it is."

She held one hand aloft. A column of flames as large as a bonfire shot up.

"Yikes!" I yelped.

She stuck her hand into the flames as if it were a perfectly normal thing to do and fumbled around. "It's in here somewhere, I think."

"Warn a guy before you set things on fire!"

"Hmm? Eh, you'll get used to it. Actually, how about you start getting used to it now?" she said. "Ah, found it."

Having located what she was looking for, she plucked a sheaf of papers from the fire.

"...A magic stash? What's up with that?" I grumbled.

"What? It's hella convenient," she replied, lining up the documents on the desk.

Paper documents. Paper you can store inside a fire. What the hell? What in the world are they made of...? Wait, no. I guess the bizarre part is the fire...?

"I want to talk to you about the next school year, so can you take a seat over here, Mr. Hitoma?" The director gestured to one of the sofas. I had been standing the entire time.

"Uh... Actually, before that, will you answer a few questions for me?" I asked.

Frankly, I still hadn't processed the absurd revelation that Haneda was the director. However, if I let myself be swept along by her pace, I was going to miss my chance to ask.

"Yeah, sure thing. But why don't you sit down first? Can't have a decent chat if you're standing." She gracefully sat down on one of the sofas.

I was torn, but I sat across from her. The sofas were swanky in a way that was different from the furnishings in the principal's office.

The principal plodded over and seated himself next to me. I thought for sure he was going to sit next to the director...

"First question—," I started.

The director cut me off. "You only get three."

"What?"

She was holding up three fingers with a smile on her face.

"Answering a bunch of questions is a real drag, and I want to discuss the coming school year. So, three."

"...What are you, a genie?"

"Hey, he's a real stand-up fella."

"You know each other?"

Well enough to know that he's a good guy?

"Apparently, he's got too much time on his hands in between gigs, and he's now addicted to mobile games."

"A real man of the people!"

The principal cleared his throat. *"Ahem!* Are those all your questions, my boy?"

"Whoops. I'm sorry," I said.

We had inadvertently veered off into small talk territory, but I refocused and took a deep breath. *Three questions... Just three...*

I had plenty of things I wanted to ask. About the director herself... About the school...

After mulling it over, I decided to ask about the school's founding. "How long has this school been around?"

The director tilted her head. "Ummm, a little while?" She turned to the principal. "When was it, Shirou?"

"It dates back to when my predecessor ruled over this region. During the Heian period, when *The Tale of Genji* was going viral."

Don't use The Tale of Genji *and "going viral" in the same sentence.*

I get what he's trying to say, though.

"That long ago, huh...?" I mused. "Around a millennium, according to the Western calendar...right...?"

"Just what I would expect from a social studies teacher." The director smiled languidly and clapped.

Did she…actually know the answer all along but gave a vague answer to test me?

Either way, it seemed that the school had existed for longer than I'd imagined.

"Okay, second question."

"Go on."

This question had been on my mind ever since I'd found out this was a school for nonhumans to learn to become human.

"Why is this an all-girls school?"

Considering the mission of this institution, it wouldn't be strange to have male students enrolled here.

"That's what you want to know? Well, it started out as coed, but it was annoying to manage. I figured I should turn it into either an all-girls or an all-boys school, and the former seemed like it'd be more fun and vibrant."

"So it was all on a whim."

"Ah-ha-ha! You could say that!" The director burst out laughing.

Despite my exasperation, I found myself accepting her answer. It was true that putting girls and boys of the same age together was a recipe for trouble. On top of that, this was far from a normal school, so its management was sure to be even more difficult. Changing it to an all-girls or all-boys environment was a logical step…maybe. To be honest, I had my doubts about the decision-making process.

"Moving on, then… I guess this is my last question…"

My final chance. I won't be able to ask anything else after this… I can't waste it…

"Besides raising nonhuman students to become human, does this school have any other purpose?"

Was the goal of Shiranui High just to guide students toward their goal of being human? Or could there be a hidden motive—?

"Ummm, there aren't really any special 'purposes,' if that's what you're asking about."

"Then what about—?"

"Mr. Hitoma," the director cut in, "I've already answered three questions."

Her countenance was stern, as if she were telling a child, *I won't go along with your antics any longer.* My words stuck in my throat.

Did I imagine the dark gleam in her eyes? It'd only been an instant. I felt as if I were being sucked into her gaze, and—

"My boy! If you have nothing else to ask, let's talk about the new school year!"

The principal's comment brought me back to my senses. His happy-go-lucky voice was somehow soothing.

The director huffed and checked over the documents. "Most of what we want you to know is written in here, so I'll just add a few more details. Okay?"

"Hey! Wait! Shouldn't you let me read over the docs first?!" I protested.

"Patience is not one of Lady Shiranui's strong suits..."

"Aw, come on. Why even bother?" the director moaned.

I agreed with the general principle, but I wished she would have a little more regard for other people's circumstances.

I had an inkling that this school, on occasion, had a tendency of over-looking the opinions of humans—in this case, me—and advancing the conversation to their own convenience. Case in point, when I was first hired, they had all the details worked out before ever explaining to me the specifics about the school. When sharing important information, it was definitely vital for all parties to have had the time to look things over!

For better or worse, I have to take things into my own hands, I thought as I read through the documents on the table in order.

Bored, the director sprawled back on the sofa and was waited on by the principal, who had at some point moved to sit next to her.

There were four pages in total.

Pages that the director had taken out of the flames.

I scanned the words written on them.

The first page was a high-level overview. The other three pages contained the details and photos of the new students being promoted into the advanced class.

The contents could be loosely summarized as follows:

- When the director assumed her student form, I was to continue treating her as the student Tobari Haneda.
- If I revealed her secret, my contract would be instantly terminated. Whomever I told the secret to would be subject to expulsion (in the case of a student) or dismissal (in the case of a teacher like myself).
- In the coming school year, two students from the intermediate class (plus one extra conditional student) would be joining the advanced class.
- The two intermediate students: Karin Ryuzaki and Machi Nezu.
- The one conditional student: Neneko Kurosawa.
- The conditional student must complete a special assignment every month in addition to their regular workload.

"What does 'conditional' mean…?" I asked. The term hadn't come up in the previous year. I hadn't realized such a system existed.

"You mean Neneko? Perfect. I was just going to talk about her," the director said, drawing close to look at the papers I was holding.

"…!" The lush curves of her body filled my vision.

Where am I supposed to look when you lean over in that outfit?! It's too late to ask this, but aren't those clothes too risqué?! Is that your personal taste?!

Seeing how flustered I was, the director teased me in her usual flippant manner. "Hmm? Something wrong, Mr. Hitoma?"

Grrr… You're doing this on purpose, aren't you…?!

"Gosh! Do take this more seriously, my boy!" the principal chided me.

Why aren't you affected by her outfit?! It should be off-limits! Anyone would be shocked by a dress like that! Besides, why am I getting scolded when she's the one who started it? This is so not okay!

But if I said any of that out loud, I would be slapped with a sexual harassment charge, so instead, I tried mentally urging the principal:

Listen! Hear my woes! I screamed internally, but he only stared back at me with his round, doe-like eyes.

"Let's cut it out with the jokes, Mr. Hitoma…," the director began.

"I'm not the one who's joking…"

Despite how dreary I felt, I nevertheless waited to hear what she had to say.

"Neneko was promoted to the advanced class, but during spring break, she ran away," the director explained.

"S-seriously?!" My heart jumped at the dramatic turn of events.

Memories of last fall's incident rushed to my mind. I had broken out of the school with Sui Usami, an advanced student, and we had been punished accordingly for it.

Neneko Kurosawa had run away over spring break, which meant that Usami and I were the forerunners of school-escape escapades. Not that it was an honor.

The details around Usami's and my crime were known only to people involved in the case and the teachers. But if the secret had leaked, if our actions had given Kurosawa the impression that breaking out of the school was easy—

Cold sweat ran down my back. My actions had been overly reckless. As a result, Usami hadn't been able to advance. I didn't regret it, but it had been a clear violation of the rules, and I had reflected on my behavior. Surely we would have found a better solution if we had looked. Instead, we—

"Earth to Mr. Hitoma! Time for you to come back from your world."

I cleared my head and found the director clapping and looking at me exasperatedly.

"Geez. You're always so quick to bury yourself in your thoughts."

She rested her chin in her hands. The principal gazed at me warmly. It was kind of ticking me off.

"All righty, about Neneko's escape. Let's see," the director said. "Actually, let's just skip it."

"Let's not," I retorted.

"Settle down now. It's to protect her reputation."

Her reputation, you say... Could there be some sort of grim circumstances behind the event? I braced myself.

"Oh, wait a second." As I scanned Kurosawa's profile, my eyes caught a certain detail. "Yesterday, under the cherry blossom tree, there was a black cat. Was that...?"

"Oops. Busted?"

The previous day, on my way back from the convenience store, I'd spotted a black cat loitering under the tree near the barrier. The cat had been nearly hidden by the blossoms. When it had noticed me, it'd leaped away and disappeared somewhere.

I had run into it outside the barrier, so I'd assumed it wasn't a student, but...

"It was a student after all...?"

"Spot-on. I figured I could fool you by saying it was in the middle of the break, but actually, the incident happened yesterday."

The director had made up this entire story in twenty-four hours—at lightning speed. She was quick at deciding.

Come to think of it, if I had captured Kurosawa in her black cat form when I'd run into her, wouldn't I have saved the director and the principal some—?

"Oh, don't worry. By the time I'd gone to see you, Shirou had already caught Neneko. No need to stress about it," the director reassured me. "It was faster for the two of us to act alone, rather than soliciting your help."

"...Hold on. Can you read my mind?" Her response had been perfectly suited for what I'd been thinking. It made me suspicious of her abilities.

"Ah-ha-ha! You're definitely the type to fuss, right? I can tell you're thinking that much even without special powers."

"A fine young man with a strong sense of responsibility, you are!" the principal added.

I felt somewhere between embarrassment and frustration at being treated like a child, but well, I supposed the important thing was that Kurosawa was safe...

The director flashed a smile at me before returning her gaze to the papers.

"Let's rewind. First of all, Neneko joined the school last year through the special enrollment system and went straight into the intermediate class. In other words, she started here the same time you did."

"What kind of system is that? Those cases exist?!"

Yet another part of the school's structure I had never heard of. What was this about special enrollment?

"In short, yes, but there are hardly any candidates who qualify. They're really, really rare."

"Conditional advancement, special enrollment... I bet there are other parts of the school system you have yet to tell me about..."

"You think so?"

She sidestepped the question, but given the circumstances, I was sure there was more I didn't know. I cast a suspicious gaze at her.

Just then, the principal cleared his throat with an *"Ahem!"* and said, "We'll only confuse you if we dump everything on you at once, my boy! We'll share everything a little at a time! When you have a question or the time is right, we'll tell you what you need to know!"

The worry that such reactivity would only lead to trouble down the line flashed through my head, but he was right that I wouldn't be able to process everything if they revealed it now. In the end, I decided not to argue.

In response to my silence, the director smiled softly and continued. "The special enrollment system is similar to what you would normally call a recommendation system. Candidates meet with me personally, and the ones I pick get recommended to a class matching their abilities. The system lets these students skip grades, so to speak."

"Okay."

The students' placement was based on their own ability, regardless of a recommendation. There could be students who immediately skipped ahead to the advanced class, and ones who started in the beginner class.

Huh? Then why—?

"Why aren't students who enter through the normal enrollment process placed based on their skill level and are instead all lumped into the beginner class?" I asked.

Students who lived close to humans in their previous environments would be able to graduate sooner if they were sorted at time of enrollment, no?

"Yeah, see, we tried that in the past. But sometimes the student's assessment and my assessment of their level don't match, right? We had trouble with some cases where we couldn't convince the student to accept my assessment... Anyway, in short, the reason is to minimize the number of customer complaints. They're a waste of time."

"The students who come on recommendation are ones who trust Lady Shiranui's judgment, so they don't make such complaints!" the principal explained.

So that's why... Yeah, I buy it.

"Back to our original discussion," the director said. "Neneko enrolled through the special enrollment system, and her grades were the best of the intermediate class. That's the background behind this runaway incident. Normally, the student would receive a large point deduction and wouldn't be allowed to advance, but...considering the circumstances and several other factors, I talked things through with Neneko and the principal and decided she would be a conditional student."

The principal, who had been nodding along, spoke again. "Ms. Kurosawa was either to advance as a conditional student or repeat a year. In the latter case, she would spend another year the same as the last. In the former case, she is able to enter the advanced class, but the workload is no joke! It's no walk in the park! That's why I recommended she be held back. But Ms. Kurosawa chose to be a conditional student! If she fails to submit even a single assignment, she'll have to go back to the intermediate class and spend an additional year in the intermediate class on top of that! It's tough! So, my boy, we ask that you follow up and make sure she turns in all her assignments!"

That was the crux of the conversation.

The supervision of the conditional advancement student's assignments.

"By the way, what kind of assignments will she be given? Also, who will come up with them?" I asked.

The additional assignments would have to be prepared by someone. Don't tell me I'm going to have to—?!

"The director and I will take care of it! They will be the same as the graduation assignments and tailored to what the student needs at that particular time!"

So I can leave this to them.

I was relieved I'd dodged the bullet of what seemed to be the most difficult job. That was a weight off my shoulders.

"Anyway, that's the story. Do you think you can handle another year, Mr. Hitoma?" the director asked, peeking up at me through her eyelashes.

A flirty move. Definitely calculated.

But it didn't feel bad to be depended on.

"I don't know, but I'll do the best I can," I promised.

*   *   *

April 8. The start of the new school year.

Starting this year, I was living in the on-campus staff dorm, so my commute was drastically easier. I no longer had to wake up earlier and get jolted around by the train for ages. Seriously… It was a huge blessing…

Thanks to that, I settled in at my desk in the teachers' office with plenty of time to spare. I got to review the files and documents on my laptop and look over my preparations for the new year and the first homeroom class.

A leisurely, valuable use of my time. I hoped to make this a routine—but then I remembered the RPG that was going to be released the day after tomorrow.

…If I can arrive at school at this early hour, going to bed a tiny bit later shouldn't be a big deal.

Such were my thoughts as I prepared for the start of the semester.

I was staring vacantly at my screen, having finished most of my work, when someone said from beside me, "Mr. Hitoma, I'm looking forward to working with you again!"

My expression softened unwittingly at the sunny and sweet voice. "Good morning, Ms. Saotome! Same here!"

"Heh-heh. There aren't any new teachers this year, so you're still the newbie!"

She chuckled softly and threw her head and shoulders back in a fake show of arrogance. She was unbearably cute as always. If I hadn't known all the facts, I might have accidentally fallen for her. Close call, close call.

Then Mr. Hoshino stopped at my desk. "Hey, Mr. Hitoma. I just got my hands on some top-shelf goods—how about a cup after school?"

"Gladly. Thank you!"

It might sound like Mr. Hoshino was inviting me for drinks at a bar, but we were talking about coffee. He must have snapped up some high-quality beans. Mr. Hoshino's hobby was brewing coffee, and he often treated me to the most scrumptious cups. Also—

"How nice! I'm so jealous! I want you to make me delicious coffee at home, too!" Ms. Saotome said.

"Fine, fine. Next time," Mr. Hoshino said.

—these two were husband and wife.

Ms. Saotome had kept her maiden name out of convenience for work, it seemed.

"The opening ceremony is going to start soon, Mr. Hitoma!" she said.

"Got it. I just need to save this real quick," I replied, pressing the shortcut keys to save the document before I closed the window.

Even though several of the advanced students I had taught last year were in my class again, I was still a little nervous. The new students, meanwhile, I'd only interacted with in social studies. I recognized their names and faces more or less, but I didn't know anything about their personalities yet.

"Done." I stood and lightly pumped myself up.

What will class be like this year?

* * *

I thought back to a year ago.

I had stood in front of this same door, jittering with nerves, just like I was now. Filled with apprehension, I had opened the door to find Minazuki and Haneda dancing to the folk song "Soran Bushi."

I wondered if Minazuki was happy and healthy.

I was hit by a wave of sentimentality as I recalled the first day of the previous school year.

Minazuki had since graduated and was now learning dance in the human world.

Clichéd as it is, encounters and farewells go hand in hand. Such is life. What kind of year was waiting ahead?

In any case, I hoped this year would be another good one. With that wish burning in my heart, I opened the door to the advanced classroom.

The first student I saw was a girl with blond hair in tight curls.

For an instant, her eyes widened in surprise—

"Um... Mr. Rei...!"

"Huh?"

Me? What does she want? ...Wait!

I frantically scanned myself over just in case, but there didn't seem to be anything weird with my appearance... Besides, I figured Mr. Hoshino would have casually mentioned if something was off...

I—I didn't miss anything...right?

But the girl with the golden curls—Karin Ryuzaki of the dragon family—was still staring at me with astonishment and trembling all over.

Why is she so surprised...?

What's going on? I don't think I've ever talked to her outside of the intermediate class... Did something shock her?

Ryuzaki charged up to me.

"W-wait... Huh?" I stammered.

She stopped less than a foot away.

I saw my bewildered expression reflected in Ryuzaki's bright blue eyes.

She was way too close, and because she was shorter than I'd realized, she had to tilt her head to look up at me. My heart pounded faster.

I thought that she was going to keep glaring at me, but instead, a look of resolve crossed her face, and she took a big breath.

"Mr. Rei! I like you! Marry me!" she declared.

"WHAT?!" I yelped.

A-a-a-a proposal…?!

Where did this come from?! Is there a rule about pranking teachers on the first day of school?!

"Hmph! Ugh!"

All of a sudden, a slight girl with long ears shoved her way between Ryuzaki and me.

"Agh!" I cried.

"Eek! What was that for, Sui?" Ryuzaki demanded.

The interloper was Sui Usami, a rabbit.

She scowled at me. She seemed to be in a bad mood…

"Tsk. You're violating public morals, Karin. I don't understand how you could possibly do this at school! And you, Hitoma. You're a teacher! Don't just stand there blushing like a schoolgirl!" she yelled. "Hitoma! Say something already!"

"Y-yes, ma'am!" I was so cowed by her intensity that my voice cracked.

Ryuzaki, however, wasn't moved by Usami's speech. "Excuse me? I was having a private conversation with Mr. Rei. *You're* the one who should keep her mouth shut, don't you think?" She smiled gracefully, but her gaze was icy.

Usami stared daggers at Ryuzaki and bristled with hostility. "What did you saaaay?!"

Animosity crackled between them. Absolutely terrifying.

The director—or rather, Tobari Haneda—was watching us and laughing herself sick. "You guys are hilarious! Mr. Hitoma, you gotta respond to Karin's proposal."

"Um, errr…," I mumbled.

"Another thing! Two little ones would be perfect!" Ryuzaki added.

"What is going on?!" I was already stumped for a response, and Ryuzaki's glib addendum threw me for a further loop.

She watched me expectantly, waiting for my reply.

"Oh, um... I'm sorry, but I can't marry you...?"

"Why not?!"

"Huh?!"

My words stuck in my throat. I didn't think she was going to hound me.

"Um... I'm a teacher, and you're my student... Come on—you just said that as a lark, didn't you?"

Since we barely had anything to do with each other, I couldn't think of any reason for her to like me. She hadn't shown any interest in me before, either... In conclusion, it must've been a prank... Although I had to admit there was a part of me that had been briefly happy.

"That's not true! I really like you!" Ryuzaki insisted.

She seemed desperate to convince me.

She can't be serious...can she? No, no, no, there's no way that's possible. I know that!

"Mr. Rei... Please believe me."

Urk...!

She looked at me with imploring round eyes, her head tilted cutely. Could any man stay indifferent when hit with such an attack?

Argh... I won't be swayed! I know. I'll recite the imperial eras. Desperate times and all that. Taika, Hakuchi, Shucho, Taiho, Keiun, Wado...

"Hmm? Mr. Rei? Hellooo?" said Ryuzaki. "What do I do? He's mumbling something."

"Sheesh! Just leave him alone!" Usami said.

"What's this? Someone's grouchy," Haneda teased.

"I don't wanna hear it, Tobari."

"Uchami, that attitude's not helping your cause, you know," one of the new students said.

"Machi—shut *up*," Usami spat back.

"*Squeak?!* Why're you being so much ruder to me?! Hold on—last year, when you left the intermediate class, didn't you make a grand proclamation about how you were gonna graduate the fastest? What are you still doing here?"

"Hmph. You wouldn't understand. I might not have graduated, but I've got zero regrets."

"Oh no, oh no... Please don't fight...," Ohgami pleaded.

"We're not fighting, Ichaki. Don't worry. This is our way of saying hello! Right, Uchami?"

"That's just what Machi is like," Usami agreed.

"Whoa!" Having finished reciting the eras, I returned to reality.

"*Squeak.* Meester Hitoma's back."

"Nezu...," I began.

"Everything okay?" she asked.

"Yeah, thanks."

"Great!" the girl with the large ears said with a smile.

Machi—Machi Nezu. She had a slight frame and big, round ears. Shorter than Usami, who had been the shortest in the advanced class last year, she was a small girl from the mouse family. She was energetic and rowdy even in the intermediate class.

What was she going to be like in this class...?

"Looks like your crush is unrequited, Karin," Nezu said.

"Ack... Well, whatever... Mr. Rei! You'll definitely end up wanting to marry me! I won't let you out of my clutches!"

Sounds like something a villain would say...

Ryuzaki's vehement declaration overwhelmed me.

"Karin will win your heart through your stomach, Meester Hitoma. It's a foolproof strategy," Nezu added.

"Awww, Machi! Tee-hee. You're sooo precious! Good girl. ♪"

"Thanks. Hee-hee!"

Ryuzaki had Nezu eating out of the palm of her hand... Patting the smaller Nezu on the head made Ryuzaki look like a mother.

It seemed that this year was going to be just as boisterous as the last.

"Okay, I'm going to start our first homeroom class of the year," I said. "Return to your seats."

The girls stopped chatting and sat down. There were a total of six students this year. Last year, the four desks had been arranged all in one row, but now they were in two rows of three.

"Hmm, let's start with introductions. My name is Rei Hitoma. I'm in charge of social studies. I like video games and sushi. This is my second year as the homeroom teacher for the advanced class. I hope to spend another fun year with you all. Thanks."

Man, I suck at self-intros, I thought as I read off the notes I had jotted down on my papers.

"Next up, let's hear from the front row, starting with Haneda in the aisle seat until we get to Ohgami in the window seat. Then on to Ryuzaki in the second-row aisle seat— Is Kurosawa sleeping?"

Sitting—no, sleeping in the second-row window seat was Neneko Kurosawa, the problem child who was designated a conditional student after her escape over spring break.

Cat ears sprouted from beneath her long black hair. She had on an eye mask and was brazenly slumped over the desk, breathing deeply, sound asleep.

She'd often napped when she was in the intermediate class, too, her head pillowed on one of her books. The books always had something to do with black magic. Today's title was *100 Simple Black Magic Spells: So Easy, Even a Kitten Could Do It!*

…What an accessible black magic digest.

"*Sigh*… Nezu, wake her up."

"Eek! No thanks!" Nezu squeaked; she was seated next to Kurosawa. "I'm a mouse. A *mouse*! I don't even want to be sitting next to a cat! We'll never be friends! Seat change, please!"

She wants to change seats…? Come to think of it, we never changed the seating arrangement last year. There are so few students, after all… Wait—maybe there's such a thing as compatibility between demi-human species? In that case, I should've taken that into consideration.

I peeked over at Haneda for help. She stared back at me, her gaze cold, as if to say, *Don't come crying to me.*

Figure it out yourself—that's what she's telling me. Fair. She might be the director, but right now, she's acting as Tobari Haneda…

I let out a small sigh. "There are no plans to change seats in the near future. Although I might be open to it later down the line…"

I left the lectern, walked over to Kurosawa's seat and knocked lightly on her desk. "Kurosawa, wake up."

Her ear twitched. She sat up slowly and removed her eye mask. She sleepily looked around the room before gazing up at me warily. "......Who are you?"

"I'm Rei Hitoma, the advanced class's homeroom teacher."

I doubted she'd heard my introduction. After I'd gone through all the effort of writing a script...

I'd taught her several times in the intermediate class, too...

"......Okay...... Zzzz."

"Don't go back to sleep!" I barked reflexively when I saw she was seamlessly slipping back to dreamland. Then something occurred to me. "Oh, are you feeling sick?"

Maybe I shouldn't have woken her up.

She stared at me, her expression still quizzical. "......I'm fine." She slowly raised both arms.

...That must be her "I'm bursting with energy" pose.

"G-great... Just, uh, hang in there a bit longer. Today's class is only some light conversation."

Kurosawa nodded. She'd already removed her eye mask and was actually awake, so I returned to the lectern, figuring there wouldn't be any more problems.

"Shall we resume the self-introductions? Haneda, you first," I said.

"Suuure," Haneda replied languidly, and rose to her feet. "Tobari Haneda. Bull-headed shrike. I like music. Doesn't matter what genre; I'll listen to anything. I want to become human to play music. Lemme know if you have any song recommendations. Let's have a good year."

A concise summary that leaves a good impression. Feels similar to mine. Excellent. That's how self-intros should be: simple. Yep.

Haneda sat down, and Usami, seated next to her, stood.

"I'm Usami. Rabbit, as you can see. I want to become human to work as a human doctor. I made a promise with someone important to me. That's why I'm going to study even harder this year."

Ever since the incident last year, Usami had started to pour even more effort into her studies, particularly in the sciences. As part of exam prep, she had been going to Mr. Hoshino, who was in charge of the math classes, to absorb everything she could. Mr. Hoshino was a great teacher. In fact, he was so exemplary that I'd wondered why he was working at this school. So exemplary that he graduated at the top of his class at an American university, according to Ms. Saotome. After receiving private tutoring from a first-rate teacher like him, Usami would surely see her academic ability shoot up. Medical school should be well within reach.

"I-I'm, uh, Ohgami. I'm a werewolf. My reason for becoming human... Until last year, it was to graduate from this half-baked existence, but now... I'm figuring things out. Actually, I have a dual personality—during the full moon, my personality changes. I need a little more time to think about how to coexist with my other self going forward. But I still want to become human. Um, I'm sorry I don't have a proper reason... The end."

"Ohgami," I said as she was about to sit down.

She straightened back up. "Y-yes?"

I should have waited until she sat to call out to her, I thought, but this wasn't going to take long. *Out with it.*

"There's nothing wrong with taking your time to find a goal. But let's have a talk about your future around the summertime—no, before then."

"I—I understand. Thank you."

Ohgami didn't want to become human while she had dual personalities. But it didn't seem like she wanted to turn her two personalities into one, either. Perhaps staying in this school ad infinitum was an option open to her. Granted, I did want to see her graduate. Maybe that was just my bias as a teacher.

"I'm next, yeah?" Ryuzaki said. "Karin Ryuzaki here. I'm a member of the noble dragon family. I want to become human in order to know what love is like. So how about it, Mr. Rei? Won't you teach me the ways of love?"

"That's out of the question."

She hadn't been discouraged at all by my refusal earlier... Unfortunately for Ryuzaki, I had more common sense and higher personal morals than she must've imagined. I could never be in a romantic relationship with one of my students. Besides, I had no desire to do such a thing. I wasn't entirely convinced she wasn't still joking, though...

"*Grrr...* Still no love flags in sight...," she mumbled.

"Come again?" I asked.

That sounded like something a gamer girl would say.

Ryuzaki pointed at me and snapped in a sonorous voice, "Mr. Rei, I'm not giving up yet! I'll definitely make you fall in love with me!"

There's a chance that she's an otaku... I kind of want to know if she is.

"Me! Me! My turn!" Nezu cut in. "I'm Machi! Machi Nezu! I'm a mouse! My little sis is in the beginner class. I want to become human to eat lots and lots of yummy food! The other day, I ate one of Roost Rep Ryouko's homemade custard puddings, and it was sooo good! Melt-in-your-mouth puddings are all the rage these days, but Ryouko's pudding was firm and had a deep milk flavor. You could really taste the eggs, too! Your classic rich pudding! The tinge of bitterness in the caramel and the sweetness of the pudding blended together in the best way possible. They were the perfect complement! A sophisticated flavor combination!"

Her self-introduction turned into a food review halfway. My mouth watered when I heard the delicious description.

Drat... Now I'm craving pudding...

"...I suddenly find myself wanting to eat pudding," Ohgami said. It seemed like we were on the same page.

"Let's make some together one of these days, Isaki!" Nezu said. "We'll ask Ryouko to teach us!"

"Yes, please!"

"Aw, I wanna learn how to make it, too!"

"I'm kinda surprised, Tobari! I didn't think that stuff was your jam!" Nezu said.

"You think?"

"Give it a rest, everyone," I told them. "The chitchat stops here." Once they got going, it seemed as if they would never stop, so I scrambled to direct the class's attention back to the introductions. "Last but not least, Kurosawa."

More or less awake, Kurosawa drifted up from her seat like a ghost. "Neneko Kurosawa... Cat... The reason...I want to become human...... is a secret."

Every student's motivation for becoming human was listed in the papers before me—including Kurosawa's, of course.

The purpose of having the students state their goal in their self-introduction was to create an environment where they could easily support one another... That was what Mr. Hoshino told me when I was hired.

Hold on. Isn't Kurosawa's reason—?

"Neneko didn't tell us why she wants to become human last year in the intermediate class, either," Nezu said to me.

"Oh, I see."

Maybe she's hesitant to share her reason. It might be better if I find a chance to hear her story in private.

"That's the kind of person she is! She puts up a front 'cause she thinks she's cool," Nezu added.

"..." Kurosawa pinned Nezu with her stare without saying a word. Her expressionless face was completely unreadable.

"Uh, *squeak*, what...?"

"......"

"S-something you wanna say?!"

".........I—"

"*Squeak!!!* Noooo! You're scaring me!! Stop it!! Helppp!!!"

"I...haven't...said...anything...yet..."

"You're staring at me! I can see your fangs when you open your mouth! I know you're thinking of eating me!"

Usami looked fed up with Nezu's screeching, and she sighed deeply. "Ugh... You're delusional. Plus, I bet you taste bad."

"That makes me mad in a different way!"

"Calm down," said Haneda. "Obviously, students are prohibited from eating one another. And any student with an instinct to do harm would be expelled immediately. Not that anyone would wanna do that in the first place, since we get to eat Ryouko's delicious food every day."

I was relieved that Haneda stepped in when it seemed like the class was about to reach a fever pitch.

Now I remember. She was supporting me from the shadows last year, too.

"But...," Nezu protested.

"Think about it. Even if worse came to worst, Mr. Hitoma would step in and protect us, yeah?" Haneda smirked, pleased. It was as if she was testing me. Her smile said, *Of course you would, right?*

"I pray it won't come to that," I answered.

At some point, the instigator of the incident, Kurosawa, had lain back down on her desk and was asleep again. Her breathing was smooth and even.

The students who had weathered last year with me: Usami, Ohgami—and Haneda, who was actually the director.

The students who had joined this year's advanced class: Ryuzaki, Nezu, and Kurosawa.

How will this newly expanded class turn out?

I have to do my best to make sure we have another peaceful year.

I hope I'll be able to help the students achieve their goals.

I hope all their dreams will come true.

But who knows?

The thoughts I'd had during the graduation ceremony came back to mind.

I secretly nursed these tender, budding hopes as I gazed upon this year's students.

Six students, each with their own unique personalities.

So began my second spring in this demi-human classroom.

The Misanthrope and the
Love Fortune of the Barren Flower

A MISANTHROPE TEACHES A CLASS FOR DEMI-HUMANS

I had a dream.

The humans in stories are always in love.
Always holding hands with someone, nestling close to each other, whispering words of love. They treasure each other, protect each other.

How nice. I'm jealous.
Someday I want someone who feels that way about me.
Someone to love me.
For that person, I would do anything.

I looked at my reflection in the water.
A dragon—massive, brawny, stronger than anything else.

I know.
I know that I'm an object of fear, not love.
This useless crown was handed to me at birth.
Dragons are special beings. Too special.
The cool night wind stroked my cheek.
There was no one to warm me up.
Not that I needed warmth. This body of mine doesn't get cold.

Nevertheless, I...
I want to be held by someone one more time.

* * *

"Mr. Rei! Have you started to want to marry me yet?" Ryuzaki asked.

"That's never going to happen," I said.

It was the middle of April. I'd been fielding Ryuzaki's bizarre proposals day after day. Classes had ended, and she'd come to declare her love once again. It had practically become routine.

"Grrr... I really thought it was about time," she grumbled.

"You sure don't give up, Karin, *squeak*," Nezu chimed in.

Usami clicked her tongue. "Tsk. What did you even come to school for?"

"C'mon, Usami," Haneda added. "This is what youth is all about."

"A teacher and a student...," said Ohgami. "That kind of forbidden love sure makes your heart pound...!"

Kurosawa had fallen asleep. "*Zzzz...*"

The other students in the advanced class had gradually gotten used to Ryuzaki's quirks, and I felt like they were chipping away at my defenses.

"I turn you down every time," I told her. "You just won't quit..."

"Nope! We're destined to be together!"

"Where does all that confidence come from...?"

"Hee-hee! I like you!" Ryuzaki launched herself at me with a flying tackle.

"...!"

I wished she would stop with the surprise attacks. It was too sudden for me to dodge, but I instinctively turned my face away.

"...Are you blushing, Meester Hitoma?" Nezu teased.

"Ugh, gross," Usami groaned.

"I'm not! You're way off base. Don't look at me like that."

Nezu's warm gaze was part exasperated and part amused. In contrast, Usami was looking at me as if I were garbage...

"...Hey, Karin, what part of him do you even like?" Nezu asked. "Don'cha think he's sullen and gloomy? Not to mention, just plain boring. I bet his casual wardrobe is full of black and white clothing. Plus, he always has bedhead… To be blunt, aren't you seeing him with rose-colored glasses because you don't meet many humans?"

Um, Nezu? That was a little too *cutting, don't you think? Some things you should really just keep to yourself.*

"Nope, not at all!" Ryuzaki said. "Mr. Rei is a catch. He's older, he's single, and he has a steady job as a teacher."

"Ryuzaki…!"

It was the first time I had been called a catch, and honestly, it was not a bad feeling at all.

Wow, I feel vindicated. I wish I could tell this to my past self when I was still in my weirdo unemployed hermit phase; it would've given me reason to live: In the future, your student is going to say you're a catch! Yes, she's a student. But that's still awesome! Your future is bright!

"Also, he's—"

Huh? You're not done?

Just then, Ryuzaki froze as if she were arrested by a thought.

"Karin? What's going on? Why're you staring at me?" Usami asked.

"What's wrong?" Nezu added.

They both looked at Ryuzaki, puzzled.

"Um, ah… Nothing. He might be lame and boring, but I still like him!"

The complete one-eighty was the coup de grâce. She thought I was lame after all…

Once Ryuzaki graduated and entered the wider human society, she would realize there were swarms of people more impressive than me in every aspect. Like Nezu said, Ryuzaki was just being hasty because this school was a bubble. Out in the real world, she would forget all about me in a heartbeat. But that was too painful for me to say out loud, so I kept quiet.

I'll try not to get ahead of myself. Go and find yourself a prince, Ryuzaki.

Come to think of it—

"Why are you so interested in love in the first place?"

I voiced the question I had wanted to ask all along.

Couldn't she achieve that goal without needing to be human? She threw the word *love* around at every opportunity on the daily... Granted, what she felt toward me might not have been love—she was like a schoolgirl in love with the *idea* of love.

Okay, not *like* a schoolgirl in love. She *was* one. Probably.

All the spirit drained from Ryuzaki's expression. "Because I'm tough as nails," she said.

That wasn't what I expected her to say. She wanted to know what love was like because she was tough? What did that mean?

"What do you—?" I started.

"Also! When I dug into human media, I ran into lots of cases where the line between platonic and romantic love blurs! That's why I want to experience it for myself!"

She had dodged my question. I felt as if I caught a glimpse of the true Ryuzaki...

After that, we talked about the media Ryuzaki had consumed—her favorite manga, movies, games, and the like.

Those were good hobbies, fairly similar to liking RPGs. Apparently, she hadn't failed to check out the RPG that had been released the other day.

There were times I didn't know how to deal with her, but her nerdy interests were right up my alley. From that perspective, I felt like we would hit it off just fine.

Karin Ryuzaki. Dragon. Enrolled for four years.
Wants to become human to know what love is like.

* * *

A certain rumor caused a stir in my neighborhood.

"The sole daughter of the ocean warden is going to school to become human."

"She lost her head over those humans who will dance over anything."

"She's as good as dead to oceanic society. The wardens are at odds over who will succeed the family."

The daughter of the ocean warden?
I had seen her before. Just once.
At the time, I thought she seemed like a sweet mermaid, nothing more, but it turned out she was surprisingly strong-willed.
Granted, that was hundreds of years ago, back in the age when dragons were still free to soar through the sky.
That little girl must have changed since then.

I grew jealous.
That's it. A way to remove this crown.
A way to get rid of my strength.
Would I be able to encounter humans like the ones from long ago?
Would I manage to understand the secret behind their warmth?
Would I be able to understand what lies behind their loneliness?

Would I come to know what love is like?

* * *

"Hey! Mr. Rei! I love you!"
That day, as every other day, Ryuzaki professed her love to me, indifferent to the fact that we were at school.
Her declarations of love were basically her way of greeting me, and I had gotten used to brushing off these confessions. "Good morning," I said.
"By the way, will you marry me?"
She offered me a perfunctory proposal. How many times did this make?
"No," I replied.
"Darn."
"Ah, Mr. Hoshino," I said.
He sure stands out.

I spotted Mr. Hoshino about thirty meters ahead of us. With his stooped back and swaying gait, I knew exactly who it was even from a distance. Granted, his tall stature drew the eye even without all that.

I could have waited until I got to the teachers' office, but since I'd run into him, I wanted to express my thanks for the coffee the other day.

"Sorry, Ryuzaki, I'm going ahead," I said.

Just as I was about to dash off, Ryuzaki hugged me from behind and stopped me in my tracks. "Huh? No way! ♪"

"Gah!" I yelped.

I can feel her pressing up against me; she has massi— Quit it with the unnecessary thoughts.

The gears were turning rapidly in my head, but in reality, I had frozen on the spot, unable to do a thing.

Ryuzaki, pasted onto my back, cocked her head. "Mr. Rei?"

I could loosely tell what she was doing based on the sensations I felt, but I wished she would stop moving. It certainly wasn't making this easier for me... Wait a second—that's not what I mean. I wanted her to let go!

That was when I heard, "Ha-ha-ha! Mr. Hitoma? Karin? What are you two doing? LMAO!!"

"Ohgami...! Help...," I begged.

I guess today's the full moon...

My thoughts turned to astronomy when I saw the sassy and flamboyant Ohgami. In front of my eyes, grinning cheekily, was the other Isaki Ohgami, whom we only got to meet on the day of the full moon.

"Lemme guess: You got captured by Karin, right? LOL! You look ridiculous!! But it's also kinda cute! Seriously, I'm dying! Ha-ha-ha! Maybe I'll try it next time!" she joked. "By the way! I can only see what Isaki sees, ya know, and I just gotta ask: Are you serious about him, Karin?! Like, capital *S* serious? Or are you just playing with him like I am?"

"I am not a toy!" I protested.

"Please! You know you like it!" she said.

Rrgh... To be honest, I didn't hate that my students were attached to me. But—

"Capital *S* serious!" Ryuzaki declared.

—it was distressing to hear one being so sincere about it.

"Wooow! Totes adorbs! I can't handle your cuteness! You're the best! I'm rooting for you! Oh, but I won't see you for another month, so let's make today count! OMG, I'm so happy!"

Oh no. I'm getting a bad feeling about this.

"This is my first time seeing you like this, Isaki. It's fun," Ryuzaki said.

"Yeah? Thanks! Let's be besties! Be friends with the other me, too!"

"...Er, I'm terribly glad you're hitting it off, but can you let go of me now?" I asked.

Yep. While the two of them were speaking, I had been securely locked in Ryuzaki's embrace. As if that wasn't enough, she had been leaning her weight on me the entire time, so my lower back—which was already weak from how sedentary I was at home—was starting to hurt more and more.

How do I put this...? I'm starting to feel the effects of age, and it is not *pleasant. Is this what being in your thirties is like...?*

"...How about just a liiittle longer?" Ryuzaki said.

Give me a break, I was thinking just as she squeezed me tight. After ten seconds, she released me and twirled around to face me. Then she grinned brightly, looking happy inside and out, and—

"Heh-heh! Thanks, Mr. Rei!" she said.

"—! Cuuute!! Geez! Karin... I wuv you! Cuties like you are irresistible! Oh man, you're *so* adorable, I just wanna cry! Wa-ha-ha! LOL!!" Ohgami hollered, beside herself.

...If Ohgami hadn't been there, I might've been in serious trouble. Who knows how I would've reacted.

However, that was something that could only happen in 2D fantasies. Reality was different.

Ryuzaki might have been in love with love, but to make a pass at a teacher... That would only end up as a black mark on both our futures.

I didn't want to get the wrong idea, and I didn't want to become the source of someone's regret.

Up until now, we'd never had any physical contact, and she'd only professed her love. While I continued to turn her down verbally, I hadn't

discouraged her attitude. But if she were to take advantage of my laxity and start sticking to me, things would have to change. Physical contact was a whole different level of problematic. If her target wasn't me but an adult who had bad intentions, her affection—serious or not—could be abused. She might do something she would regret.

One of these days, I have to find out exactly what she's thinking. No—today.

* * *

"Hell yeah! Karin! Operation Seduce Mr. Hitoma is a go! Strategy one! Let's do this!" Ohgami cheered.

"I won't disappoint you, Isaki!" Ryuzaki replied.

"You're acting like idiots again…," Usami said.

I could hear everything. They had been whispering about their operation after the morning's homeroom class, as well.

What in the world is going to happen…? I hope it won't turn into anything weird…

It was the end of second period, which was my world history class.

I had just finished answering a question from the studious Usami. She glared coldly at Ryuzaki and Ohgami, who were keyed up with excitement.

Ryuzaki shuffled to me, holding her textbook, and shoved her way between me and Usami. "Mr. Rei! There's something from class I wanted to know more about. Can I ask you now?"

Wow, what a classic approach… I could see right through to her real intentions, but I couldn't refuse to answer.

"What is it?" I asked.

"Huh?! Oh, ummmmmmm…" She hesitated.

A minute passed.

…Figure out what you're going to say ahead of time! Even if it's just a ruse! You tripped right out of the gates!

A look of panic crossed her face, and she turned to seek help from

Ohgami a little ways away. Ohgami whispered, "Anything is fine!" but it was perfectly audible from where I was.

"Are you dumb, Karin?" Usami sneered in irritation, her arms crossed.

Ryuzaki froze beneath Usami's withering glare.

Ah, this is when I should step in and ease the tension. Go for it.

"Usami, she's not doing this out of spite—," I began.

"Yeah—you might be right, Usami. Maybe I *am* dumb…"

Ryuzaki's inane comment stopped the room cold.

Your serious expression doesn't match your realization.

"Grrr… We messed up before, but this time I've got it! Karin—on to strategy two!" Ohgami shouted.

"Strategy two. Okay!" Ryuzaki replied.

…I told you, I can hear everything.

During lunch, I was in the teachers' office, munching on some bread my mom had sent me from back home. She had bought a mountain of it at the spring festival again. She'd told me that now that I'd moved out, a portion of that bread was for me. That was why, for the last several days, all I had been eating was bread.

Ryuzaki and Ohgami were in front of the teachers' office, it seemed.

"Eating lunch together is a standard move! Off you go!" Ohgami told Ryuzaki.

"Yes, ma'am!"

Snickering broke out around the office.

What the hell? Did they do this on purpose? It's humiliating.

My throat had gone strangely dry. I reached for my drink, a health drink that had been all the rage lately. Apparently, it contained ten thousand beneficial microbes. It was blatantly suspicious, but it had been making the rounds on my social media feeds, and I found myself buying one on a whim. *What kind of drink is it going to be?*

Ryuzaki burst into the office. "Mr. Rei!!! Come out here!!"

"Ack!!"

My microbes! Nooooo!!

It was as if she'd come to challenge me to a duel. Her flashy actions drew the gaze of all the teachers. *How did she plan to talk her way out of this if I wasn't here?* I wondered.

Sitting at the desk in front of me was Ms. Saotome, who beamed. "Someone's popular," she said.

That's great and all, but what about my poor desk that's now smeared with microbes?!

…It was likely that the piles of papers on my desk were perfectly placed to block her view of the disaster scene.

Then the challenger Ryuzaki came charging at me. "Mr. Rei! Eat lunch with— Um…did I come at a bad time?"

"……Yeah," I grumbled.

As she could see, my desk had turned into a pool of probiotics.

I was thankful that at least my papers had been spared.

Sadly, I now had cleanup duty to attend to.

* * *

"Oh no! School's already over! Sorry I'm such a disaster, Karin!" Ohgami moaned. "But we still have one more shot!"

"Go home already!" I said.

"Geez, Mr. Hitoma! I think you should take some of the blame here, TBH!"

After school. Somehow, the day had felt longer than usual.

The other students had already left the classroom. Ohgami and Ryuzaki were the only ones left. It had been a truly bizarre day. I had no idea what I'd gotten wrapped up in.

"Ryuzaki, I need to talk to you. Can you stay for a while?" I asked as she was about to leave with Ohgami.

Ryuzaki turned around. "Huh?"

Then Ohgami stopped. Her ears sprang up as if she had been struck by a realization. Her expression turned guilty as she came to stand between me and Ryuzaki.

"Um… Mr. Hitoma… If you're going to lecture her about today, well, I was the one behind all of it. Karin didn't do anything wrong…"

I see. She thinks I'm making Ryuzaki stay behind to lecture her.

"She's not in trouble, Ohgami," I reassured her.

"Oh! Are you going to confess your love?!" Ohgami asked.

"Gosh! Should I mentally prepare myself?!" Ryuzaki said.

"Not in a million years!" I yelled.

Sheesh... Here I am, impressed by how much she cares for her friend, when she turns around and says that...

Uncomprehending but accepting, Ohgami mumbled a quiet, "Hmm?" before saying, "All right, Karin! I wanna chat with you some more, so I'll wait for you in the library and read a fashion mag." She waved and left for the library.

Now then—just me and Ryuzaki.

I had a ton of things to say, but with Ohgami gone, the room was quiet, and I didn't know where to start.

Man, I should just be direct...

"Ryuzaki," I said.

"H-here!" She stood up straight and faced me. Her voice was shaking.

She was jittery, as if she was anticipating I was going to ask her out. I'd already told her a second ago that wasn't happening! Her nervousness was infectious. I let out a small sigh.

"About this morning..." *God, this is hard to talk about.* I instinctively averted my eyes. "You shouldn't cling to me, okay? And...I don't know how serious you are, but I can't reciprocate your feelings, so I would like you to stop proposing to me as a joke."

I said it...

At first, I had only planned to convey my disapproval of the physical contact, but that wasn't the root of the problem.

The issue was the way she acted as if she had a crush on me. Never mind that she was only teasing; if she kept this up day after day, the same consequences would be waiting for her at the end.

In that case, I had to succinctly turn her down now before she misunderstood.

Ryuzaki looked at her feet. She was shaking lightly. "No."

"...What?" My voice sounded weak and pathetic.

She raised her head and glared at me. "No. No, no, no, no, no! I'm not going to stop telling you how I feel!"

"What?! Why—?"

Her tearful but piercing gaze distressed me.

Is she actually more sincere than I thought—?!

"Okay. Then first of all, why me…?" I asked.

"Because—"

"You said I was a catch before, but honestly, that's painfully untrue. In the human world, there are tons of men who are more handsome and successful than I am—they have more friends, they have great personalities, they're diligent, and they're not annoying. They're literally everywhere! If you want to become human and fall in love, then one of those guys would be much better than—"

"No! That's not the point! I—I know what you did. I know you broke out of the school with Sui…!"

"How?!"

Why does she know that…?!

That information should be a secret to everyone except the people involved… Was she watching us?!

We had taken precautions at the time, but we couldn't possibly have thought of everything. Or could we have been seen by someone else? If word got out among the students—

"Sui can be oblivious. She didn't notice at all that I was tailing her when she left the dorm. It seemed like she was keeping an eye on her surroundings, but she basically has zero bestial instincts… It's amazing she was able to survive as a rabbit. Was she someone's beloved pet? That's nice… I'm so jealous."

Mystery solved… Ryuzaki was the one who saw us.

I neither confirmed nor denied Ryuzaki's assumption. Usami *couldn't* live in the wild. She was formerly a stuffed animal.

"I saw the human who Sui met up with—I saw *you*, Mr. Rei."

We locked gazes. I couldn't look away from her gentle, lovely eyes.

"At the time, you were teaching a few of the intermediate classes as well, so I had an idea of what kind of teacher you were. A typical meek human—that was my impression of you. But that day, you were amazing. You were cool. It looked like you were a bit hesitant, but you still chose to leave the school with Sui, right? That's when I fell for you."

"That's…the reason?"

Thinking back to that time filled me with mixed emotions.

What was it about me that day that could have made her like me?

Ryuzaki chuckled. "Yeah. I want to become human so I can fall in love. And I want to fall in love because I want to be cherished by someone. When you asked me before, I couldn't tell you, but when I saw the way you acted on behalf of your student despite your uncertainty, I fell for you."

"…Isn't being uncertain lame?"

"When one is uncertain, it's because they're trying to find the best course of action, right? I think that's pretty cool."

"That's a flattering way to put it."

"To me, that's the truth."

What was there to say to such a declaration? I couldn't see how that had made her like me, but I couldn't refute her feelings, either.

"You're a wonderful human who knows how to care for others," Ryuzaki continued. "A long time ago, there used to be a person like that near me… Mr. Rei, while we're here, will you take a walk with me down memory lane?"

She dropped her gaze, recalling a memory from a time long gone.

"This story takes place back when I could live near humans. Before that, I never felt hindered by my solitude. I lived in a cave in the mountains. Thanks to my abundance of magic, I never needed to eat or sleep. Every once in a while, I had to chase off the humans or animals that came too close. That was my everyday life.

"Then one human approached me."

From there, Ryuzaki told me a long tale of her past.

The human who came to her cave was an elegant young lady in a dress unfit for the treacherous mountains.

Ryuzaki tried to drive the woman away as always. However, the woman was injured and in no state to return home.

With no other choice, Ryuzaki decided to live with her in the cave.

The woman told her many stories about the human world.

It turned out that she was a princess who had been cast out from her kingdom:

"The princess treated me as if I were precious. That was a first for me... Do you know how amazing it feels to be stroked, Mr. Rei? Also, phrases like 'good morning,' 'good night,' and 'thank you'—they were completely new to me. Words...for a person other than myself... I still remember our last day. The prince of the neighboring kingdom came to my cave. I don't know what he'd been told, but he thought I had kidnapped the princess and was holding her captive. He came with a massive army—"

The prince turned his sword on the dragon—Ryuzaki—to fight for the princess, whom he loved. A by-the-book development. But Ryuzaki hadn't kidnapped the princess at all. She was never the prince's enemy to begin with.

"I didn't know what to do. He was pointing a sword at me, so I fought back, but there was no way an attack by a human could hurt me... Besides, the princess could've been caught in the cross fire. It was dangerous..."

In the end—the one who settled the fight was the princess.

After the prince rushed in for one final strike, he and his largely inferior army were nearly decimated.

The princess then ran to the prince and cast a spell to heal him. She turned her pleading face to the dragon.

"*No more. Don't hurt him anymore,*" she said.

"Just like that, the princess and the prince returned to the lands where humans lived. She forgot about me. That was the first time I had the thought: 'I'm jealous of the prince. The princess cares for him, protects him, holds him. If I were weak, she would stay with me forever.' That's what I believed... From that point on, I tried to live with humans and other races. But I'm too strong. The others feared me and ran from me. They recoiled from me, attacked me. It was always the same thing. I'm stronger than anyone else, so no one would even think to cherish me..."

Time passed; the human world developed further. Humans, droves of them, came to the cave in the perilous mountains where Ryuzaki lived.

She didn't want to hurt them anymore, so she ran. She moved to the mouth of a volcano enshrouded by poisonous smoke.

"I became no more than a rare cryptid sighting. That was around the time I heard the rumors that the ocean warden's daughter had enrolled in a school to become human."

Ryuzaki was talking about Minazuki. I had heard she was from a prestigious family. They were so renowned that the rumors even made their way to Ryuzaki, who had hidden away from the world...

"'That's it,' I thought to myself. If I became human, I would be on equal footing with them. I could stay beside them. I could be cherished by them...! I knew about it from the princess's stories. That feeling is called love, right? And when you live side by side with another person, that's called marriage, right? ...This is all the princess's fault. I started to yearn for that warmth. My strength as a dragon and the strength of that desire— they're incompatible. I don't want to live as a dragon anymore. The princess and prince fell in love, and that's why the princess left me. So I'll become human and fall in love with someone, too. I want to find another human dear to me... I want to be cherished, to be loved. That's the reason I'm here. And—"

Ryuzaki took one step toward me.

"—the one I found was you, Mr. Rei."

Here in this classroom after school were the two of us—and she was gazing at me, her eyes swimming.

"You meet us where we are, even though we aren't human. You talk to us like equals... That's why I like you. That's why I want to be loved by you... You're the one I want."

Ryuzaki's hand was trembling. I could no longer call her feelings a misunderstanding. However—

"...Sorry, but I'm still a teacher."

"Dating a student is out of the question?"

"...There's that, too. But the reason I care for all my students—including you—is because I'm a teacher. So for me to...um...treat someone in a special way, to...love them... I just don't think I can do that."

I was awful at this. I hadn't conveyed my point at all. Cut me some slack; no one had ever confessed their feelings to me before...!

The tension drained from Ryuzaki's body. She looked fed up. "If you're going to turn me down, can you at least do it properly?"

"...Sorry."

How firm was I meant to be in a situation like this? I was still her teacher; I felt that I shouldn't hurt her feelings on purpose. I had nothing more to say to her.

She watched me falter and smiled in surrender. "I get it. I'm sorry to trouble you. It's okay. I'm used to being alone."

Her last words—likely added to give me peace of mind—weighed heavy in my heart.

No—I don't want her to be alone. I didn't mean to make her say that. Then what do I do? Am I being a hypocrite? I'm the one who's abandoning her. I can't reciprocate her feelings, so consequently— Dammit! I don't know anymore.

Anyway! It might be hypocritical. I might hurt her feelings some more. It might be for my own satisfaction.

This scares me. But I don't want to leave Ryuzaki like this—looking so forlorn, accustomed to being alone even though she doesn't want to be.

"Ryuzaki," I said.

She tilted her head slightly, and her hair rustled softly.

I took a breath—slowly, so that my voice wouldn't shake. "I won't fall in love with you. But I don't have to be in love with you to want to stay by your side. As your teacher, I won't let you go off on your own—not until the day you graduate."

Ryuzaki pierced me with her stare. I couldn't tell what she was thinking, couldn't read her expression.

What should I do? Did I overstep?

"You don't play fair, Mr. Rei. But that's...what I love about you."

Her feeble, tearful smile made my chest tighten painfully, likely from guilt. A person with more romantic experience might have rejected her outright, severed ties, made her hate them—and by doing so, have her forget that this even happened. That, too, was a form of kindness. But that person wasn't me.

I didn't want her to regret falling in love, even if I was the object of her affections.

I didn't want her to think she shouldn't have even tried, the way I had in the past.

Ryuzaki slowly began to speak. "Listen, Mr. Rei. I understand I have no chance with you. But I still like you. I just do. So as long as I don't overdo it, can I...continue telling you I like you? Until I graduate, at least. Until then, allow me to keep on liking you. Heh-heh. I'll take full advantage of your kindness! You said you won't let me go off on my own, right? Of course, I know my love won't bear any fruit. Anyway! Ah— no need to respond! Well, Isaki is waiting, so I'm gonna go! See you tomorrow, Mr. Rei!"

"Huh? Wait—"

The second half of that speech was way too fast!

Ryuzaki said her piece, picked up her bag, and fled the classroom.

I dropped my gaze to my right hand, which was reaching for nothing.

Um... Uh, I think I got my message across.

My feelings were still a tangled mess, but pushing the conversation further would likely only lead to us talking in circles. *Will things really be all right the way they are, though...? Ugh...*

Self-loathing welled up inside me. I let out a small sigh.

"...Guess I should go back to the teachers' office," I mumbled to myself.

The attendance list I'd left on the lectern, my small pencil case: I picked them both up and left the room.

Out in the hall, I heard voices from a distance. From the library? My curiosity piqued, I walked toward the voices.

"Auuugh! Isakiii! Mr. Rei dumped me!"

"Aww, Karin! I know it hurts. I know you're sad... But you did your best! You're amazing! Let's talk our fill until the day is over!"

"Yeah, okay...!"

Those were Ryuzaki's and Ohgami's voices. My chest tightened when I overheard their conversation.

It'll be all right. Ryuzaki has friends.

Surely she'll meet many other people, and she'll forge a bond with someone again.

She'll graduate and become human. Her world will widen.

What was I doing during that stage of life…?

Guess I was still in school, same as now.

My thoughts drifting, I headed back to the teachers' office.

* * *

"*Yaaaaawn…* Mmmm… Sleepy…," I grumbled.

Such a massive yawn was permissible since I was on my way to school. That was what I believed.

To my sleep-deprived body, the morning sunlight was so bright it hurt. The previous night, unusually for me, I had booted up a dating sim.

I had bought it because it was a well-known classic, but since it was a genre I rarely forayed into, it had been gathering dust on my shelf.

I could see why it was so highly rated. The storyline was excellent. To be honest, before I had been disdainful, thinking it was one of those games where the protagonist was wooed by and fawned over by the heroines. However, the protagonist undergoes a series of decisions that causes him to grow. Strangely enough, I found myself empathizing with him, and I played through the game until I reached an ending.

That was why I was sleep-deprived. *I might be better off spending my lunch break sleeping rather than eating…*

"Mr. Rei! Good morning!" Ryuzaki called out to me.

"Ryuzaki…"

She greeted me as she always did. Faced with her usual smile but less than usual salutation, I felt a touch wistful. *But that's for the best*, I thought as I remembered how every morning up until now, I'd been greeted with a marriage proposal.

This is fine.

"Hey, good morn—," I started.

"Also, I like you just as much today!"

"...!"

She went for a follow-up attack!

Ryuzaki looked at me—I was rendered speechless by the surprise attack—and grinned. "I'm going on ahead, Mr. Rei!" She ran right past me.

The sunlight that glittered off her golden hair seemed completely different from the harsh rays that had stabbed my eyes moments ago.

The light was endlessly warm, soft, and gentle.

The Misanthrope and the Gluttonous Hero

A MISANTHROPE TEACHES A CLASS FOR DEMI-HUMANS

If there's a god out there, then why did they give me this trial?

My little sister was lying on her side in front of me, bound with packing tape and unable to move.

Through a slit between the layers of tape, I could see her mouth sipping breaths of air.

"Squeak..."

She's alive.

I brought a piece of food I had just picked up closer to her face. She twitched her nose, checking what it was, then opened her mouth to receive it.

Thank goodness. She can still eat.

Luckily, humans rarely came here.

My sister was immobile, stuck to the ground with tape.

But that was okay.

Just—

As long as we have food, we'll survive.

* * *

The Golden Week holidays were over, and I had slowly grown used to this new advanced class. Ryuzaki continued to profess her love for me, Usami was hard on herself and others as always, Ohgami was studious, and Haneda idly shepherded the class from the shadows.

However, I wanted Nezu to fix her habit of eating her food before lunchtime. And Kurosawa often napped in class, although once she was woken up, she stayed awake...for about ten minutes.

I was impressed that she had managed to be promoted to the advanced class with such a lifestyle, but her grades were just as excellent as the other new students'. Ryuzaki conversed about world history as if she had seen the events with her own eyes. Sometimes, I thought she might even be more knowledgeable than a specialist like me. Nezu was surprisingly strong in the sciences and had a particular interest in chemistry. Kurosawa was the biggest shock. Even though she slept through most classes, she was versatile and had a good grasp of every subject. In that way, she resembled Usami. If pressed to find a difference, I would say Kurosawa was more arts-focused and Usami more sciences-focused.

I was just about to leave the teachers' office when a beautiful woman with white hair who was wearing a lab coat—Ms. Saotome—called out to me.

"Yoo-hoo, Mr. Hitoma! Are you heading to your end-of-the-day homeroom?"

"Hello, Ms. Saotome," I replied.

She's as wonderful and sunny as always...

She was holding something. A package?

"This arrived for you just now!" she said. "There's some food inside, according to the label. Tomorrow's Friday, so I thought it would be best to give it to you as soon as possible! You can tell your students about it, too! Heh-heh! Getting packages is so much fun! Here you go!"

A package for me? The only thing that came to mind was the special-edition release of a game with bonus content that was going on sale next week. But that would be delivered to the staff dorm, not the teachers' office...

I didn't know what it was, but I took the package—small enough to be held with both hands—from Ms. Saotome.

"Oh." After seeing the sender's name, I realized what this was about. "Looks like Minazuki's doing well in her new school."

The package was from a former advanced student who had graduated last year: Kyoka Minazuki.

* * *

"You're late, Hitoma! You can't shirk your duties just because it's homeroom!" Usami scolded me.

"*Squeak?* Meester Hitoma? Whatcha got in your hands? What a cute basket! Are those cookies inside?"

Sharp. I expected no less from Nezu.

"Yeah, I got a package and a letter from Minazuki, who was in last year's advanced class," I explained.

"Oh gosh. From Kyoka…?!" Ohgami lit up all of a sudden. I remembered the two of them being particularly close.

"…What did Kyoka say? Does it seem like she's doing well?" Haneda asked, her voice gentle. Her expression, which was brimming with affection, seemed more befitting of the director rather than Tobari Haneda—

"Mr. Rei?" Ryuzaki said.

"Oh, my bad."

Crap. That was sloppy. What just happened? Did I almost let myself be enchanted by her? No, that can't be it. The dating sim I played must be getting to my head.

"Hitoma! What did Kyoka write?!" Usami demanded.

"Oh, um… She's learning to dance at school and having fun every day. Lately, she's taken an interest in musicals, apparently."

"Yes, Kyoka's a really good singer," Ohgami said.

"Really?" I hadn't known. Maybe she had sung for the class before.

"Singing is an indispensable communication skill between mermaids," Haneda explained. "That's why Kyoka's musical intuition is better than anyone else's here. Kyoka can't do this anymore now that she's human, but if you layer a mermaid's song on top of the unique sound produced by their fins, you get this mesmerizing soundscape… Granted, it's fatal to humans. That's why mermaids were feared as sirens in the past, and why they live deep in the ocean now."

"Interesting..."

She knows so much...

"Oh, also, Minazuki has been going to a lot of musicals," I continued. "This is a souvenir from one of the shows."

The title was *The Little Mermaid: The Remake.* Minazuki enjoyed it, finding it novel to see mermaids through a human's perspective. The cookies she sent were based on a present the mermaid protagonist gave the prince. Minazuki gave them to us because "You're the most important people to me!"

What a considerate souvenir.

"They're fish-shaped! Cute! Can I have one?!" Nezu exclaimed.

"Yeah, I'll pass them out," I said. "Hmm? 'There's a fun surprise inside. Please enjoy them with everyone!'...?"

"What's that supposed to mean? Aw, whatever! She's probably just saying it's fun to eat yummy food! Come on, Meester Hitoma! I wanna eat one already!"

"All right, all right..."

I took off the plastic wrapping around the basket.

Let's see. There's ten in all... I'll hand out one each.

I distributed the cookies among the students evenly.

"Yay! Thanks for the grub!" Nezu stuffed the cookie in her mouth the moment I gave it to her.

"Machi, you glutton," Usami said.

"But it's a gift!"

"We're still in homeroom!"

I stepped in. "It's not a big deal, Usami. This is all I had to share with everyone anyway, so we'll let it slide."

"You're too soft... Hmph!" Usami sniffed.

Despite her complaint, Usami also opened her wrapper and took a bite of the small cookie.

"*Munch, munch...* Hmm, not bad," she said.

"Guess I'll eat mine now, too," Haneda mused.

Ryuzaki jumped in. "Me too!"

"........*Munch.*" Kurosawa took a bite.

"I-I'll eat mine, too!" Ohgami said. "Hee-hee! The shape is so adorable."

The students chatted as they snacked on the cookies. The conversation mostly revolved around Minazuki: Had she made friends at her new school? Granted, this was Minazuki; no need to worry about her in that regard.

"Hmm, so Neneko is the only one here who doesn't know Kyoka... N-N-N-N-Neneko! Are you okay?!" Ohgami cried.

I looked over at Kurosawa and saw that her mouth was cherry red.

"Huh? What happened?!" I asked.

"........What?" She tilted her head in puzzlement, her face blank as usual. Maybe she hadn't realized what had happened to her.

"Neneko's cookie...smells super spicy," Nezu commented.

"Huh? The cookie?!" Usami yelled. "But mine was delicious! It was completely normal!"

A super spicy cookie? I scrambled to check the tag on the basket.

No matter how I looked at it, there was nothing unusual about— No, wait!

RUSSIAN ROULETTE COOKIES! TWO FIERY SURPRISES IN TEN!

"Aghhhhhh!!!"

What on earth did you send us, Minazuki?!

She likely didn't mean any harm.

She probably just wanted us to have fun playing Russian roulette. But still!!!

"K-K-K-K-Kurosawa!!! Don't force yourself!!!" I said.

"........Force?"

I was panicking, but Kurosawa was cool and unfazed.

Am I wrong?!

"A-are you good with spicy food...?" I asked.

"...No clue..."

She doesn't know? Maybe she doesn't have a strong sense of taste.

Wait—no one's taste buds are that *dull.*

"*Squeak*... Neneko, give me that," Nezu demanded.

Kurosawa stared fixedly at Nezu, but then abruptly held out the cookie.

"Thanks!" Nezu took the red-hot cookie.

She can't be...

"*Ahhh—nom!*"

"Nezu?!"

I thought she might've wanted to eat it, but I can't believe she actually did!!

"A-a-a-are you okay?!" I asked.

"Mmmmmm, spicy and scrumptious!!" she exclaimed.

"Y-you have nerves of steel...!"

Naturally, applause broke out around the classroom.

Have I ever thought of her as this dependable before...? Nope, never.

Nezu, grinning smugly, gave us two enthusiastic thumbs-up. Her expression was like that of a warrior with a storied history in battle.

Usami side-eyed Nezu, looking somewhat repulsed. "Machi... You really will eat anything..."

Nezu leaped onto the desk, stuck the landing, and declared, "*Squee-hee-hee*... Wherever there's food...there's me, Machi!"

"Hey now, get off the desk," I said.

For a second, it looked like Nezu was standing on a stage beneath a spotlight. She was getting carried away.

"Isn't there anything you don't like?" Ryuzaki asked.

"Hmm? Foods I don't like, huh? Hmm, fancy grilled beef and sushi aaand high-end desserts. I *hate* fancy-schmancy desserts...... Eep."

"Don't tell me you're scared of *manju* buns," I said.

"Yeah, I am. I'll collapse and start foaming at the mouth."

"She's just saying that to wheedle a bun from you!" Usami insisted.

Even while we were ribbing one another and joking around about the classic *rakugo* play, I didn't fail to notice Kurosawa starting to nod off.

"Hey! Kurosawa! Sleep after you go home!" I barked. "...Oh, also, why

don't you have another cookie, since the one you got was spicy? There's still a few left."

"……*Meow?*"

Acting as a pillow beneath her head was a book titled *Black Magic Through Manga!* Another handy-dandy guide…

Having been woken up right on the cusp of dreamland, Kurosawa looked a little dazed, but she stared at me and nodded.

"*Squeak?!* Why?! No fair! I want seconds, too…!!" Nezu whined.

"You already got two cookies," I retorted.

"One and a half!"

"Same thing!"

That was when I noticed something.

"Two surprises in ten…?" I muttered.

In other words—of the four cookies left, one was a fiery bomb…?!

Having realized the horrible truth, I froze with the box in my hand.

"Meester Hitoma? What's wrong?" Nezu asked. "Aren't you gonna have one?"

"Nezu… You see, one of the four is going to be super spicy…"

"Hmm? It's this one!" she said as if it was blatantly obvious.

"How do you know?"

"Heh-heh! 'Cause I'm a mouse! There's no way it would escape this superior nose of mine! A mouse's sense of smell is way, *way* better than a human's, so— Ah."

"…Nezu."

She had admitted something that I, as a teacher at this school, could not overlook.

"Eep!! Meester Hitoma? You heard wrong! I—I—I didn't say anything…!" she cried.

I felt sorry for Nezu, whose eyes were swimming with tears, but I had to do my job.

"Nezu, unhuman-like behavior means…a point deduction," I told her.

"*Squeak?!* You're awful! You tricked me with a leading questiooon!!"

"*Sigh*… What an idiot," Usami muttered.

"*Zzzz…*" Kurosawa snored on.

* * *

Sis's breathing was getting shallower by the day.
Our food supply was dwindling, too.
Why? Why…?!
At this rate—I'm going to lose my little sister.
No way.
How could this be happening when I wanted her to live so badly?!

But there was nothing more I could do. I knew that.
These hands of mine, powerless as I was, couldn't remove the tape.
I couldn't do anything about the fact that Sis's health was waning.
I knew nothing.

I want to be strong.
Like humans.

If I were human…
…saving my sister would be a snap, wouldn't it?

* * *

After morning homeroom, I was chatting with the students in the advanced class, when suddenly a quiet knock came at the door.

The door then opened to reveal a small girl.

"Um, is Machi here…?" she asked.

"Oh, aren't you—?" I began to say.

"Chiyu! Why're you here?!" Nezu cried, rushing toward our surprise visitor.

The girl's hair was the same color as Nezu's, and their uniforms were similar, too.

Her name: Chiyu Nezu.

Smaller than Nezu, she was one of the beginner students.

"Machi, I, um, accidentally took one of your textbooks," Nezu (junior) said, and passed a Japanese literature textbook to Nezu (senior).

"Do you and your little sister room together, Machi?" Ohgami asked.

"Bingo! I asked to be roommates with Chiyu when I joined the intermediate class!"

I see.

There were several room arrangements in the student dorm.

First, the single rooms. These were given to intermediate students who had excellent grades. Otherwise, they were reserved for advanced students. Unless students demonstrated a certain level of independence, it was too risky to let them room alone.

Next, the double room. They were for intermediate students, but it wasn't a requirement for both occupants to be intermediate students. Beginner students were permitted to stay in a double so long as the intermediate student looked after their younger roommate and assumed responsibility in case of an emergency.

Lastly, the group room was for students who weren't eligible to stay in singles or doubles. These students lived under close supervision by Roost Rep Ryouko.

"Long time no see, Chiyu."

"Karin... Thanks for the snacks the other day."

"Chiyu!" Nezu squealed. "You said your thanks properly. Good job!!"

"Eh-heh-heh..."

It was endearing to see Nezu's little sister so happy at being complimented.

Nezu (junior)—Chiyu—was particularly young even among her beginner-class peers.

"...Wait a second—how are students' ages determined?" I mused.

"Ages don't mean anything at this school," Usami told me.

"Whoops. Did I just say that out loud?"

"It's creepy the way you mumble to yourself."

"You replied to me, so I'm no longer talking to myself, right?"

"You're *so* annoying."

Her point-blank reply left me speechless.

"Oh no… Don't fight…," Ohgami pleaded. "Um, about our ages, though… I believe they're different from how many years we've been alive…"

"Really?" I said.

I had been informed about the nitty-gritty details of the school system, but I realized now that I hadn't heard anything about the students' ages. Granted, that information had nothing to do with teaching.

"As long as they're in this school, the students stop aging—at least, that's what I heard from the director," Haneda said.

So you heard it from yourself. In any case, I was curious about several things.

"Okay—for example, if a student enrolled here right before their life span was over, would they stay alive? What would happen when they graduated?" I asked.

"Yeah, they'd stay alive," Nezu answered. "Students don't age while they're here, so hypothetically, they would keep on living. But our biological clocks resume once we leave the school… Basically, y'know, after we graduate, we become eighteen-year-old humans with eighteen-year-old bodies… That is to say, the school sends us off to our new life in a healthy and unencumbered body."

"I see… In effect, your life span is prolonged."

Then it wouldn't be strange if students wanted to become human in order to extend their life spans. I hadn't encountered any such student, though. Not that I knew the goals of every single pupil at the school.

I found myself glancing at Haneda.

This was just my personal assumption, but I believed that the director would disqualify such candidates; their goal, at the end of the day, wasn't really to become human. And all prospective students were vetted by the director—

"…What?" Haneda asked me.

"Um, it's nothing…"

Knowing that Haneda was the director, I found my thoughts kept going in unnecessary directions. *Mm... That's no good... No good at all... I have to get myself out of this funk...*

"Okay, Machi, I'll wait for you in the library like always!" Chiyu said.

"Gotcha! Thanks for bringing me my textbook, Chiyu."

The younger Nezu sent a little wave in her sister's direction before turning to me and dipping her head in a shallow bow. She then scampered back toward the beginner classroom.

"It's unusual to meet a pair of siblings attending the same school," Ohgami remarked.

"Well, I consider her my younger sister, but who knows if we're actually related."

"I see. How long have you been together?"

Ohgami's circumstances were different but still bore some resemblance to a sibling relationship. I wondered if that was why she was asking.

"As long as I can remember! Actually, we had way more brothers and sisters, but...it's hard for us little guys to get by!" Nezu said. "You're a fellow pocket-size pal, Uchami, so you get it!"

"Y-yeah... I hope Chiyu will be promoted soon, too."

"Yep! I want us to become human quickly and live together! I'll probably get there first, so while I wait, I'll make sure to stock up on tons of yummy food for the day Chiyu becomes human."

Her merry reply was bursting with hope and anticipation.

Machi Nezu. Mouse. Enrolled for eight years. Wants to become human to eat lots and lots of yummy food.

* * *

It was sweet.
A different smell than the usual ones.
I brought it to my sister like I always did.

For a little while, Sis was only drinking water.

The food with the sweet fragrance was soft. If I ripped it into small pieces, maybe she would eat it.

I gently brought it near her mouth.

I saw her nose twitch. Then she opened her mouth a tiny bit. I slipped the sweet food inside.

She chewed slowly, then swallowed.

I will never forget what she said next.

Her mouth moved soundlessly, but I still heard her loud and clear:

"'S yummy..."

From that day on, she started eating again, little by little.

I don't know what that sweet food was.

But it saved my little sister.

It saved me, too.

* * *

"Meester Hitomaaaaa, I wanna go hoooome," Nezu whined.

"No can do," I said.

Nezu and I were alone in the classroom.

Spread out in front of Nezu were supplementary worksheets—almost entirely blank—with a five-hundred-word essay and fill-in-the-blank questions dealing with fundamental vocabulary.

"But I'm starving! I want something to eeeat!"

With the way she was dragging her feet and whining at her desk, Nezu was acting just like an elementary school student.

"Who was the one who couldn't wait for lunch and ate in the middle of my class?" I asked.

"...I thought I was gonna get away with it."

This rascal... She's not sorry at all... Besides, considering how few students are in the class, she was inevitably going to get caught...

"Shape up... Next time, I'll skip the extra work and jump straight to docking points. This time, I'll let you off if you turn in the assignment."

"*Squeak-squeak...* Okay. For a change of pace, I'll boost my motivation to study with some pumped-up tunes."

"What?"

Crunch, crunch, crunch, crunch.

"Are you seriously eating rice crackers right now?" I said.

"Aw, come on. Eating helps me think!"

Is food the only thing on her mind...?

"*Sigh...* Look, I have other work to do, so I'm heading to the teachers' office," I told her. "I'll come back here in a while, but if you finish your work before that, find me in there."

"What if I don't turn it in?"

"Point deductions."

"*Squeeeak!*"

I could hear the dissatisfaction in her voice, but sad to say, it was the natural course of action.

I left Nezu to work through her assignment in the advanced classroom alone and went to the teachers' office on the second floor. As I slowly walked down the stairs, I caught sight of a short and slight figure.

"Meester Hitoma."

I heard someone call my name. It was Chiyu.

"Where's Machi? Do you know?" she asked.

She must have come to pick up Nezu.

I knelt down to her eye level. "Yeah, Nezu...uh, Machi—Ms. Machi? Anyway, your sister has some review work to do, so she'll be going home late. She should be back in an hour...or, actually, a little longer than that..."

"Okay. *Squeak...* I get it. Then I'll do my homework in the library."

"Good girl. If only Nezu—I mean Machi was as levelheaded as you."

"*Squeak...*"

Ah, crap! I didn't mean to bad-mouth Nezu in front of her sister! I crossed a line, no matter how you look at it.

Chiyu hung her head dejectedly.

"S-s-s-s-sorry!" I stammered. "Obviously, I know Machi has lots of great qualities, too! Um, for instance, she seems to enjoy her food more than anyone else!"

Really? That's the first example that came to my mind???

But I genuinely believed that was her best talent. On the other hand, there were other—

"...Machi is my hero," Chiyu said.

"Your hero...?"

She looked up at me, her eyes blazing with pride.

"Yep. When I was a mouse, a bad thing happened to me," she explained, her voice gentle as if she were holding something precious. "I got stuck to some tape that a human threw out, and I couldn't move. I thought I was gonna die. If that was it, then that was it, I figured. But Machi didn't give up on me. She fed me, protected me from the rain and meanies—that's why she's my hero." She smiled proudly.

I get it now. Chiyu thinks of Nezu as—

"I see... Sorry. Make no mistake: Your big sister has a good head on her shoulders. She's an awesome superhero."

"Eh-heh-heh..."

Nezu, more than anyone, had a talent for devoting everything she had to the stuff that she liked. Although...this time, she had gone a little overboard, earning herself after-school lessons.

"Thanks, Meester Hitoma." Chiyu bowed, then went up the stairs to the library.

* * *

"...Hey, hero," I said.

"*Gnmm—zzzz...* Hee-hee... I can still eat... *Munch...*"

I thought that my impression of Nezu would change after hearing Chiyu's story, but that wasn't the case. After finishing up most of my work in the teachers' office, I had headed back to the classroom, only to find Chiyu's hero drooling in her sleep, her mouth moving like she was chewing.

"Reallyyy? You're sure I can have this...? Hee-hee..."

Her greed was showing...

Gah... I guess I should wake her.

"Nezu, wake up." I knocked lightly on the desk. The same way I woke up Kurosawa.

"Hmm? *Squeak!!* My *Summer Limited-Edition Special Deluxe Soft and Flaky Shaved Ice: Miracle Mochi Reborn! Strawberry Condensed Milk, Topped with Freshly Swirled Soft Serve*! Where is it?!"

"That's some feast you're having!!"

"I even got extra strawberries, mochi, and whipped cream, and a bonus drizzle of chocolate sauce on top."

"What kind of café is this...?"

I'm not sure you can call that shaved ice anymore...

"Anyway, seems like you had a blast in your dream. Are you done with the assignment?" I asked.

"Eep!" she squeaked.

...That's the reaction of someone who didn't finish their work.

"Fine. I'll check what you've done so far for now. Show me."

"Urk... Here." She handed me the supplementary worksheets I had assigned her.

There was drool on one corner, but...no use crying over spilled milk.

I scanned the sheets.

Hmm... Seems like she took it seriously before she fell asleep.

More than 80 percent of it was filled in, and she only had to write the conclusion for her essay.

"Okay, it looks good," I said. "Just a few questions left. Hang in there."

"Mm'kay, I'll do what I caaan."

Based on her lackadaisical attitude, it didn't look like she had any motivation, but when I returned the sheets to her, she got to work. Rather than run away and seek distractions when faced with a task she didn't want to do, she was the type to go all out on her passions and neglect everything else.

"By the way, I ran into Chiyu after I left you earlier," I told her.

"Is she in the library?"

"Yeah, she said she'd do her homework while she waits for you."

"*Squeak...*"

Learning that Chiyu was waiting for her kicked Nezu into overdrive. Her whole vibe changed, and she made rapid progress on the assignment.

"Done!"

"Already?!" I exclaimed.

"I only had a teensy bit left! Plus, Chiyu's waiting."

"All right. Wait—let me check it over quickly. Hang on a sec." I stopped Nezu as she picked up her bag and turned to leave. "You really care for Chiyu."

"Of course! She always, always supports me! Chiyu's my light of hope! Also, she's a pro at sniffing out delicious food! Just the other day, she found some loquats growing in the mountains! We promised to pick them together!"

"Wow, I didn't know there were fruit trees in these mountains... Okay, your assignment is good to go. See, Nezu, you can do it when you put your mind to it."

"You bet I can!"

"Yeah, yeah, you're a superstar, all right. Anyway, if you're sick of getting extra work, stop eating during class."

"Ack... I can't make any promises."

"Why not?!"

I didn't want to dock points if I could help it, so I'd given her an assignment instead, but that was work for me, too. *Students don't know how rough teachers have it! They just don't get it!*

"Well, Meester Hitoma, see ya tomorrow!" Nezu said, dashing out of the room while I was otherwise preoccupied with playing a tragic heroine.

Maybe if I introduce different global cuisines during world history class, she'll take an interest in the subject. Actually, that seems more suitable for geography class... Cuisine brings to mind local ingredients...and—

My idle thoughts were interrupted by the pitter-patter of running feet in the hallway. A second after, a loud *bang* reverberated through the advanced classroom. Nezu rushed in, having violently shoved open the door.

"...! Meester Hitoma...!"

"N-Nezu? What's got you so worked up...?" I asked.

Did she forget something? Doesn't seem like it.

She collapsed against the wall, thoroughly shaken up.

"Chiyu's...," she started.

Chiyu? Come to think of it, they're not together. But Chiyu said she would be in the library—

"Chiyu's gone...!" Nezu cried. Her face was drained of color. Tears sprang to her eyes.

"M-maybe she went home first?" I offered.

"She wouldn't do that! She's the one who said she wanted to go home together because she was worried about being eaten by another student! Do you really think a scaredy-mouse like her would leave by herself?!"

"I guess not... Do you have any other ideas?"

"I would've gone to find her if I did!!" Nezu was inconsolable.

I was worried about Chiyu, but I decided that I had to calm Nezu down first.

"Nezu, I'll do everything in my power to help. Now—take a deep breath. Clear your head, and let's assess the situation."

She looked at me helplessly. Then she closed her eyes. She breathed in deeply and sighed out slowly before opening her eyes again.

Her expression was one I had seen earlier. She was in focus mode. She tightened her fists and brought them to her chest, almost like a boxer, to psych herself up.

"...Thanks, Meester Hitoma."

"Let's start by ruling out what we can. Does Chiyu carry a phone?"

"*Squeak...* Beginner students are only allowed kid-friendly phones, and I didn't think Chiyu needed one yet, so she doesn't have one."

"Ahhh... Got it."

To be honest, I was pretty shaken up, too. Nezu was afraid that Chiyu would be eaten...but with the principal and director around, I figured that wasn't a problem. However, if Chiyu had wandered away from the building or main roads and into the forest, and if she'd kept going and accidentally crossed through the barrier, I didn't know what would happen. An hour had passed since I'd last spoken to her. That was plenty of time for her to have left the barrier if she'd wanted to.

What if—? No, we'll rule out what we can and then decide our next steps.

"…Nezu, let's split up for now. You look for her along the road to the dorms and in your dorm room, and I'll search the school. I'll also ask the other teachers if they've seen her."

As a last resort, our best option would be to leverage the principal and director's OP skills to determine her location.

"This is my number. Call me if you need anything," I said.

Nezu nodded. "Got it." She gave me the number to her on-campus cell phone.

"…Do you think Chiyu's okay?" she asked me with a quivering voice. She was putting on a brave face, but she must have been anxious.

I shouldn't say anything reckless, but—

"I believe that Chiyu…is safe."

But the words *don't worry* didn't come so easily. I hoped she understood what I wanted to tell her.

"Chiyu is my light of hope," Nezu said.

Hope.

The image of Chiyu saying that Nezu was her hero came to my mind.

"As long as Chiyu is with me, I can do my best—she's the only thing that's kept me going all this time. If she's gone, I won't know what to do. Is she really okay? She's not going through anything scary, is she? I'm nothing without her, Meester Hitoma. Why do the powers that be always try to take her away from me? All I want to do is live a normal life. All I want is to eat good food with Chiyu and talk about how yummy it is and share a laugh. That's all…! This is my fault. I wasn't by her side. I took my eyes off her. I—!"

"Nezu," I blurted out.

She looked at me with tears spilling from her eyes, no longer able to hold them in. "…Meester Hitoma." Her face scrunched up even further. "Save…Chiyu…!"

I had never heard her scream with such anguish. She spent more time with Chiyu than with anyone else. Cared for her, cherished her. That was why she was in such pain.

"Nezu," I repeated.

There was one thing I had to tell her before anything else.

To the Nezu who had worried and worried all alone until she had broken down.

"...It's not your fault Chiyu is missing. You didn't do anything wrong."

Nezu's eyes widened into saucers. "—!" Her face contorted in anguish. A large tear slid down her cheek. "What do you mean? What do you mean I didn't do anything wrong? Then what do I do? Who do I blame? Where can I vent these painful feelings? If there's no villain to blame, I will always, always be in pain!"

Had I looked the same way to others back then?

"You don't need to be the villain. You did nothing wrong. Nothing," I said.

I wished someone had told me the same.

"...Nothing wrong, you say... Okay, then who should I blame?!" she yelled.

"You don't have to blame anyone." I pushed on. "I understand wanting to blame yourself. I'm the same. But if you do that, those who care about you will be sad. So...when anything bad happens, you should tell the people around you... That's how humans live, I think. By supporting one another."

Once I said that, I had a realization.

Huh. Even though I ran away, there were probably lots of people who were supporting me.

It might have been overdue, but I knew now. And going forward—

"...Keep it a secret from Chiyu. Don't tell her I blamed myself and that I cried," Nezu said brusquely, wiping away her tears. "Sorry for breaking down on you. We'll...find Chiyu for sure. Geez! I'm gonna let her have it when we do!" She flattened her lips into a tight line and stared at me imploringly. "—! I'm going to the dorm!"

She spun around and ran down the stairs.

What were the right words to say? I wonder...

I watched her until she disappeared before starting my search on the third floor, where the advanced class and library were.

* * *

"Did you find Chiyu, Mr. Hitoma?!"

"Ms. Saotome..."

After parting ways with Nezu, I'd searched the third floor with no success. Next, I'd gone to the teachers' office and explained the situation to Ms. Saotome and got her to help. She'd then searched the places I couldn't enter, like the girls' bathrooms and changing room, concentrating her search around the gym, while I'd checked the main building and annex. However, neither of us had found Chiyu.

"The principal just returned, Mr. Hitoma. I think we should consult with him about the next steps to take," Ms. Saotome suggested, her expression grave and concerned.

"Right... Perhaps we should... Thank you, Ms. Saotome. Nezu went to look for Chiyu in their dorm room, and— Ah, pardon me for a moment." My phone started ringing in my pocket.

I picked it up. "Hello. Rei Hitoma speaking."

"Meester Hitoma... What do we do...? Chiyu's not in the dorm, either...," Nezu said on the other end.

"...I see."

I had thought maybe Chiyu had returned to the dorm first, but...

We might seriously be in trouble.

"Got it. Listen to me, Nezu. I'm going to speak with the principal about what to do. Please wait in the dorm for now. Once we decide on a strategy, I'll call you right away."

"She could have gone into the forest! I'm gonna go look for—"

"I know you want to help, Nezu. But it would be a problem if you go too far and we can't reach you once we figure out where Chiyu is. I know it's tough, but please stay where you are for a little bit."

"...Fine," she agreed, if discontentedly.

Thank goodness...

"I'll call again."

"ASAP!"

"Okay."

I was sure she had plenty more to say to me. However, she kept all that to herself for now, accepting that the best course of action for her was to wait.

"Did Machi have any luck?" Ms. Saotome asked me worriedly, having stood by during our phone call.

"...She wasn't in the dorm, either, apparently. I'm going to go consult with the principal. Thank you for your help, Ms. Saotome."

"Not at all! It's nothing! I'm concerned about Chiyu, too... We might have overlooked somewhere, so I'll keep searching the building!"

"Thank you." Seeing her smile made me a little less anxious.

Yes, I was scared, too.

I was the one who had given Nezu the extra assignment. If I hadn't, maybe Chiyu wouldn't have gone missing. Plus, I was likely the last person to see Chiyu. Had there been something I was supposed to have noticed?

Stop. Torturing myself isn't going to get me anywhere.

I smacked my face to psych myself up.

Ms. Saotome blinked in surprise when she saw that.

"I'm off to see the principal!" I told her.

"Good luck!" she said as she saw me off.

* * *

"Excuse me," I said as I knocked on the door, and then I entered.

It was tasteless as usual.

The principal was working through some documents at his desk.

"I have a general grasp of the situation, my boy," he said.

"Huh?"

But I haven't said anything yet.

"I have ears like the devil!" he told me. "Chiyu, from the beginner class, is missing. Is that right?"

"Y-yes. I was hoping to ask for your advice on what to do…"

I was shocked by the speed at which the conversation was moving. Was super hearing a special ability of crow *tengu* like the principal…?

"I see. In that case…we will treat this as an emergency, and I'll release the restraints on my powers."

The principal stood from his chair. He slowly closed his eyes and laid his hands over them.

The atmosphere was oddly tense. What in the world was going to happen…?

The principal began to chant. "Lo, forest. Lo, wind. Reveal to me, Shirou Karasuma, that which is unseen—crow *tengu* secret technique: Second Sight!!"

Th-that's frickin' AWESOME!!

A secret technique triggered by a chant?! What's it gonna do?!

The principal's eyes snapped open wide. Reflected in his pupils was a crest like a revolver's cylinder.

This is my first time seeing a power like second sight in real life!

Wind whirled around the room even though the windows were closed. The papers on the principal's desk fluttered but stayed put thanks to the paperweight over them. When the vase on the coffee table looked in danger of falling over, I scrambled to hold it down.

This lasted for ten seconds or so.

The principal closed his eyes again, and the wind stopped. I let go of the vase.

"She's in the forest, about three hundred yards north of the dorm…," the principal explained. "Still inside the barrier, on top of a tree."

"That's much farther than I thought! How did she get there so quickly…?"

And on top of a tree, of all places—Chiyu knows how to climb?

"Thank you. I'm glad to have confirmation that she's safe. May I contact Nezu—I mean Machi?" I asked the principal.

"Yep. Go for it, my boy."

Having received permission, I called Nezu immediately.

She picked up on the first ring. She must've been waiting with her phone gripped in her hands. *"Meester Hitoma?! Did you figure anything out?!"*

"Yeah. First, Chiyu's okay."

"—! Thank goodness…"

I could hear the tension flood out of her through the phone.

"Do you know where she is?!"

"According to the principal, she's in the forest, three hundred yards north of the dorm somewhere."

"Got it! I'll head there right—"

"Hold on, hold on. I only told you an approximation. The principal is going to pinpoint her location now, so let's go together. It would be bad if you passed her, wouldn't it?"

"Squeak… *Okay, you better run over!"*

"Yeah… Let's meet in front of the dorm. I'll be there right away," I promised.

"Run at full speed!" She then hung up.

Damn… I'm nearly at the age when running more than a hundred yards is agonizing. I have no choice, though. It's been a while, but the situation demands that I sprint at full power…

"Sorry to keep you waiting, Principal Karasuma," I said.

"It's all right! Well, let's get going, my boy."

"Say again?"

He's going to come along?

…I wasn't in tip-top shape, but I was pretty confident I could outrun the principal.

I only needed him to tell me the location, but I didn't know how to turn him down respectfully and still ask for his help. Of course, he was the one who knew precisely where Chiyu was, so it would be reassuring for him to come along…

"Um, Principal Karasuma…," I said hesitantly.

"Do you know what the fastest mode of travel is among land, air, and sea, Mr. Hitoma?" he asked.

"Hmm? What do you—? Wait. What?!"

The principal smiled at me and tipped himself forward, falling toward me. I caught him without thinking.

Crap. This might be another emergency! What should I do?!

"Principal Karasuma! Please get a hold of yourself! Principal?!"

No response. It wasn't a joke. The principal lay unresponsive in my arms and was gradually getting stiffer.

This couldn't possibly get any worse—

"Calm down, my boy!" someone said.

"Huh? Where—?" I yelped.

"Above your head!"

It was the principal's voice.

"What?!"

I looked up to where the voice was coming from and found a pure-white bird flapping above me.

This bird—it was the one that always perched on the principal's shoulder.

"No way—," I muttered.

"Hmm? I think you've already guessed, but this is my true form!"

"THE BIRD IS TALKING!!!"

"Oh, you can set that body down wherever, Mr. Hitoma. It's my favorite one!" the white crow said happily.

Weird. At second glance, it seems to have grown bigger than when it's on the principal's shoulder...

"Could you open the window for me?" he asked.

"Oh, uh, yes."

Unsure what else to do, I did as the crow directed.

When I turned back around, the crow had grown as large as me.

"Ack! You're massive!"

He was menacing. A beast of a bird. Seriously terrifying.

What's gonna happen to me?!

"When I'm free from the principal's body, I grow really big!"

"I-isn't that a little *too* big...?"

He was closer to the size of an ostrich rather than a crow.

"It's more convenient this way! All the better to carry you!"

"What?"

Carry me?

"Now, dear boy! To the dorm we go!! We're off!"

"Huh—? Wait. Agh!"

The crow circled behind me and grabbed me firmly by my shoulders. My body was lifted into the air.

No way. Not again—!

I remembered this feeling of weightlessness; it brought back memories of when Haneda took me up to the roof last year and scooped me up, bridal style. This, however, was different.

The principal carried me the way an eagle does its prey. I wanted to point out that he was a crow and not an eagle, but I was too shaken up to actually say anything.

"Okay! One nonstop flight to the dorm coming up!!"

"EEEAAAHHH!!!!!"

The two of us soared through the window and out of the office.

* * *

We flew—well, *he* flew carrying me, half-unconscious from the shock, for around thirty seconds before we spotted Nezu.

She hadn't noticed us yet.

For good reason: She had her gaze fixed on the road leading from the school to the dorm. Her face was stony. There was no way she would imagine we were going to fly. I certainly wouldn't.

But for real, this was terrifying. I was on the verge of tears the whole time. My breathing was weird, and I was sweating out of every pore.

With great flaps of his wings, the principal sped up. Nezu glanced up and met my eyes.

"M-Meester Hitoma! How can you be playing around while I'm here worrying my butt off?!"

"I'm not playing around! I'm scared out of my wits!" The principal set me down on the ground, but unable to catch my balance, I collapsed. "Oof!"

It wasn't a huge deal, although my suit was covered with dirt. The principal landed next to me.

"What's the deal with this bird?!" Nezu asked. "It's humongous! Did it mutate or something?! Spooky!!"

"Machi," the crow said.

"*Squeak-squeak!* I-it can talk? Smart bird... Meester Hitoma, are you a bird whisperer?"

"No, this is—!" I started to say.

But the crow finished my sentence: "I'm the principal!"

"Really?!" Nezu darted uncertain glances at me.

I wanted to explain to her, but I didn't have the luxury. My brain had gone helter-skelter the way it did after riding a roller coaster. My head spinning, I finally managed to stand up.

Nezu sidled up to me. "Is this the same principal I know, Meester Hitoma? The old-timey-speech guy?" she asked.

"That's, uh, some nickname," I replied.

I bet she has a secret nickname for me, too.

"...Ah, I thought you knew that this was my true form, my dear," the principal said to Nezu.

"Huh?! Did I?"

"I neither publicize nor conceal my true form. I've flown around like this several times. I thought it was common knowledge among the students, but it appears that I was wrong?"

"I definitely didn't know. But if you're really the principal, why did you come in this form—? Wait! Is Chiyu in danger?!" Nezu cried.

"That much I'm afraid I don't know. In any case, let us go to Chiyu. Get on my shoulder, my dear!"

"Will do!"

"Um, and me...?" I asked.

"I'll carry you the same way as earlier."

"No, that was pretty awf— Aghhh!"

Thus, the principal flew through the forest with me and Nezu in tow.

* * *

"So this is what it's like to be in the sky…," said Nezu. "It's amazing! Right, Meester Hitoma?"

"Nghhhhh…!!"

"You look like you're having fun, *squeak*!"

"What makes you think that?!" I cried.

"It's written all over your face—" Then she screamed. "Chiyu!!" Gone was her nonchalance.

"What?! Where?!" I asked. I hadn't seen Chiyu yet, but Nezu had found her, apparently.

"On top of that tree!" Nezu cried.

Which tree? I thought, but then I saw Chiyu. She was in a roughly ten-meter-tall tree in the direction the principal was flying. She had climbed quite far up. When we got closer, I could tell that she was clinging to the tree so that she wouldn't fall.

Chiyu noticed us, turning teary eyes our way.

"Chiyu!" I called.

"Chiyu! We're coming to help, so don't move!" Nezu said.

Chiyu was trembling, but she nodded.

"Let's land for a moment," the principal said.

"Save her, Principal Karasuma!" Nezu pleaded. "I'll do anything! Please!"

"Of course, my dear," he reassured her.

We dropped in altitude. The principal landed at the base of the tree Chiyu had climbed.

"Whoa!" I cried as I was tossed to the ground. Once again unable to catch my balance, I collapsed.

"Machi, you can choose to wait here with Mr. Hitoma or fly up with me," the principal offered.

"I'm going with you, of course!" she declared.

"All right. In that case, Mr. Hitoma, please wait here. Machi and I are going ahead!"

The principal hoisted Nezu onto his back and lifted off with a flap of his wings. Accompanied by the sound of the wind, he flew to where Chiyu was crouched.

I wondered whether two people could ride on his back, but since the Nezu sisters were both small, they should've been able to fit, if barely.

The principal must have thought the same before offering to take Nezu.

"Chiyuuu! Come here!" Nezu called. "Principal Karasuma! A little closer!"

Down on the ground, I could see Nezu desperately stretching out her hand from atop the principal's back. I was secretly sweating bullets. *If she leans out that far, she's going to fall.*

"M-Machi…!" Chiyu cried, stretching out her own hand as far as it would go.

The principal eased his massive body as close to Chiyu as possible.

"Chiyu! Jump! I promise I'll catch you!" Nezu urged.

"What?!" I yelped. "Are you sure?!"

"Yes!"

I couldn't help but be anxious at her overly daring plan, but Nezu seemed certain she would be able to catch Chiyu.

Preparing for the worst, I moved to stand right beneath Chiyu.

Chiyu steeled herself, screwed her eyes shut, and—jumped to her sister!

There was a *thud.* The principal's body rocked.

"Are you two okay?!" I called. I couldn't see them from where I was. *It looks like they're both on the principal's back, but…*

"See, Chiyu, I caught you like I said I would," Nezu told her.

"Bwahhhhh!" came Chiyu's relieved sobs from above me. "Machi!!"

"Thank goodness," the principal said. "I'll land slowly. Grab on tight, you two!"

He drifted closer to the ground. It seemed that the rescue mission was a success. *Phew…*

"Don't go so far forward, Chiyu," Nezu cautioned. "It's safer close to me."

"Won't that put you in danger, Machi...?" Chiyu asked.

"Nezu, stay alert until you land!" I yelled.

"That's right. It's dangerous, so hold still," the principal added.

Chiyu and Nezu were seated as if they were riding a tandem bike, with Chiyu near the principal's head and Nezu near his tail.

If Chiyu sat too far forward, she would be too close to the wing and shoulder joint. There was a risk she could fall from that position...

"I'm fine!" Nezu said. "I rode all the way here on the principal's back, so— *Squeak?*"

"Machi...!" Chiyu cried.

"Nezu...!" I hollered.

From the ground, I saw Nezu wobble on the principal's back. She looked like she was going to fall. Nezu and the principal immediately rebalanced themselves. However, Chiyu was on his back, too, so if he leaned too far, Chiyu would be the one in danger!

They were slightly less than five meters above the ground.

In that case—

I extended both arms toward Nezu. "Nezu! Over here!" I shouted.

"...! Meester Hitoma!"

She grasped what I was trying to do and immediately set herself up to fall safely.

"Mr. Hitoma! I will take care of Chiyu. I'm leaving Machi to you...!" the principal told me.

Chiyu was in a crouch, securely settled on the principal's back. Good. I wasn't confident I could catch both of them.

They dropped farther in altitude before Nezu fell from the principal's back. She was two meters from my arms.

At that height, we might be able to pull off this stunt without any injuries—!

"Oof!!" I groaned as Nezu slammed into my arms with a *thump.*

"Meester Hitoma?"

I had managed to catch her, but my newly thirty-year-old body was even more frail than I had thought. My torso, back, and hips were unable to endure the impact of her fall, and I collapsed into the thickets. Thankfully, since I had fallen backward, Nezu was unharmed.

"Are you okay, Meester Hitoma…?" Nezu asked.

"Y-yeah…for the most part…"

She was sitting astride me and looking worriedly at me.

Ah, there's a leaf in her hair.

What's up with my luck today…? Does the earth have something against me?

Through all the tumbles and falls, I was covered from head to toe with dirt—now with leaves added into the mix, I felt as if I had become one with nature. My back hurt, but it didn't seem as though I'd strained anything, which was a relief.

The principal and Chiyu made a safe landing.

As I struggled to sit up, the principal said, "Don't force yourself, Mr. Hitoma. I'll have Haruka come check on you, so take a breather for the moment."

"Oh, all right…"

"Haruka" was Haruka Karasuma, the school nurse and the principal's daughter.

Hold on. How long is Nezu going to stay on top of me? I'd like her to get off soon.

The principal smiled at Chiyu. "I'm happy to see you safe, my dear."

While I had been busy eating dirt and grass, Chiyu had ridden back down on the principal's back.

"Principal Karasuma, Machi, Meester Hitoma…" She looked at each of us with watery eyes. Her voice was trembling. She was having trouble finding words.

"Chiyu…," Nezu said, shooting to her feet.

She had finally gotten off me. I thought about telling her off jokingly, but the atmosphere was too tense for that.

"Chiyu, why…why did you do this?!" she yelled. Chiyu twitched at Nezu's sudden outburst. "Why did you come here alone?! What you did was dangerous! Without Principal Karasuma and Meester Hitoma, I might not have found you!"

"I-I'm sorry… But, Machi—"

"You caused so much trouble… And I… Do you know how worried I was…?!"

Tears were streaming down Nezu's cheeks. She grabbed Chiyu's hands and squeezed them tight. It was like she was trying to reassure herself that Chiyu was actually there.

"Wa…wahhhhh!! I'm sorry. I'm so, so sorry, Machi!!" Chiyu was sobbing uncontrollably.

Nezu hugged her close. "…Think about what you did wrong and tell everyone you're sorry, Chiyu."

Chiyu looked as if she was trying to say something in between sobs. Nezu stroked her sister's back softly as she held her.

"Huh? Are you holding something?" I asked, spotting a yellow fruit in Chiyu's hands, which were locked around Nezu's back.

Is that a—?

"*Hic…* This is…," Chiyu muttered.

Nezu released Chiyu and looked at the fruit in question. "A…loquat…?"

It was a large loquat with shiny skin. It looked like it was at the peak of its ripeness.

"*Hic…* You finally got into the advanced class. You're doing your best every day… You were studying hard today, too, so I thought you'd be happy if you had something yummy to eat when you got back," Chiyu explained while wiping away her tears. "That's why I…looked for it…by myself. And—"

Nezu's eyes seemed to sparkle. "…You did that for me?" she said. She tilted her head down slightly and mumbled, "I see…," quietly under her breath. Then she faced Chiyu again.

"You did it all for me," she said.

"But I…!"

"Chiyu." Nezu looked directly at Chiyu with kind eyes. "Thank you. You must have been scared in a place like this all alone. And even so, you tried your best. You're brave. But you know, we all really care about you. So when you do dangerous things without thinking, it makes us sad. I was beside myself worrying if you had hurt yourself, and if that happened,

no food would taste delicious until I knew you were better. So—can you promise me, if there's a next time, you'll take me with you?"

With tears still dripping down her face, Chiyu responded with a deep nod.

Nezu smiled, looking every bit the big sister. "Smart girl! I knew you would understand, Chiyu!"

"Sorry… I made you worry…"

"Yeah. I'm sorry for getting angry," Nezu replied.

"Principal… Meester Hitoma… Sorry…," Chiyu then added.

"We're happy you're safe, my dear!" the principal said.

"It's such a relief," I told her. *Seriously. I'm so glad she's okay.*

Gurrrrgle…

Suddenly, from Nezu's direction, I heard a funny sound that was completely at odds with the atmosphere.

"*Squeak-squeak…* Now that I don't have to worry anymore, I'm *starving*," Nezu groaned.

"Nezu… You were so cool up until now…," I said.

What a waste. However, seeing her act like her usual self took a load off my mind.

"Machi! Let's eat this together when we get back to the dorm!" Chiyu said.

"Sounds good! Hmm, a loquat, huh…? I got it! Let's make jelly! We can ask Ryouko to teach us!"

"Okay!"

"What do you think?" Nezu turned and asked.

The principal and I exchanged glances.

Which 'you' does she mean?

Noticing our confusion, Nezu clarified, "Both of you. Principal Karasuma! Meester Hitoma!" She held out the loquat Chiyu had picked. "Once the jelly is done, we'll share some with you! It's a…thank-you and an apology for today. I don't want to just focus on remorse. I wanna show you how happy I am, too!" The bashful Nezu was being sweeter than usual.

Next to her, Chiyu was nodding enthusiastically.

The principal beamed. "Thank you, Machi. I'm looking forward to it!"

"…What about you, Meester Hitoma?" Nezu asked, peering worriedly at my face.

"Happy"… Not just remorse—how very Nezu. That must be how she brings smiles to everyone around her.

My answer was obvious: "Thanks. I can't wait."

Nezu's face instantly lit up. "I swear it's gonna be delicious!"

"I'll do my best to help, too!!" declared Chiyu.

The two of them jumped up and down as they chatted excitedly about their plans to make the jelly together right away, tonight.

The forest air had taken on a trace of early summer, but it was still somewhat cool.

A refreshing loquat jelly, homemade by the Nezu sisters. Better break out the fancy tea my parents sent me.

A Misanthrope
Teaches a Class for
Demi-Humans (2)
Mr. Hitoma, Won't You Show Us the Light of Hope...?

The Misanthrope and the Blossom's Morrow

The buzz of the cicadas' song filled the air.

It was the break between classes. As I walked to my next class, I gazed absently through the windows. It was a dazzling, sunny day without a single cloud in sight. The invigorating, triumphant blue sky expanded over the school.

In the forest where the school was, one could feel the pulse of nature, so the seasons felt richer and more tangible to me than they used to. It was the first time I had heard the cicadas this year.

Such was the scene this early June day.

"Ah, um… Mr. Hitoma…!" I heard someone call.

The one who had stopped me was Isaki Ohgami, a teenage werewolf girl.

"U-uhhh… I wanted to discuss my future aspirations, or, um, share them…I guess…," she told me.

"Right, of course. How's after school today?"

When she heard my reply, her expression went slack with relief, and she smiled. "That would be great. Thank you." She bowed and padded off to her own classroom.

Ohgami's future aspirations.

In April, during her self-introduction, she'd said she was still figuring out why she wanted to be human. I had given her until summer began; I wondered how she felt now.

* * *

"We want to become two separate humans."

Those were the first words out of Ohgami's mouth when we met after school. She jumped straight to the point. Her resolute expression put both her conviction and anxiousness on display.

"I see. Instead of becoming one person, you'll live on as two," I said.

Isaki Ohgami, werewolf.

Before coming to this school, she'd turned human only on the night of the full moon. Her personality would change, too. The docile lupine Isaki and the vivacious human Isaki—their goal in the beginning was to collapse their personalities into one. However...

I had to admit, I was relieved to hear both Ohgamis would live on.

Hold on. Huh?

"You want to become two separate humans... Right now, you're two people in the same body... So you're saying each of you will have your own bodies...? Am I getting that right?" I asked.

"Y-yes..."

"...Is that possible?"

"Oh! Actually, the director explained a lot of things to me when I enrolled, and it's not impossible to separate our personalities into different bodies, apparently...!"

"That's really something..."

The director is seriously OP. Is there anything she can't do? Ohgami should've just aimed for that from the start... Ah, but—

"You didn't like the sound of that at first?" I asked.

"That's right... I thought it would make me uncomfortable if there was someone who was so similar to me..."

In a doppelgänger sense, I guess?

"I see..."

I didn't think it was particularly weird...or did I? Identical twins were pretty much the same thing... Twins were together since birth, so maybe that was different.

"But I realized it would be okay after talking with the other me... So I'm thinking of becoming a separate person from full-moon me...!"

Ohgami was gripping her hands tightly in front of her chest as a show of resolve, but they were trembling. She must have arrived at this answer after a lot of thinking and worrying.

"Okay, got it," I said. "I'll let the principal and the director know."

"Thank you very much!" She broke into a broad grin. Her eyes were shiny with what might have been tears of relief.

Good for her. The other Ohgami must be happy, too.

"So then what will you do when you're human? Up until now, your goal was to study at a private liberal arts college. Has that changed? And what about the other Ohgami's aspirations—?"

"...Huh?"

Hearing the sudden panicked edge in her voice, I took my eyes off my papers to look at Ohgami. Her face, which had been relaxed up until a second ago, was steadily growing paler.

Whoops. Don't tell me—?

"What do I do, Mr. Hitoma...?" Ohgami cried. "I didn't think that far ahead...!"

* * *

According to Ohgami, she had picked a goal that sounded appropriate without much thought. She was of the mind that as long as she could become human, anything was good enough.

Granted, there were plenty of students in your average human schools who picked their path half-heartedly to delay having to make a choice. It wasn't anything *bad*, but...

Ohgami declared, "I—I want to think about my future properly! Then I'll decide what to do...!"

Wow, look who's fired up.

She was usually quiet and meek, but for once, she was speaking clearly. She must've been highly motivated. Her journey started with finding what she wanted to learn, what she wanted to do going forward.

One obstacle after another.

Thus, Ohgami began the search for her goal as a human anew.

* * *

The next day after school, me and Ohgami were discussing her future again.

"Ughhh... Mr. Hitoma... I'm toast... I don't know up from down anymore...," she moaned.

"I know. It's not the kind of question you can answer right away," I replied.

"Agh..."

Ohgami's drooping ears twitched softly. The cuteness of it was kind of cathartic, though I felt guilty about that since she was down in the dumps.

"But I even asked everyone in class what their aspirations were," she said.

"Wow, good for you! That's great!"

"And what I got in response was—"

Usami: *"I want to be a doctor, so I have to take medical entrance exams! My current grades aren't nearly good enough... I'm going to work my butt off from now on!"*

Haneda: *"Hmm... I want to go to a college for music and major in composition, I think? It's fun to make something from nothing."*

Nezu: *"You want to know my aspirations? I wanna study food science, research what makes food delicious, and contribute to culinary culture!"*

Ryuzaki: *"Umm...a—a bride...? Maybe? Huh?! Oh! Like* career *aspirations...?! Ahem. I'm going to a college where I can study world history! I'm interested in what humans were up to when I was a dragon. Also...Mr. Rei teaches social studies, you get what I mean...?"*

Kurosawa: *"Zzzzzz..."*

"Everyone put serious thought into what they were going to do...!" Ohgami whined.

Has Kurosawa seriously thought about it, though...?

"Ughhh... Is there anything I want to do...? What *do* I want after I become human...? I'm not like everyone else; I don't have anything I like or am good at. I don't have any particular goals..."

"That's normal, you know," I told her.

"Huh...?"

"When I was in high school, I had a hard time deciding what to do with my life, too...," I explained. "Actually, my dad is a teacher. It wasn't as if I was following in his footsteps, but that's the environment I grew up in, so I ended up in education and somehow got my teacher's license, and now I'm here."

"You *somehow* got your license?"

Ooh, she's sharp. Truthfully, I had studied my butt off—or more accurately, the college I'd gone to had worked me like a dog. But for the purposes of the message I wanted to convey, I left that out.

"More or less! What I'm trying to say is, thinking about your future is important, but you don't need to force yourself."

Especially for people like Ohgami. It was highly likely that overthinking would only cause her to miss the forest for the trees.

"Agh... You're right... It's not good to rush...," she said. "Thank you. I feel calmer now... *Sigh.*"

Hope I didn't end up bumming her out... Although... Hmm, I can relate to her restlessness...

"I wonder what *she* thinks...," Ohgami whispered.

"Hmm?"

"Oh, I'm sorry. Just talking to myself."

The soft-spoken words were for Ohgami's ears only, but at the same time, they seemed to be directed at someone else. I was sure she wanted to consult with the other Ohgami. However, her other half appeared only during the full moon. She had no choice but to wait. The next full moon was in a week.

"I want to meet her...," Ohgami mumbled.

Come to think of it, the rest of us got to meet Full-Moon Ohgami once a month, but Ohgami couldn't meet her other self directly... My heart squeezed painfully at the realization. The one who wanted to meet with her preppy alter ego was Ohgami herself.

That day, we called it quits.

For the week until the full moon, Ohgami was slightly more absent-minded than usual.

* * *

The June full moon was called the "strawberry moon," apparently. That was what the TV anchor lady said during the morning news.

The trendy Ohgami was due to come to school that day.

As I was walking down the hall to the classroom, I reflected on the conversation I'd had with Ohgami about her future aspirations.

I'll have to talk to Ohgami about her future and her goals today... But how do I bring it up...? Hmm, I guess I'll pull her aside after school again—

"Morning, Mr. Hitoma!!" Ohgami called out to me just as I was thinking about her. "Hey! You and Isaki talked for *ages* about our aspirations! Now you know—we're gonna become two people! Awesome, right?! Oh, and in the future, I wanna work in the beauty industry!"

"Whoa! Talk about a quick resolution!!" I exclaimed.

She had answered everything I had planned to ask her as part of her morning how-do-you-do.

"Huh? Whaddaya mean?" Ohgami asked.

"Oh, um, don't worry about it..."

I was so shocked that I'd accidentally said what I was thinking out loud...

"Oh yeah? Okay, whatever. Anyway, listen to this! The other Isaki wrote a *ton* about the future in our exchange diary. She's seriously the cutest! She seems pretty torn, though," Ohgami said. "Personally, I just want to do something I'm interested in. Remember when I was Karin's sidekick that one time? In April, I think? You know—you were involved and all that jazz. Anyway, that's when I realized that it's suuuper fun to see a person's sweeter side. I thought it'd be nice to help more and more people, and that's how I decided what I want to do! That's my future aspiration!"

She giggled and flashed a peace sign. It didn't seem like she was troubled at all about her future. Quite the opposite, in fact: She was overflowing with passion over her interests.

"Okay, I got it," I said.

"Good! Thanks, Mr. Hitoma! Can I count on you to look after the other Isaki?" she asked.

"Yeah… I plan to do whatever I can to help."

"Okay. Great to hear! Besides, you know how Isaki said she didn't have any interests or special skills or goals? I don't think that's true at all!"

"Oh yeah? How do you see her?"

"She's super kind! She's serious and hardworking! I love that about her!" Ohgami declared. "Ah, yeah, did you know, Mr. Hitoma? I don't have a lot of time to do what I want, right? So Isaki has been compiling the latest trends for me! Look! She wrote it all down in this notebook! Talk about a huge time-saver! It makes me so happy to think she did all this for me! Angels like her are one in a million! I wonder what I can do to repay her… The way Isaki cares so much for other people is amazing! I want to learn from her! And that's the thing! That's her spark! It's not just that she did something for me. It's the fact that she's thinking about me that makes me happy! And it's not just me, either. I think she pays attention to everyone around her. Plus, she does it naturally. It's wonderful. It feels like love! That's it! I think I said everything I wanted to! I can't wait to see what Isaki decides to do in the future!"

After saying her piece, Ohgami up and disappeared… *What a free spirit…*

She'd left in the direction of the classroom. Maybe she had already gone in.

I get it now…

The usual Ohgami was more of a supporting character, if I had to say, and was very considerate toward others… It was true that she often helped out in subtle ways, like refocusing the conversation when it was derailed.

Man, I could stand to learn a few things from her…

Afterward, in class, Ohgami told me about her plans to enter the beauty industry in more detail.

Specifically, she wanted to go to a cosmetology school. She also said, "I want to get certified as a nail tech and a stylist, too!" Seeing her shining with her hopes and dreams for the future, I found myself hoping that her dreams would soon come true.

* * *

The next day was the day after the full moon.

Ohgami appeared in the teachers' office, her hair in her usual braid. "Um, Mr. Hitoma…"

What could she want?

"Yeah? What is it?" I asked.

"Um, about your talk with the other me yesterday…"

Oh, this must be about her future plans.

"Ah, sure. It's a bit awkward to talk here. Let's go to another—"

"That's okay! I don't want to bother you! It'll be quick, so I don't mind talking here…!"

"A-are you sure?"

"Yes…"

My effort to be considerate might have stressed her out instead.

Ohgami took a small breath.

"I heard what you talked about with Isaki… I decided what I want to do in the future, and I wanted to let you know: I'll continue on to a private liberal arts school. But I won't do that just to go with the flow. I want to study literature, with a focus on memoirs, letters, and other such writings. That way I can study communication through written records of people's lives. That's how Isaki and I have been talking all this time."

Then she added bashfully, "Isaki said so many nice things about me. I don't know what to say."

Full-Moon Ohgami had really laid it on thick. It had sounded practically like she was bragging about her S.O.

"To be honest, I was torn between literature and social services. But I think Isaki's impression of me is a result of being able to properly convey my thoughts and feelings to her… And, um, her compliments are maybe a little off the mark… Anyway, that is my future aspiration." She chuckled shyly and bashfully made a peace sign.

It was the same pose as Full-Moon Ohgami's, but different.

"Okay," I said. "I got it. It suits you."

"Heh-heh. Thank you."

Having made her report, she looked refreshed and more confident than usual.

Ohgami had found a new road forward through the other self who was inside her. The everyday life we humans lived was waiting for them after graduation. I was sure that both Ohgamis would cross many more mountains as they walked forward, step by step.

A Misanthrope
Teaches a Class for
Demi-Humans 2

Mr. Hitoma, Won't You Show Us the Light of Hope...?

The Misanthrope and the Summer
Vacation in the Forest

A MISANTHROPE TEACHES A CLASS FOR DEMI-HUMANS

It was a place for which there was no map.

A place so closely and carefully guarded that no one would find it.

The place where it all began.

* * *

T-minus one day until summer vacay!

In fact, with the closing ceremony over, all I had left was the end-of-the-day homeroom.

My head was already filled with thoughts about my plans starting the next day. The next installment of a survival game franchise I had been waiting forever for was finally being released. The developers must've gotten a grasp of the players' demands during summer vacation.

Becoming self-sufficient, expanding your base, making weapons, taming gigantic beasts... New character traits and appearances to choose from and new items as well. On top of that, I heard the map is bigger, too. Man, they really understand!

As I was daydreaming on my way back to the advanced classroom, a shout from behind startled me from my thoughts and stopped me in my tracks. "Meester Hitoma!"

"Ack! Oh, it's you, Nezu," I said. "Why'd you scare me like that...?"

She twirled around to stand in front of me, a twinkle in her eyes. "There's something I wanted to do over summer vacation after becoming an advanced student!"

"O-oh yeah...?"

"So I wanted to ask—"

Oh no. I have a bad feeling about this.

"—will you be our chaperone?"

I knew it!!

I'd gone to the river past the barrier last year. What a throwback… Frankly, it sounded like a pain. Plus, it was hot.

But I went with the class last year, so it's hard to say no now… What should I tell her…?

After debating for a little while, I realized I hadn't heard anything about her actual plan. Maybe it was more chill than last year's outing.

"…So what is it you want to do?" I asked Nezu.

"I wanna go camping and have a barbecue in the forest with the class!"

That's definitely going to be more tiring than last year!!

You can't fool me. I know very well that in situations like this, the guy is made to do all the heavy lifting.

…Well, whether or not they ask me, I'll feel the need to help out if I'm around, so it's fine. But I'd rather not go in the first place if I can avoid it. Sounds exhausting…

I was lost in my thoughts, getting reacquainted with the magnificently garbage side of myself, when Nezu called me back.

"Meester Hitoma?" She was looking at me with her head tilted quizzically.

"Oh, um, yeah. How about you ask the others what they think? About camping and barbecue and whatnot," I said.

"Okay! You're right! Thanks, Meester Hitoma!" she replied, then darted ahead of me toward the classroom.

Whoops. I forgot to warn her not to run in the hall.

Camping and barbecue… Considering the oddballs in the advanced class, they'll probably all agree to go. Haneda will be gung ho about the plan, Ohgami and Ryuzaki will go with the flow, and Kurosawa and Usami won't be bothered to argue.

* * *

August 12.

"It's great that everyone was free," Haneda said.

"*Squeak!* I can take credit, right?" Nezu asked.

"Don't misunderstand. I'm only here because Tobari said she would hold a tutoring session." Usami sniffed.

"*Squeak!* Really?"

"I came because...well, Mr. Rei's here."

"I'm rooting for ya, Karin!" Ohgami said.

It was past midsummer, but the heat was still fierce at this time of year.

The entire advanced class and I were gathered in front of the student dorm.

"Wa-ha-ha! You look like a limp noodle, Mr. Hitoma! I seriously can't!!" Ohgami cackled.

"Ohgami... I see it's a full-moon day...," I said.

It'd been a month since I'd last seen Ohgami's flashy alter ego. She was rocking a bare midriff, dressed as if she were going on an actual vacation.

"Your casual outfits are way too cute!" Ohgami gushed. "I wanna go clothes shopping with everyone sometime!"

Since it was summer break, we were all dressed casually, me included. It was a novel sight.

Ohgami had plenty to say about everyone's clothes:

"Usamiii! You look so fresh with that frilly white top! And those shorts and sneakers look *so* easy to move in. They're perfect for the occasion! You're killing it with this fit!"

"And, Machi! Those overalls are literally the best thing ever! It's like they were made for you! Gotta love the rough-and-tumble look!"

"I'm loving Tobari's sporty getup, too! The oversize T-shirt is actually super feminine and gives off major camping vibes!"

"Nothing beats gingham in the summer, right, Karin? It's fabulous! All those ribbons! And the lace! I can't handle the cuteness! The crop top is sexy, too! We're low-key twinning! Let's do a full-on twin outfit next time!

"And let's just take a hot sec to talk about Neneko's dress! Is it a set with your bolero? Even your parasol is black. Everything matches! It's lovely! The slightly sheer fabric gives it an ethereal look. Totes adorbs!"

Ohgami's torrent of compliments had everyone gaping like a fish. She really was passionate about fashion... Head over heels for it.

"And you, Mr. Hitoma... Um, don't you have anything better?" she said. "A T-shirt and jeans is fine and all, but isn't that a bit *too* basic? I wanna see a little more spark! Like a slightly flashier shirt, or...shirts with loud, colorful patterns are mad trendy right now. They're super cute! Or, like, put some thought into the color of your pants. You're tall and have a surprisingly decent build. You just gotta spruce yourself up more! Oh, accessories might suit you pretty well, too!"

"What, like a silver bangle or something?" I asked.

"Bulky much? I'm thinking more like a subtle chain necklace!"

Ohgami had answered my glib question more seriously than I had expected. Unsure what to say, I muttered, "Oh, okay..."

Awkward rejoinders are a bad habit of geeks like me...

"Now that we're all here, let's get going," Haneda declared.

"*Squeak!* I'm so excited!" Nezu chirped.

We set off into the forest. The road we were following was more of an animal trail than anything. It just met the bare, bare minimum for a road. It was my first time taking it.

Our goal was slightly southeast of the midpoint between the dorm and the hot springs. Apparently, there was a small clearing in that area. The information came from Haneda, so it should be accurate. She was the one leading us there, too. I took up the rear and was responsible for making sure the students didn't stray.

Since our destination was inside the barrier, we didn't need to apply for the rings, which was a load off my mind. There was no need for me to be on edge on the road. Last time, we had gone outside the barrier, so I'd had to look after the rings *and* the students...

It'd been a year since then. Minazuki, who had been with us at the time, had already graduated and was now living as an outstanding human.

Will someone be leaving us this year, too? I wondered.

The thought brought me a twinge of sadness.

* * *

I had a dream: One day, I wanted to relax in a hammock, rocked by its gentle sway.

"C-can it be…?!" I gasped.

"…Mmngh… *Zzz.*" Kurosawa yawned.

"It's a hammock. I figured it'd set the mood," Haneda said.

While Ryuzaki, Ohgami, and I were setting up the tents, and Nezu and Usami were preparing the food, Haneda and Kurosawa had been busy by the trees. I'd been curious about what they were up to, but who would've thought—?

"…Sleepability, solid B," Kurosawa said contentedly, swaying in the hammock.

"Yeah? Good!" Haneda replied.

I was a smidge jealous. No, very jealous. *Extremely* jealous. I wanted to do that.

"Oh my freaking gosh!!" Ohgami exclaimed. "I've never seen a hammock before! It looks so fun! Let me try next!"

"……*Zzzzz.*"

The hammock was already becoming Kurosawa's territory. Actually, it was amazing that she could sleep through the ruckus Ohgami was making…

The hammock was strung up in the shade under the trees. It looked comfortable.

"Also, we set up the grill for the barbecue and collected firewood!" Haneda reported.

"Thanks," I said. "The tents are up, too."

There was a large family-size tent for the students and a personal tent for me. The latter was simple and modest—it only needed to be unfolded—but the big one was the real deal and a pain to set up. The frame had to be anchored to the ground with stakes. We were all supposed to be beginners at this stuff, but Ohgami and Ryuzaki both outmatched me in terms of skill. I didn't know how to feel about that.

In a video game, a tent could be set up with the press of a button, but there wasn't anything so convenient in real life...

"Hey! Hitoma! Stop standing around and help with the food!!" Usami boomed from behind me.

"Usami, what the—? Don't point knives at people!" I yelped.

"Enough! If you don't come here already, I'm going to crush you!"

"Who has a crush?!" Ryuzaki shouted.

"Ugh, I'm so not in the mood. You help, too, Karin," Usami said.

"Nooo! Oh, fine—as long as I can be with Mr. Rei!"

Ryuzaki... She jumped into the conversation herself, right in front of a stray bullet...

"Seriously... I can't believe the prep isn't done yet!" Usami griped.

"Sorry, Usami, but what should I do?" Haneda asked.

"Get the pot for the rice ready."

"'Kaaay."

"I wanna help make the rice, too!" Ohgami declared, so she and Haneda got down to work together.

Next to Usami, who was cutting the corn, Nezu was chopping the onions, sniffling as she did so. "*Squeeeak!* Stupid onions! Sure they taste good in any dish! Sure they can do it all, from seasoning to playing the starring role! But they've gotten too big for their britches! *Squeeeak!!*"

Good luck, Nezu. Don't give up. The barbecue you've always wanted is just a step away.

* * *

"I'm stuffed!! That was delicious!!" Nezu said, sitting in the hammock and patting her belly in satisfaction. She looked exactly like an old drunk in a dive bar. I wanted to hand her a toothpick to complete the ensemble, but I had to be content with my imagination.

While Nezu was lazing about, Ohgami went over to her and hugged

her tight. "Good for you, Machi! Great suggestion! I had a lot of fun, too."
Ohgami was the tallest in the class, and Nezu, who was the shortest, was
swallowed up in her embrace.

"Ichaki! Heh-heh-heh… Actually, the fun's not over yet! Ta-daaa!! The
go-to barbecue finale: s'mores!!"

"For real?! *Sa-weet!!*" Ohgami squealed.

Where did those marshmallows come from?! She didn't have them a min-
ute ago!

"What's wrong, Mr. Rei?" Ryuzaki asked. "Do you secretly hate
marshmallows?"

"No, that's not it!"

"C'mere and roast your marshmallow, Mr. Hitoma," said Haneda.
"You can sandwich 'em between these graham crackers. Dig in."

"Ooh, sounds delicious." My mouth was watering just thinking
about it.

Usami and Kurosawa had gotten the jump on us and were already
toasting their marshmallows over the fire. A sweet scent filled the air.

Mmmm, the smell of burnt sugar is making me high… The charred bits
are tasty, too… Maaan, who cares where the marshmallows came from…

"Wa-ha-ha! You look so dopey, Mr. Hitoma! LMAO! Say cheese!"
Ohgami cackled.

"…Whoa—!"

The sound of her phone camera snapped me out of my daydreams.

Her phone hadn't left her hand the entire day, and she'd been snap-
ping photos like a maniac.

"What are you going to do with that photo?" I scowled.

"What do you mean? We're making memories. Besides, I wanna show
the other Isaki!"

I couldn't tell her to stop after hearing that. But wasn't the other
Ohgami seeing everything anyway? I figured that even if they were seeing the same thing, they experienced it differently.

"Hey, why don't we go to the hot springs after we rest a bit?" Haneda
suggested. "The girls' bath is only open till nine, so we don't have time to
waste."

"Yay! This'll be my first time going to the hot springs with everyone! I can't wait!" Ohgami said. "By the way, how much groping will y'all tolerate before you draw the line?"

"How can you ask that with a straight face?" Nezu said.

"I just gotta say, Karin: Your boobs are freakin' huge!" Ohgami squealed.

"Hey, did you forget I'm here? Save that talk for the baths," I pleaded.

If this were the classroom, I could have slipped out. But unfortunately, in the forest, I had no place to run.

"Fiiine," Ohgami replied. "Ha-ha! That must've been too *stimulating* for you!"

"Whuh-oh, Mr. Hitoma's a closet pervert," added Haneda.

"Quiet, Haneda," I spat.

"Wa-ha-ha! He's blushing! LOL!"

"I...think it's kind of cute...," Ryuzaki said. "I like that side of you, Mr. Rei...!"

"*Sigh...* Pathetic," Usami groaned.

"*Zzzzz...*"

"Enough already! Hurry up and go take your bath!" I yelled.

Having my chaste feelings toyed with made me itch with mortification. You might wonder what a man my age was doing acting like a young maiden—and I did, too, to some extent—but I...wanted to keep living the dream.

Nezu walked up to me, a smile on her face. "Meester Hitoma."

That's a smile as pure as the Virgin Mary's... Maybe she understands my feel—

"A closet pervert's just as bad as a regular pervert."

For the briefest instant, I thought: *You're just asking to be smacked.*

* * *

The hot springs: paradise in the heart of the mountains!!

The hours were divided by gender, with the men's baths open from ten PM to six AM and the women's from seven AM to nine PM.

In the hour between operation times, students cleaned the baths as part-time jobs.

It was my first time going to the hot springs! I'd wanted to go ever since moving into the staff dorm, but it was out of the way, so I hadn't yet had the chance.

The students had set off a short while earlier.

It was getting dark, so I was a little worried. Well…even if anything were to happen, Haneda was with them, so it would probably be all right.

In any case, I was thrilled to finally get to go to the hot springs I had been curious about ever since I saw them mentioned in the job listing. Ohgami had mouthed off about groping and whatnot, but she must've been trying to hide her own embarrassment. Surely she wouldn't actually do that to her classmates.

I wondered if they were enjoying themselves. I sure would when it came my turn!

* * *

"Hee-hee-hee! Karin! Can I touch your boobs?!" Isaki asked.

"Isaki…," said Usami. "You're being kind of a sleaze…"

"But the bigger they are, the more exciting it is, no?!" Isaki protested.

"You want to? I don't mind," Karin said.

"Score!" Isaki cheered. "Thanks, Karin! Wanna cop a feel of mine in return?!"

Usami sniffed. "Do you even hear yourself…?"

"I would love to, Isaki!" Karin replied.

"You would?!" Usami cried.

"Now, then… Without further ado, pardon me…," Isaki said. "Whoa, these things weigh a ton!"

"Yeah, they do… I don't pay much attention usually, but they float in the bath, see? That's when I notice it. Like, how heavy they are usually, I mean," Karin explained.

"Sounds rough," Usami said.

"Yours seem like they wouldn't give you any trouble at all," Karin said back.

"You trying to start something?" snapped Usami.

The hot springs were filled with a gaggle of advanced students.

I kept an eye on Isaki and her blatant sexual harassment while I engaged in a leisurely soak.

As the director, I built this place for my own amusement.

It was an open-air bath, which meant I could look up at the night sky and the stars I had alighted in the past.

To have somewhere I could relax and enjoy the view—that was why I built these baths.

It was a little rowdy at the moment, but I didn't hate it.

Machi was rinsing herself off in the shower area. Isaki and Karin were... fondling each other's chests. What *were* they up to? From the fragments of their conversation that I could hear, it seemed they were discussing their breast sizes and shapes and tactility. I briefly thought about joining them, but I wasn't in the mood; I was content to just watch. Usami was off to the side, looking on with a mixture of disgust and fascination.

Oh, and Neneko—she was sitting in the corner of the spring with only her feet dipped in the water.

I waded over to her. "You're not coming in?"

"...No... I hate...water...," she mumbled.

"Awww, it feels great, though."

"...It's wet. And uncomfortable."

"But you'll stay here with us, at least?"

"..."

Is that silence a yes?

"Make sure you don't get too cold," I said.

"...I know," she replied.

I returned to my earlier spot.

Neneko seemed aloof, but she'd still keep us company.

I hadn't thought she'd even come camping with us, but she actually filled out all the registration forms and paperwork beforehand. As expected of a student whose grades rivaled Usami's. I'd pulled out all the stops when creating the form, too. Taking Neneko's prior efforts into consideration, I could forgive her for dozing off while we were setting things up. She was trying to fit in with the class in her own way.

"Uchami…!! You and me! Sauna battle!!" Machi had finished scrubbing herself and was squeaky-clean.

Business as usual. I watched over them with a smile.

"I refuse to participate in such a worthless activity." Usami sniffed.

"Oh-ho? Are you scared of losing? Heh-heh!"

"Your attempts to provoke me are lame. What are you, five?"

"The one who runs before the fight ♪ has less than a child's might. ♪ I'm talking 'bout you, Uchami! ♪" Machi sang.

"What'd you saaay?! That song is slander! You're the worst!!" Usami shouted.

"Mad about it? Then meet me in the sauna!"

"You asked for it!!"

Oh, Usami… She played right into Machi's hands. Machi took full advantage of how Usami's a sore loser… Usami can be so easy sometimes.

I looked up at the sky again.

Wonder what Mr. Hitoma's up to.

* * *

The noisy students were finally asleep. Blessed silence fell over me.

When they had come back from the springs, they had been dead on their feet.

Usami and Nezu had overexerted themselves in their sauna battle. Nezu must have egged Usami on. Usami had won through sheer stubbornness, I had heard, but I wished she would put that willpower to more productive—and less dangerous—feats.

Ohgami and Ryuzaki had carried the exhausted combatants back to the tent. Kurosawa had made a beeline for the tent, grumpier than usual; it seemed that the hot springs hadn't been to her taste. Haneda was looking after Usami and Nezu and making sure they were staying hydrated. I wasn't allowed in the student tent, so her help was a godsend.

Then, after the day's shenanigans, late at night...

The soak in my long-yearned-after hot springs should have relieved me of all my exhaustion, but maybe because my circadian rhythm had been thrown out of whack over summer break, I couldn't sleep. Instead, I left my tent and sneaked into the hammock for a little rest.

The gentle sway of the hammock made me feel at ease.

Will I catch a cold if I fall asleep here? I never want to leave this spot, though.

I stared up at the cloudless sky.

Is there life to be found on the stars?

Ack. I sound like a middle schooler.

My face grew hot with embarrassment.

There were downsides to growing up, too. Your worldview certainly expanded, but consequently, you saw things that were better off not being seen. I had encountered loads of situations where "ignorance is bliss" was applicable.

Whoa. A shooting star.

A streak of light blazed through the night sky.

When had I stopped making wishes?

The starry sky was far higher and wider than it was in my head.

When...had I given up on having my wishes come true?

It was always a given that the stars were out of reach, but I was different back then.

"Mr. Hitoma. You're still awake?" asked a voice from beside me.

"Haneda?"

When did she get here?

She was wearing the same clothes from earlier. Maybe she'd changed back into them?

"I could ask you the same," I said. "I thought everyone was asleep."

"They are. Machi's even having a feast in her dreams."

Yep... I can easily imagine that... I'm glad she's still in such good spirits, at least.

"There's a place I want to go," Haneda added. "Come with me?"

"Are you sure?"

"Yep. It's this way. Let's go."

She turned on her heel. I had no idea where we were headed, but I followed her, feeling adventurous.

Haneda walked off into the forest, in the opposite direction from the dorms and hot springs. We were moving farther to the southeast. There wasn't so much as an animal trail. It was creepy in the lightless forest despite the light from the full moon. A seedling of fear sprouted in my heart.

Out of nowhere, I took a blow to my forehead, like I had been punched. "Oof! What?!" I cried.

"Oh, whoops. You ran into a tree, huh? Makes sense with your height," Haneda said. "Sorry I couldn't warn ya. Are you okay?"

Tree? Oh, that's what it was... I wasn't paying attention...

"Y-yeah, I'm fine... Thanks for asking..."

I wasn't used to walking in the forest, so I had no idea what to look out for... For the moment, I decided to watch where I was going at least...

After we walked for a while longer, I saw a building of sorts.

"Is that a shrine?" I said.

It was old. The shrine building was wooden, and its roof was overgrown with plants, but it hadn't rotted. It was as if someone came regularly to maintain it, to preserve it.

Haneda spun around to look my way. "This is where the school began."

The wind blew through, and the forest clamored in response.

"Here...?" I asked.

"Yeah. At first, we held it at Shirou's shrine."

Shirou's shrine? Does that mean this shrine is where the principal was enshrined as a crow tengu...?

"This sure takes me back—it all started when a dryad declared she wanted to become human," Haneda said. "I didn't think anything of it. I just turned her into a human and sent her off into the human world. But it didn't go so great."

She took a seat on the stairs leading up to the main hall and started to reminisce. Her eyes looked off into the past. They seemed to say, *How precious those times were.*

"It was strange. Nothing went well. I listened carefully to all the dryad's stories. The reason was because they hadn't understood human customs and culture. That's when it hit me: You just needed the right preparation before diving in and becoming human."

Haneda leaned against the railing, tilted her head up, and met my gaze.

"That's how this school began."

"...What happened to that dryad?" I asked.

"She never acclimated to being a human. But she's still here in the school," Haneda answered. "You know the cherry blossom tree?"

The cherry blossom tree. I'd seen it every day last year; it was next to the barrier.

No way—

"All the nobles who had tended to her—to Sakura—died, and they left behind one son. She wanted to become human for his sake."

I guess that tree had the same wish as everyone else.

I had thought there was a strange atmosphere around it the first time I'd laid eyes on it, but I assumed that was because it was growing near the barrier.

"Did you notice, Mr. Hitoma? This is the center of the barrier. It's the nucleus of the school."

"The nucleus..."

"Yep. That's why I come by to check up on it every so often. Well, I say 'check,' but there's nothing I really need to do. I just have to recall my original resolution."

"The other students can't find this place?" I asked.

I was thinking about the incident with Chiyu a while back. I'd also heard that the students often explored the forest.

"Nope," Haneda replied. "There's normally a second barrier around the shrine, but I released it since I was coming today. That's why they can't find it. It'd be a problem if a student carelessly touched anything in the vicinity. They might get hurt."

"Oh, that's the concern?"

"Huh? You thought I was worried about the barrier or the buildings? When I'm personally and thoroughly tending to their protection? They'll be fine, obviously. Anyway... Yeah, I suppose a student powerful enough to meet my criteria could get through the barrier. Like Karin, maybe? She makes the cut, but just barely."

"Got it. I have no idea what you're talking about."

What does she even mean by "powerful"? I don't understand the criteria she's basing this stuff on. Wait a sec—

"Am I allowed to be here...?" I asked.

From what she's explained, isn't this place super dangerous? I don't think a regular person like me should be here...

"You're with me, so it's fine," she replied glibly.

Absolute confidence.

The director who oversaw everything about this school made this proclamation without a shred of doubt.

"I wanted to tell you some things, Mr. Hitoma," she said. "About this place."

She stood and smiled under the guise of a student.

"Thanks for this! In return for listening to me ramble about the past, I'll show you something cool."

Haneda lifted her index finger into the sky. Then she brought it down to the ground. And then—

"Wow."

A shooting star.

Was the one I saw in the hammock earlier also her doing...?

"Did you make a wish, Mr. Hitoma?" Haneda asked.

"A wish...?"

There's no way mine would come true.

But Haneda's...

"A wish," she said. "I wished for your wish to come true."

It sounded like your ordinary pickup line, but those words pierced my heart.

She had wished for me in my stead.

My wish.

I want to like humans. A wish too absurd for me to say.

The stars were out of my reach.

But Haneda was different.

A phoenix was surely able to touch the stars.

My wish was futile.

But…if I wasn't alone—if I was with Haneda—I might be able to make it come true.

A Misanthrope Teaches a Class for Demi-Humans 2

Mr. Hitoma, Won't You Show Us the Light of Hope...?

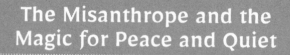
The Misanthrope and the Magic for Peace and Quiet

A MISANTHROPE TEACHES A CLASS FOR DEMI-HUMANS

Alice stayed in bed the entire day again.

I jumped into the bed to get her to pay attention to me.

Her lithe body rolled toward me, and we collided, her taut skin against mine.

Alice maintained her youthful looks through magic, and she'd lived far longer than her appearance would suggest.

She was always clothed in black with a big black hat perched on her head. She spent her time lazing around, munching on cookies even when she was in bed.

"*Sigh.* Isn't there anything fun to do around here?" she mused out loud, showering me with crumbs from the cookie she was eating.

I rubbed my head clean and meowed my agreement.

"Hmm? You think so, too?"

Yeah. You can only spend so many years doing the same routine. I'm bored out of my skull.

Alice was a witch. Until several hundred years ago, she had devoted herself to magical research, but it seemed she now knew everything she'd wanted to know. She'd recently been amusing herself with human pastimes but had been starting to tire of them over the last couple of years.

"Hmm, come to think of it..." Alice stood up—or to be more precise, she used magic to float—and drifted toward the mountain of parchments in one corner of the room. "I heard a while back that *she* started something fun."

She?

It was the first time in ages that Alice had talked about a living being other than me.

She rummaged through the parchments and drew a large sheet from the stack.

"Where was it? Hmm... Yep, found it!"

Words I'd never seen before were scrawled across the page.

Is this Japanese?

"How 'bout it? Wanna check this place out for me?"

* * *

Monday mornings were always gloomy.

The weather was on the fritz. Clouds covered the sky, and it looked as if it was about to rain at any moment. Future misery was inevitable. Plus, even though it was only late September, it was already chilly. I slightly regretted not throwing on a jacket when I had left my apartment. Anyway, my less-than-stellar win-loss record in the FPS game I'd played the night before was probably dragging my mood down, too.

They were definitely cheating... How dare they desecrate the sanctity of the game... I won't let this disrespect go unanswered...

While I was distracted by my internal raging on the way to school, I heard a student call out to me from behind. "Mr. Rei! Good morning! I love you!"

"Oh! Morning, Ryuzaki," I replied, switching immediately into work mode.

"I was wondering: Do you watch any Sunday morning anime?" she asked me out of the blue.

"Hmm, I used to, but I'm not familiar with the recent ones."

"That's too bad! The show in the superhero time slot has an interesting storyline! I think you would like it, too! Unfortunately, I have to wait a week for the newest episode, since they have to be checked by the school..."

Ah, that's right. The director filters all the media the students consume. Must be a pain.

"The anime in the shoujo slot afterward is wild, too!" Ryuzaki added. "Its selling point is hand-to-hand combat, which is a nice change of pace from the usual!"

"I can't believe that's in the shoujo slot..."

Isn't that a little too violent? Shoujo anime isn't all hearts and sparkles anymore, I guess...

I was feeling the generation gap.

"Which reminds me: Humans nowadays can't use magic like they used to, huh?" Ryuzaki said.

"Huh? Is this about shoujo anime? You're talking about the old magical girl shows?"

"No, it just reminded me... I used to be able to fly when I was a dragon... Those were the days. There were lots of people who could use magic back then, you know? The princess I talked about before was one of them, too. I was just thinking how there are so few humans who can use magic now..."

"...Humans *can't* use magic, though."

Ryuzaki gave me a blank stare and tilted her head. "What?"

Just then, a black entity drifted between us. "Witches...aren't... human."

"Gah!" I yelped. "You scared me..."

The one who had materialized out of nowhere was Kurosawa.

She looked drowsy as usual, but for once, she had taken the initiative to speak first.

Her book of the day was *Learn with Diagrams! Serious Black Magic from A to Z: A Primer for Complete Beginners.*

"...Witches...can't...live in the...human world...because of...their powers..."

"So the princess who came to my cave wasn't a human but a witch?" Ryuzaki asked.

Kurosawa quickly averted her gaze. "......Probably."

"You know a lot about witches," I said to her.

"......Not really."

With that, she plodded off ahead.

I figured she had an interest in the occult since she was never without a book about black magic…

Neneko Kurosawa. Cat. Enrolled for two years. She dodged the question during her self-introduction, but the reason she wanted to become human: "Because I was asked to."

* * *

I returned to the teachers' office after the end-of-the-day homeroom only to be ambushed by a teary-eyed Ms. Saotome.

"Waaah! Save me, Mr. Hitoma!" she cried.

"What's wrong?" I asked.

"It's just…the projector in the new AV room might be broken…"

"No way!"

If I remembered correctly, that projector had been purchased around when I started teaching here. It should've been practically as good as new.

"I didn't do anything to it! It just broke on its own!" Ms. Saotome insisted.

"Hmm… What exactly is broken? Like the screen won't turn on?"

"Yes! Good guess! That's precisely the problem…"

"Got it. Let me take a look."

"Yay! Thank you! I knew I could count on you!"

There were two AV rooms in the school: the old one in the main building and the new one in the annex. I followed Ms. Saotome to the latter.

* * *

"Sorry to trouble you, Mr. Hitoma!" Ms. Saotome said.

"Don't worry! It's totally okay!"

When we had gotten to the AV room, the first thing I had done was check if the projector was plugged in, then if all the cables were connected.

I had taken a look at the input cord and noticed it wasn't properly connected. All I'd done was plug it into the right place.

"I'm really sorry...," she said, nearly beside herself with remorse. "I can't believe I called you out for something like this... I should have double-checked..."

"It's fine. Inputs and outputs are confusing. I get it," I replied sincerely to placate her. "By the way, are the AV rooms used for classes?"

I hadn't used one before, so I figured I would ask for future reference.

"No, this room will be used for the special training tomorrow for teachers. The principal told me to get it ready."

"What training?"

"I don't know the details. Apparently, the principal picks who will attend. He asked me to make sure all the equipment is working."

"Mysterious."

The final checks could have been done the day of. How thorough. Was the training so important?

"In any case, you're a lifesaver, Mr. Hitoma! Thank you so much!"

Guh! Don't look at me with such sparkling eyes. Be still my heart! Ms. Saotome is married! She's married!!

I managed to rein in my emotions by picturing Mr. Hoshino. *Phew.*

"Anytime," I finally said. "Feel free to ask me for help whenever you need it."

"Yay! Thank you!"

Her smile is so radiant...

Every time I talked to Ms. Saotome, I felt as if her sheer loveliness purified the corruption inside me... There wasn't going to be anything left of me at this rate...

"Let's go back to the teachers' office!" she suggested. "Thanks again!"

"I'm glad I was able to help."

The AV room was on the third floor of the annex. To return to the main building, we either had to cross the hallway on the second floor connecting the two buildings or enter back through the front entrance on the ground floor. Ms. Saotome and I went downstairs, heading toward the second-floor hallway.

"Huh?" I said unwittingly.

We were approaching the art room on the second floor.

I hadn't noticed when we came, but the door was open.

The blackout curtains were drawn, so the room was dark. However, it seemed there was someone inside.

Without thinking, I stopped and peered in to see Neneko Kurosawa in front of a canvas.

Seeing me stop, Ms. Saotome said, "Mr. Hitoma? What's wrong?"

"Ah, errr, um…" I dithered, unsure what to say.

While I fumbled for a response, Kurosawa noticed me. "……Mr. Hitoma."

"Why, it's Ms. Kurosawa!" Ms. Saotome exclaimed. "I see. I'll go on ahead, then!"

"Wait—Ms. Saotome?!" I cried.

"See you later!"

She ran off back to the main building, leaving me gaping in surprise.

Things quickly became awkward between Kurosawa and me.

"…Here, Mr. Hitoma." Kurosawa called to me from the art room. She gestured to a chair. "……Come sit."

She stared at me with eyes like the full moon. Her gaze was compelling—or should I say, demanding. Drawn by the command in her eyes, I entered the room.

"P-pardon me…," I mumbled, seating myself in the chair she had indicated. It was positioned perfectly to see the canvas. "Is that…?"

"Meow."

She had painted a picture of a black cat.

"A portrait?" I asked.

"……Yeah."

"Do you like drawing?"

"…I guess. This is…an…assignment…"

"Really?"

"…For my…conditional advancement."

I see.

The director had mentioned this when we'd talked over spring break. Kurosawa had escaped during our time off, which normally would have resulted in a major point deduction and a demotion. However, she had opted for the assignment-heavy "conditional advancement" route instead.

Was she always sleepy because she was busy with the extra workload?

The door to the adjacent art prep room opened. "Oh-ho, is that Mr. Hitoma I spy?"

Out stepped Shiki Emoto, the art teacher.

"Hello," I said.

Mr. Emoto had a sturdy build, although not as sturdy as the principal's. His shoulder-length black hair was parted in the middle. He was wearing a long robe—black like Kurosawa's clothing—and a paint-splattered denim apron over it.

"Did you come to check in on Kurosawa?" he asked me.

"Y-yes."

Damn, I just blurted that out. He might think I'm overstepping my bounds. You've got it all wrong, Mr. Emoto. I'm not here to make sure she's doing her assignment. I'm just looking out of curiosity. Just seeing what the assignments are like. Don't get me wrong. I swear, I'm not here because I think your supervision is lacking, or that I don't trust you to handle Kurosawa alone!

That's what I wanted to tell him, but I didn't know how!

While I was busy thinking in circles, Mr. Emoto spoke to me. "Mr. Hitoma."

"Ack! Y-yes...?"

I-it's all right. I've mentally prepared for a scolding about my behavior...!

After shoring up my resolve, I collected myself.

"Are you interested in modeling?" he asked.

"...Come again?"

All the tension rushed out of my body at the unexpected question.

What did he just say? M-model?

"Um...what do you mean?" I asked.

Did I mishear?

"You know, a model… Like for a drawing."

Nope, I heard him right.

"Kurosawa is just finishing up her portrait, see? I figured you could pose as her next subject. You're kind of shadowy. Her theme is 'black,' so I think you'd be a good fit…"

Kurosawa had stopped what she was doing and was staring my way, the gears turning in her head. After a second, she gave a short nod to indicate her agreement.

"That's settled, then! Every week, Monday," Mr. Emoto said. "Glad to have you on board as our figure model."

"Settled? Already?!" I cried.

"Kurosawa agreed, right?" Mr. Emoto looked over to her for confirmation.

"……You won't do it?" she asked me.

Ack… Don't look at me with those eyes.

"…From when to when on Mondays?" I asked.

I *might* be a bit of a pushover.

"After classes end until six PM," Mr. Emoto said. "You don't have to hold one pose the entire time, by the way. You're even free to do your paperwork, if you want."

"That's generous…"

Seems pretty chill, then…

"One more push should do it, right, Kurosawa?" he whispered.

"……One…more," she mumbled back.

I could hear everything they were saying.

Kurosawa stood. "…Mr. Hitoma." She walked to me and gripped the hem of my shirt. "……Please."

I noticed Mr. Emoto pumping his fists behind her.

Their plan to butter me up was all too transparent, but oh well.

"*Sigh…* Fine. After class on Mondays until six, right?"

From that week on, I spent my Monday afternoons with Kurosawa in the art room.

* * *

Today was a special day.

For once, Alice was in a great mood.
She baked me a cake.
The outside air, which I hadn't felt for ages, was pleasant. The soil beneath my paws was cool to the touch.
I heard birds chirping in the distance.

The sky was blue and perfectly cloudless.
The trees were a lush, inviting green; their leaves gleamed.
The flowers were vibrant; their rich colors seemed to declare their joy.

I couldn't see anything like this from Alice's house. It felt as if the tapestry before me was mocking me to my face.

Today was the day I left this place, the day the world turned its back on everything I am.

* * *

The next day, for some reason, I ended up in the AV room.

"Okay, everybody, we will now begin the special training program: Humans and Their Analogous Species."

"A training session with the director herself. What an honor...," I mumbled.

The course Ms. Saotome had been asked to prep the room for had just one attendee...and that attendee was me. Haneda had led me here after homeroom, and before I realized what was happening, the session had already started.

The only two people in this spacious AV room were me and Haneda in her director form.

"Did we need this whole room if I'm the only attendee?" I asked.

"It's fine, it's fine," the director said. "Besides, I wanted to use the screen. Just surveying the equipment, y'know?"

Makes no sense, I thought. But it was true that I'd never have come to the AV room if it weren't for this training.

"Let's get started. Anyway, I call it training, but it'll be pretty casual. Sit back, relax, and pay attention."

"Okay."

The director nodded lightly and pressed the button at her fingertips.

A little ditty played from the speakers: "*Da-da-da-da-dum! ♪ Ba-dum-dum! ♪ Ba-dum-tss! ♪*"

"Um?" I spluttered.

Displayed on the screen was a video of me sorting through my papers.

"Whoops. My bad. I sneaked a video of you humming when you were in a good mood."

"Next time, don't!"

"Incidentally, Mr. Hoshino was right there with me."

"*Another* witness to my humiliation…?!"

"So that concludes the introduction…"

"*What* introduction?"

This is a little too *casual.*

I was internally shaking my head in disapproval when a slide with the actual topic of the training popped up on the screen.

"Let's continue to the meat of today's schedule. The motivation behind the theme of the day, 'Humans and Their Analogous Species,' is the conversation you, Karin, and Neneko had about witches," the director explained.

"You were listening?" I said indignantly.

"You were standing in the hallway," she rebutted.

For a second, I'd thought she had eavesdropped on us, but now that she mentioned it, we *had* been in a public space. In that case, there wasn't anything unusual about the fact that she'd overhead…or was there?

"Anyway, I figured knowing this information would help you in your teaching as well. Admittedly, the line between human and analogous species is pretty thin. First, a few accessible examples to start us off. The main ones are werewolves like Isaki and mermaids like Kyoka, I suppose.

Ah! *Yuki onna* spirits like Yuki and crow *tengu* like the principal count, too."

"So species whose original forms already resemble humans?"

"You catch on quick. I expected nothing less. Exactly right: Students from analogous species tend to progress through this school particularly quickly. Their physical abilities are similar, too."

"I see…"

Most of the points deducted from beginner and intermediate students are because of unhuman-like behavior, now that she mentions it… Same for Nezu's recent point loss…

"There's something I'm curious about," I said.

"Hmm? What's up? Go ahead."

"Do aliens, time travelers, interdimensional beings, or espers exist?"

"Ahhh, that's your inner nerd speaking, I'm guessing."

She smirked, as if to say, *I was waiting for you to ask*, then clicked to the next slide.

"I'll introduce them in the order I planned—first, espers. They're known in the human community as individuals with extraordinary magical ability, right? But real ones are extremely rare. Folks who claim to have esper powers are usually either your normal sleight-of-hand magicians or quacks. This is a little off topic, but powerful magic wielders normally live in special communities. You also get witches and wizards who live in remote areas with their familiars—most of the time, at least."

On the slide were pictures of a fraud and a real witch with a simple explanation. I wondered idly what magical abilities meant. Was it like having an OP sixth sense?

"Next, time travelers," the director continued. "If you can travel faster than the speed of light, you could cross the bounds of time, in theory. As far as I know, they don't exist. Same with interdimensional travelers."

There went any hopes I had of being reincarnated into another world… I had fantasized about it a little… I wanted to see what it was like to be OP…

"…I can tell exactly what you're thinking," she said.

"No! I'm not thinking about anything!"

"Time travelers and interdimensional beings might exist. I might just not know about them, so cheer up." She patted me on the head as if I were a kid.

So humiliating...

It was embarrassing to have my head patted at my age. Not even my parents did that anymore.

"What else—? Right, aliens. Well—" She grabbed me with the hand stroking my head and forced me to look up. "There's one right here."

"...You're too close," I mumbled.

She was a mere handspan away. Her hair falling on my face tickled. I smelled a sweet scent. Was it her shampoo? And...her chest was pressed up right against me. Was it on purpose? Right against my collarbones.

Man—what do I do? Am I allowed to point it out?

Seeing my distress, she grinned mischievously. "Exciting, right? My training. Like it?"

"...Honestly, I'm in a bit of a bind."

I couldn't concentrate like this. The director wasn't in her student form but her adult form. How do I put it? The premise was different, so my feelings about being hugged were different, too. I was super conflicted. What was I supposed to do?

"Heh-heh. Okay, okay. Is it still a little too early for you?" she teased.

She let go of me and returned to her place by the screen.

I was half-relieved and half-wistful...

The presentation about other species resumed, covering everything from elves to dwarves, and even *kappa* water sprites.

"The end. So? Got the gist?" the director asked me.

"More or less..."

There were more species than I had imagined. I hadn't wrapped my head around everything. It was all very fantastical.

"Sure, that's good enough for now." The director nodded briefly. "Your impression might change once you meet them in person."

In person—

I remembered what she had said earlier.

"You're an alien?" I asked.

"Depends how you look at it. I don't know where I was born. I've been alone for as long as I can remember. I was roaming around the universe and ended up here."

"It's a miracle you picked Earth of all places… The chances must've been astronomically low…"

"Yeah, totally," she said nonchalantly, as though it had nothing to do with her.

Maybe that detachment was the result of having lived as long as she had.

"Oh, by the by, a witch is gonna come for a visit soon. I want to introduce you to her. Sound good?"

"What?! Sure."

Her sudden declaration shocked me; this was a real witch we were talking about!

She might have planned this training in preparation for the witch's visit. But why me? Did our guest want to meet a human?

Can witches fly? Flying scares me, so I don't need a repeat performance. I'd love to see a flying witch in action, though. A classic scene in fiction come to life! Man, I'm such a sheep.

Then the director said, "She's Neneko's guardian."

"Whoa…"

Wait… Is this a parent visit…?

I crashed straight back down to earth from my high. I hadn't even known parental observations were a thing in this school…

"She's a bit of a pain, but I have faith in you!" the director added.

"Please don't," I begged.

"A pain" how? You can't gloss over such a dreadful announcement with a smile. What do I do if she's one of those helicopter parents who brags about their kid on social media…? I definitely won't be able to stand my ground…

"All right. That's the end of the training," the director declared. "If you remember what analogous species are as a whole—the examples, and the fact that they learn human abilities and advance faster than other species—that's enough."

"Okay, got it," I said, though I was a nervous wreck because of the bomb she had just dropped on me.

Kurosawa's witch guardian… I wonder what she's like…

* * *

The next week passed as usual, and my first Monday after school with Kurosawa rolled around. I brought my laptop to the art room so that I could work. I couldn't write tests with a student around, of course, but I could create worksheets for class. One blessing of this school was that there were few annual, school-wide events. The sports and cultural festivals were held only once every three years, which cut out a large swath of work. In other words, teachers like me could spend the majority of our time on the subject we were in charge of rather than general administration. That said, the toughest part of the job was that the students were all female and demi-human…

The quiet room amplified the clacking of my keyboard keys. Kurosawa painted in silence, glancing between her canvas and me.

The uniquely acrid smell of oil paints filled the air.

I'd never done any oil painting before. My vague impression of it was that it was pretty badass. Back in high school, I had picked music for my arts elective because it'd seemed more chill, so my exposure to art classes in my life had ended in middle school. That being said, as a social studies teacher, I could at least draw a map, but that was the extent of it. Nothing legit.

Kurosawa moved her hand leisurely. She might've actually been more focused than she was in my class, which was a little maddening.

"……What?" she said.

"Oh, uh, nothing," I replied. I had stopped typing when my thoughts had turned to Kurosawa. "Um…do you like art?"

On the floor all around her were paintings that were presumably hers.

The black cat from the day before, a silhouette clothed in what looked like a black dress, a landscape of the black forest depths, a still life of a black book, the list went on—colorless paintings encircled her.

"......It's fine," she said in response to my question.

"...Oh."

End of convo.

It's my bad for interrupting her when she was in the zone. Yeah, let's just leave it at that. She doesn't hate me, I'm sure. Pretty sure...

Just as I was about to return to my work, I heard Kurosawa mumble, "...I don't like colors." She paused what she was doing and turned her gaze slightly downward. "...They...deviate...from what's normal."

For an instant, it had looked as if she were about to cry, which threw me off. However, she was as expressionless as usual.

What does "normal" mean to her?

Surrounded by black paintings, she looked as if she were frozen in time.

I failed to respond to the sudden, emotionless words that had tumbled out of her mouth.

* * *

My after-school sessions with Kurosawa in the art room continued for several weeks. Her painting was almost complete.

One Wednesday, after end-of-the-day homeroom, Haneda asked me, "Got a sec, Mr. Hitoma?"

"What is it?"

The other students were getting ready to head back to the dorm.

Haneda's terribly dazzling smile gave me a sense of foreboding. I'd seen it several times in the past, and every time, it had been followed by an upsetting announcement.

"You made me a promise before!" she declared.

"...?" Had I? I tilted my head, her words not ringing a bell.

"Did you forget?"

"Hitoma's already a geezer," Usami cut in. "He forgets things easily."

"U-Usami! He's not that old! Thirty isn't that bad!'" Ohgami said.

I was usually grateful for Ohgami's considerateness, but this time it kind of stung...

You're trying so hard... Thanks...

"But Mr. Rei has a baby face, don't you think?" Ryuzaki said.

"Yeah, *squeak*! With a uniform on, he could pass for a high schooler!" Nezu added.

"Pretty sure that's impossible...," I grumbled.

I wouldn't be fooled. Flattery like this was a trap. You can't fall for it. I had seen plenty of netizens meet with nasty ends that way.

"*Mreow?!*" Kurosawa yowled, bolting up from her desk, where she had been sleeping.

"Gah!" I yelled in surprise.

She seemed shocked. Her breathing was labored. I'd never seen her so awake before. The other students had frozen in surprise as well.

Looking distressed, she scanned the room. But three seconds later, she sighed, and her shoulders slumped in disappointment.

"......I was wrong."

Haneda went up to the somber Kurosawa. "Neneko? You okay?"

Kurosawa sighed again as if she was double-checking something. "...Yeah... I'm going back."

"O-okay," I said. "Don't push yourself!"

She stooped over to snatch up her bag, then drifted out of the classroom more listlessly than usual.

"I'm worried. I'm going after her," Usami said. "Neneko! Wait up!"

"I-I'll go, too!" Ohgami said.

"Me too!" Ryuzaki chimed in.

The three of them ran off after Kurosawa.

I wondered what had happened. A nightmare, maybe?

Nezu popped out from behind me, where she had hidden at some point. She had a fistful of my suit jacket. "*Squeak*... She scared me with that outburst... I thought she was threatening me... Geez. What's with her?"

"Yeah, I'm worried, too," Haneda said.

"I'm an emotional mess of worry *and* fear!"

"Really?"

"What do you mean, 'really'?! I was terrorized by cats in my days as a mouse!! Of course I'm scared!"

"Mm, I don't think Neneko's like that, though."

"How would you know, Tobari?! ...I mean, I don't know, either! Her thoughts are a complete mystery! She doesn't talk. I can get all up in her face and she just ignores me! She won't even fight me! That means she sees me as—as prey!!!"

I don't think that's it...

It was true that Kurosawa was exceptionally unassertive. I agreed with Nezu that Kurosawa's thoughts were a "complete mystery." Naturally, it was impossible to fully understand another person, but Kurosawa... It felt as though she had shut the door herself.

"*Sigh...* Chiyu's waiting. I'm going home," Nezu announced. "See you, Meester Hitoma! See you, Tobari!" She dashed off like a cartoon character.

Only Haneda and I were left in the classroom.

"Why don't we go to the principal's office?" she suggested.

* * *

We got to the principal's office and found its occupant in a huff.

"Yeesh! You're late!" the principal said to us.

I went with the flow and followed Haneda here, but come to think of it, what's this "promise" she was talking about...?

"Sorry," Haneda replied. "Is *she* in my office?"

"Yep, indeed! She's impertinent as always!"

It was rare to see the principal acting so pointed...

Just how eccentric was this visitor?

"Calm down," said Haneda. "That's just how Alice is."

"Alice?" I echoed. An image of a certain wonderland popped into my head.

"The witch. Neneko's guardian," Haneda told me.

"Oh!"

I remember!

The day of the special training, I had been told a witch was coming.

Haneda opened the door to the director's office in the back of the room. "Long time no see, Alice. How's it going?" she said.

"Waaah! Lady Shiranui!! I've been bored out of my mind without you!" the visitor cried.

Her penetrating voice reminded me of the pretentious young ladies who were popular antagonist tropes these days.

My crappy intro to her might have biased my first impression, though.

The woman named Alice was about my height and dressed in a black robe and a pointy hat. Her long silver hair was beautiful like the Milky Way; the thin braids framing her face swayed back and forth. Her narrow eyes were as dark as her clothing.

She was far younger than I had imagined.

"Ah, is he my little one's homeroom teacher?" she asked Haneda.

"Yep. This is Mr. Hitoma."

"Huh."

Zero interest!

Her gaze flicked over to me. I thought she might have been assessing me, but she quickly returned her attention to Haneda.

Haneda was practically draped over her. They must have been extremely close.

"Lemme introduce you," Haneda said to me. "This is Neneko's guardian, Alice Medea."

"I-I'm Rei Hitoma, Neneko's homeroom teacher. It's my pleasure."

"Neneko?" Alice said quizzically. "Ohhh, that's the name she ended up with?"

"Yep," Haneda replied.

"Ha-ha! Anyway, enough about that. This form of yours, Lady Shiranui! It's pint-size and simply marvelous! Like a babe in diapers! Adorable!"

"Ha-ha-ha, thanks."

Was that a compliment?

"Besides, how long are you going to stick around this dump? *Tengu* and those lame-ass species are a giant bore. You came to me for advice when you first set up the school, so I thought you were gonna stick close to me. What the hell?"

"Yeah? Didn't I tell you I already picked this location as my base? You were a big help back then. Thanks again."

"Ughhhh! I love you!"

What am I watching...?

Alice the witch had plopped Haneda onto her lap. She was hugging Haneda from behind and being outrageously flirty. I was extremely uncomfortable. I wanted to leave. Why had they summoned me?

"*Ahem!* So? What did you come here for, Alice?" the principal cut in. He had moved to stand beside me when I wasn't paying attention.

"Excuse me? To see Lady Shiranui first and foremost, and to ask my kitty's teacher how she's doing while I'm here. Problem?" Alice sneered.

"Now you know. So what do you think about Neneko, Mr. Hitoma?" Haneda asked me.

Roped into the conversation all of a sudden, I froze like a deer in the headlights. "U-um, oh," I stammered. "She's good. I've warned her about her frequent naps, but it doesn't affect her grades at all. She's one of the top students. She's diligently doing the assignments for her conditional advancement, and—"

"What do you mean, 'conditional'...?"

Alice's expression clouded over, and she narrowed her eyes.

Was I not supposed to mention that? My forehead grew clammy with cold sweat.

When I failed to respond, Haneda stepped in. "Some stuff happened."

But that did nothing to alleviate Alice's sour mood.

"Okay? What *kind* of 'stuff' happened?" she demanded.

The pressure.

Terror seized my body; it was as if I had run smack into a wild beast. The air felt thick and oppressive. My breathing became shallow.

Crap. My legs are buckling. What's happening? My body feels heavy. Everything hurts.

No longer able to muster any more strength, I came crashing down to my knees.

"Hold up, Alice. Undo your magic. It's affecting Mr. Hitoma," Haneda said.

The witch threw me a cold look. "Tsk. This is why I can't deal with humans," she spat.

Her words sounded far away.

All of a sudden, the weight came off my body.

"So? What happened?" Alice asked.

"Neneko ran away," Haneda answered.

"Are you serious?"

"Yeah."

"Why?"

"Who knows."

"I'm sure *you* know, Lady Shiranui. Tell me," Alice urged.

"Hmm... Nope."

And there it was: Haneda's signature smile that left no room for argument.

"...I hate that about you," Alice said.

"Is that so? You're only saying that to get my attention, and I *love* that about you."

"God! You meanie!" she huffed, pouting like a child. "Fine, whatever. It's better for that kiddo to leave the nest sooner rather than later. Turn her into a human quickly, if you'd please."

"That depends on Neneko," Haneda said.

"...Why do you want Kurosawa to be human, Miss Alice?" I asked.

"What? You're still here, human? Is Kurosawa my cat? By the way, you can call me Alice."

"Yes, Neneko Kurosawa is your cat...ma'am," I said.

I have never been on a first-name basis with any woman in my life. That "ma'am" had just slipped out. She was looking at me as if I were an idiot. She must have seen right through me.

"Ahhh, Neneko Kurosawa. A fine choice of name, Lady Shiranui," she said.

"Heh-heh, thanks!" Haneda replied.

So it's the director who comes up with the students' names. I'd been wondering.

Not all the students must've had Japanese names before. I'd realized that much already...

"Right. What was your question? Why do I want her to be human?" Alice asked me.

"Yes."

"That was just something to keep me busy," she said. "But that cat—she's been by my side for too long and started to gain magical powers. I noticed in the nick of time. So at first it was a lark. I didn't have any real intention of letting her go. But it's no good if she actually gains powers... That's why I reached out to Lady Shiranui and had her take the kiddo in."

"Why would it be bad for her to wield magic?" I asked Alice.

"At a certain point in time, she'll cease to be a cat."

"She won't be a cat anymore?"

"Yeah. Wait—actually, it's more like she'll turn into a *nekomata*, I think. That sound right, *tengu*?"

The principal nodded. "That's correct."

Alice turned from the principal back to me. "And there you have it. That would cause problems. It's one thing if she were going to turn into a higher entity like me, but *nekomata* are shadows of their formal bestial selves. They can't control their magic and end up rampaging and destroying against their will. Do you think that little one will be able to handle such a fate? To prevent her from absorbing any more magic, I brought her to Lady Shiranui to turn her into a human."

"That's right," Haneda said. "Alice asked me for a favor. Neneko agreed to it, too, so she was enrolled here. Students' life spans freeze inside the barrier, and they stay the same way they were when they first entered. Therefore, she won't gain any more magic."

"So Kurosawa agreed to it," I muttered.

Then why did she run away? She risks turning into a nekomata *outside the barrier's protection.*

Don't tell me she was trying to turn into a nekomata *on purpose?*

No, that was impossible. According to what Alice said, Kurosawa wouldn't be able to control her own magic, which would make life tough in various ways. The risk was simply too great.

"Can I tell Kurosawa I met with you today, Miss Alice?" I asked.

"Seriouslyyyyy? No way," she groused, but then said, "Wait... Okay... Fine."

"Aliiice, which is it?" Haneda pressed.

"I'll look like a mother hen! That's so uncool!" Alice protested. "But she probably found out I came the moment I released my powers, so I guess...I'll roll with it."

"Huh? Didn't you come to meet with me?" Haneda said.

"Oh! ...Yeah! Of course! Go for it, human! Tell her I came by! Don't hold back!"

"Y-yes, ma'am," I replied.

What the heck? She's a big ole softy on the inside...

The principal watched Haneda and Alice exasperatedly from the sidelines. Come to think of it, the director had been in her Haneda form this entire time.

"Let's call it a day," Alice said. "I'll be staying in this area for the time being, so come visit me, Lady Shiranui!"

"Will do. I'll reach out," Haneda promised.

With a snap of her fingers, Alice disappeared in a plume of smoke.

So that's what magic is like... It's more straightforward than I pictured.

It was leagues simpler than the chanting I'd seen the principal perform a while back.

"What did you think of Alice, Mr. Hitoma?" Haneda asked me.

"...She dotes on Kurosawa more than I thought she would. I'm relieved."

"You bet. Interesting, right? Especially since the person herself is blind to her own tendencies."

At first, I had thought she was indifferent, but she seemed to care for Kurosawa in her own way.

That was the reason she had enrolled Kurosawa into this school—so that the latter wouldn't end up a *nekomata*.

However... In that case, Kurosawa's reason to become human should've been "to not turn into a *nekomata*" or "to protect myself from magic." Why did she say that it was because she had been asked? Had she really agreed to come here?

After that conversation with Alice, I was left with one burning question.

How did Kurosawa feel about Alice?

* * *

It was Monday, after school in the art room.

I told Kurosawa that Alice had visited.

Kurosawa's paintbrush came to a stop. "...Mistress...came," she muttered. "I knew it... That *was* her......"

She clammed up.

The day I had met with Alice—the moment Kurosawa had jumped out of her seat: Was that because she had sensed Alice's powers?

"Can I ask you something?" I said to Kurosawa. She slowly turned toward me. "Do you want to be human?"

She took a small sip of air.

She paused. Then—

"If that's...what Mistress wants..."

Deep in her golden eyes, which she averted, I could see a flicker of conflict.

"Do *you* want to be human?" I repeated.

The uncertainty in her gaze grew. She sighed and slowly closed her eyes. "......I don't...know."

Her voice trailed off, so soft it would've been inaudible anywhere other than the quiet art room.

"I'm...not...normal...," she continued. "I was...no good...as I was..."

She spoke as if she were carefully choosing and wringing out every word.

"I...have to...become...normal..."

It sounded as if she was trying to persuade herself.

"What do you think 'normal' means?" I asked.

Kurosawa's hand tightened around her paintbrush. "…What Mistress… wants me…to be. That's……normal."

I was unsure how to respond. Silence fell between us.

Considering the course of our conversation, I was positive that Kurosawa knew that wasn't what I had meant.

That meant she didn't want to answer. *In which case, I shouldn't pry any further…right?*

"…Do…you think…colors…are essential…Mr. Hitoma…?" Kurosawa asked.

"What?"

The palette she was holding had only black and white paint on it. She dipped her brush into the black paint with a practiced motion.

"Everyone else's normal…has…lots of color…" She silently touched her brush to the canvas and painted a black streak straight down. "Mistress too…"

It sounded as if she were resigned.

I thought back to the conversation we had the first day I sat as a model for her assignment.

"I don't like colors… They…deviate…from what's normal."

That was Kurosawa's answer.

Her normal was different from what everyone else wanted to be normal, and she didn't want to conform to the standard.

She had told me her wishes from the start.

"…I like your paintings," I said.

Although the canvases were covered primarily with black, they were filled with vitality.

The artist of said paintings stared at me fixedly.

I continued. "Your works might not have color, but I can see you inside them. I can tell they're the world you see with your eyes. You and I might see different colors, but different doesn't mean wrong. So—I don't believe colors are essential at all."

Kurosawa's normal and my normal; if she was black, what color did I appear to be?

She said nothing, her gaze focused on her canvas.

* * *

"Ahhhh, building games are sooo relaxing," I said.

It was late at night, minutes away from a new day. Building games were the best for whiling the time away.

My Mondays after school, spent accompanying Kurosawa on her assignment, had wetted my creative appetite. For the first time in a while, I found myself wanting to design buildings. I was playing God and raising buildings left and right from the myriad of building blocks on the field. The game in question had a good Architect Mode, where the player could make whatever they liked without collecting the materials first. However, Survival Mode was my jam. I was part of the faction that liked to build with items that were carefully collected with their own hands. Having a few restrictions nurtured a fondness for the final product, in my opinion.

"All right, looks good."

I had collected a decent amount of materials, and I still had inventory my past self had stocked up for me.

Good job, past me. Time to make the biggest magic sword this world has ever— Huh? What?

My phone, charging beside my bed, vibrated.

It's still going... Is it a call? But I was just getting to the good part...

Since the room was spacious—God bless—the bed was slightly far from me. I got up from my beloved gaming chair and walked over. **Shiranui High** was displayed on the screen.

The school's calling me at this hour? I've got a bad feeling about this.

I picked up. "Rei Hitoma speaking."

"Sorry for the late call, my boy, but it's an emergency." It was the principal. *"Kurosawa planned a second escape across the barrier."*

"Again?!" I cried. "Where—?"

"Luckily, we caught her. She's safe. However, we will have to announce what her punishment is. I understand if it's too much to ask, but can you come to my office?"

"I'll go right away."

I hung up and got ready to leave.

Ugh, crap! Just gotta look decently presentable!

If they were going to make an announcement, that meant this was the only chance I had to give an opinion. By the time the next day rolled around, it would be too difficult to reverse the decision.

I scrambled to put on a T-shirt and jacket. Jeans and sneakers I could run in should do for the bottom.

Literally anything is fine. Is Kurosawa already in the principal's office? Why did she try to escape again? The punishment for a conditional student can only be— Don't think about it!

Nothing's been settled yet!

I rushed out with my laptop and the lights still on. However, I made sure to lock the door before I sprinted off toward the school.

* * *

Five minutes later, I arrived at the principal's office.

"S-sorry for the wait…!" I spluttered. My lack of stamina had me gasping for air.

"Thanks for coming here so quickly, my boy," the principal said. "Just have a seat for now."

Kurosawa was in the room, too.

I sat down on the sofa, still struggling to catch my breath.

"I'll cut to the chase. This runaway attempt is Kurosawa's second offense. From the school's perspective, we can no longer defend her. The punishment will be—expulsion."

It was the logical but most severe punishment.

Kurosawa listened submissively. Perhaps she had already accepted the outcome.

"…Aren't there any alternatives?" I asked.

"Her conditional advancement was the alternative. For a second attempt—" The principal hesitated.

This incident was akin to a parolee's repeat offense.

The situation was dire.

"Mr. Hitoma," Kurosawa said, turning to face me. "...I'm...okay."

What do you mean, "okay"? More importantly—

"Why did you run?" I asked.

Her first attempt over spring break. A second attempt today.

Kurosawa looked straight at me. "The colors... I wanted to erase them." Her words were deliberate and precise. Underneath her soft voice was a strong resolve.

"...I don't...want to become human."

There was no indecision in her words.

She had chosen to drop out.

Then why—?

I balled my hands into fists, reining in the part of me that wanted to interrogate her.

There was plenty I wanted to say, but I couldn't let emotion take over my speech.

I didn't want to attack her. I just wanted to understand.

I exhaled slowly. "...I recognize you want to drop out because you don't want to become human." I chose my words carefully. What was the best way to phrase it? I had no idea. However, I wanted to understand her. "... But why did you try to run away? Was there a place you wanted to go?"

"I..." She turned her face down. It looked as if she was struggling to speak.

Crap. I might have said the wrong thing.

This would make it the second time a student I was responsible for had dropped out. It was painful for me, too. That was why I wanted at least to understand, but was that self-serving? Should I have sent her off without asking anything?

Kurosawa was a cat. A magical cat. Once she left the barrier, there was a chance she would turn into a *nekomata* and lose control. She, more than anyone else, should've grasped the peril she was in. So why had she deliberately chosen to leave the barrier in order to drop out of school? I didn't get it. Why would she expose herself to such danger?

Kurosawa had yet to look up.

"...I thought...Mistress would come," she said.

"Miss Alice, you mean?" I asked.

One of the principal's eyebrows twitched when he heard the name.

"Yeah...," Kurosawa replied.

Had Kurosawa assumed that Alice would come if she put herself at risk? Or was it that she had known that Alice was near and had gone to see—?

No. That wasn't it. She missed Alice, and—

"What are you doing here—" the principal started to say all of a sudden.

Huh?

Purple smoke drifted up behind me and Kurosawa.

Then I felt an overwhelming pressure. I remembered this feeling.

"—Alice?" he finished.

"Can't *tengu* keep their mouths shut? That's why you're considered beasts." It was Alice's voice.

"These are extenuating circumstances and all that," said another voice.

Apparently, Haneda was here, too.

My body was heavy. I couldn't turn around.

The director whispered something to Alice, but I couldn't hear.

Alice sighed. At the same time, my body felt light again.

"...Mistress," Kurosawa said.

"A little cheeky for you—a mere cat—to be calling me out, don't you think?"

Alice and Haneda—ah, she was in her director form—were leaning against the wall behind us.

Alice had her arms folded and one leg bent, and she was propped against the wall. She seemed cross. "So? What are you gonna do? The only future waiting for you at home is one as a monster, you know."

"I did...some research...," Kurosawa replied.

"You did what now?"

"On black magic... I searched...for a way...to suppress...myself..."

Kurosawa looked down at her feet.

The books she always carried around—but all of those were written by humans, sold by regular bookshops. On top of that, they were targeted toward amateurs and only contained the basics...

"What way? Find anything?" Alice asked.

"......No," Kurosawa said.

"Then it's impossible," Alice spat.

"But I don't...want to be...human... That's why..." Kurosawa slowly lifted her head. "I wanted you...to end it all...Mistress."

A beat of silence.

The meaning of her words dawned on all of us in the room collectively.

Kurosawa had planned to leave the barrier, become a *nekomata*, and have the witch—

"Excuse me? Do you even know what you're saying?" Alice demanded.

"I do," Kurosawa said brusquely, intercepting Alice with a proclamation of her will.

She rose to her feet sluggishly and walked toward Alice.

"You picked me up... Raised me... Gave me magic...... And now... you're here... So..."

Her gaze was cool and piercing.

She and Alice were nearly touching.

She gripped Alice's clothes as if she were begging for attention and brought her lips close to Alice's ear.

"Alice. You must...take responsibility."

Her words were as sweet as poison—as if she was saying, *You started it. You must end it.*

Kurosawa, expressionless as always, drew away from Alice.

"...What if I say no?" Alice's voice was shaking.

"You can't." Kurosawa refused to let her run.

"Wh-why not? I—I don't get it... You agreed. You said you would become human. Why would you say something like this out of nowhere...?"

Their gazes locked for a heartbeat.

"Mr. Hitoma...over there... He taught me..."

Me?!

I had been tossed into the fray without warning. All eyes were on me. Only Kurosawa hadn't turned.

She continued. "He said I didn't need...to be the 'normal' you want from me... What I want... My normal... I just need you, Alice. Nothing else."

At that moment—she made a face I'd never seen before.

"Alice. I just need you."

A broad smile. The normally poker-faced Kurosawa was smiling so tenderly it tugged at my heartstrings.

This was the ending she had chosen.

"...*Haaah*..." Alice sighed deeply and mumbled in resignation, "Fine, I get it. Why would you force me to do this?"

"Because...the world, to me, is...black," Kurosawa answered.

"Ugh. That makes no sense... If we had more time, I might have figured out a solution to your problem... Why didn't I notice earlier?"

A laid-back voice interrupted the pair's conversation.

"You could do something if you had the time?"

It was the director.

"Um, m-maybe...," Alice said. "One can control their magic to a certain extent. Then, even if they turn into a monster, they can stop themselves from running wild. If I can teach her to have such control..."

"Three years, then," the director declared. "For the next three years, I'll prevent Neneko's magic from growing any stronger. Can you figure something out in that time?"

"Y-yes...!!" Alice said.

"Okay, good. What do you think, Neneko?"

When she heard her name, Kurosawa's ears perked up, but it seemed her head had yet to catch up to the rapid developments. She looked between Alice and the director. "......I might...be able to stay...with Alice... forever?"

"Yeah. If everything goes well," the director replied.

"Really...?"

Kurosawa turned a hopeful gaze on Alice.

"It won't be easy, but it'll be better than your situation now," Alice said. Her words were cold, but she couldn't hide the hint of a smile tugging at her lips.

Perhaps Kurosawa had noticed as well; she was smiling faintly in return. "I...want to...be with you...! I want...to study magic...with you...!"

Those words were filled with her dreams for the future.

It wasn't the end.

Kurosawa would live on together with Alice.

The director appeared satisfied with Kurosawa's response. "Work hard," she said. "Good luck."

"Who...are you? Have we...met before?" Kurosawa asked.

The director might have been in her adult form, but they had still been classmates for half a year now.

"This is the first time we've met like this. I'm Director Shiranui." She bowed humbly, which wasn't like her at all. Maybe she was just playing around.

"Oh, the talking light...from the interview...?"

"Yep, yep."

That's the form she went with...? I mean, I guess it was convenient for an interview.

"This is the real you...?" Kurosawa asked the director.

"Mm, more or less."

"Lady Shiranui," Alice said, "how do you plan to halt the growth of her magic?"

"There are two ways." The director held up two fingers. "One, I can lend a ring like the one Mr. Hitoma is wearing. Then she can learn to control her magic at home with you. The second way is for her to live in the shrine in the forest and learn there." She then suggested cheerfully, "That's the method I recommend, since there's a second barrier around the shrine to prevent other students from entering. Plus, I can help her if anything goes wrong."

"Aw, man! I don't wanna owe that *tengu* a favor!" Alice protested. She gripped her head, conflicted. It looked as if she would rather pick anything else.

She and the principal really don't get along...

In contrast, the principal just seemed fed up with Alice's overreaction. He sighed. "I am not quite willing, but since it is Director Shiranui's proposal, I'll go along with it."

"...You won't nag?" Alice asked.

"I will not complain if you remember your manners," he said.

"That's *exactly* what I'm talking about," she retorted, glaring back at him.

The director pressed Alice for an answer. "So? What will you do?"

Alice scowled. She took a moment to think, peeking at Kurosawa and the principal.

Then, having made up her mind, the witch finally spoke.

"...Fine! Ugh... I hate to ask *him* for anything, but...I'll have her use the shrine for a while!"

The director beamed. Her expression read, *Now we're talking!*

"Good, that's what I thought you'd say," the director said. "In that case—"

She reached out her hand toward Kurosawa, her bracelet gleaming.

"Neneko Kurosawa. You are hereby dismissed," she declared.

For an instant, Kurosawa's body was engulfed in orange flames.

The flames soon disappeared, leaving a small black cat with golden eyes where Kurosawa had been.

* * *

Kurosawa's sudden withdrawal was a big shock to the other advanced-class students. Nezu took it especially hard. "I barely even got to talk to her!" she sputtered in outrage through tears.

I explained what I could about Kurosawa's situation.

The entire time, Haneda stared out the window, a faraway look in her eyes.

* * *

"God, what a dump!" Alice exclaimed.

"What happened to minding your manners?" the principal said.

"Can I use magic on the shrine? Or is it a non-magic zone?"

She treats magic like it's smoking...

"Not on the building itself, because it'll affect the barrier. That's why we had Mr. Hitoma come along as a custodian!" the principal declared.

Yep. You heard that right. I was tasked with cleaning up the shrine since I used to be Kurosawa's homeroom teacher.

"Fine. I want it sparkling clean," Alice said.

"Understood."

The black cat in Alice's arms meowed. Maybe she was cheering me on.

Oh, I forgot to ask.

"Kurosawa... I'm not sure if that's what I should call you anymore, but anyway... The painting you did of me in the art room... You finished it a while ago, right? I was curious how much you'd done, so I asked Mr. Emoto. He told me—"

"Hmm? Your portrait that Kurosawa was working on? She finished it ages ago! But she really took her time. Maybe she was fussing with the finishing touches? Or she has a crush on you? She withdrew from the school, so I guess we'll never know."

I didn't know what Kurosawa was thinking, and I didn't care what the truth was. I only wanted to treasure the time we had spent together.

Kurosawa watched me with her golden eyes.

"Thank you for drawing me, Kurosawa," I said.

The color Kurosawa named as black—the color inside me. In life, we experience a variety of colors. That's what she taught me.

She blinked, hopped down from Alice's arms, and padded over to me. Then she rubbed up against my feet and let out a quiet *mew.*

A Misanthrope
Teaches a Class for
Demi-Humans ②

Mr. Hitoma, Won't You Show Us the Light of Hope...?

The Misanthrope and the Tobari from Days Gone By

A MISANTHROPE TEACHES A CLASS FOR DEMI-HUMANS

I was jealous.

Of living. Of killing. Of feeling the emotions that drive those desires.

To love, to hate, to grieve. Humans are inconvenient. They are always busy.

I wanted to keep on witnessing the moments when a human's heart was moved. And I wanted to experience one such moment for myself.

* * *

Winter was here.

A month had passed since Kurosawa had dropped out of school. It was already October, and the end of the year was creeping up on us.

Classes were over for the day. I was in the director's office.

"Okay, Mr. Hitoma. Lemme give you a rundown on Neneko's recent progress," the director said to me. She was still in her student form.

"Please. Thank you," I replied.

I'd been whisked away to the office after asking offhandedly how Kurosawa had been doing. Apparently, she and Alice were plugging away at their research, holed up underneath the shrine.

At the moment, Kurosawa was like a cup of water, filled to the brim. Trying to scoop out the water would only cause the cup to overflow the moment the spoon dipped in. The director's powers were currently keeping the water frozen.

In the meantime, Kurosawa was learning how to chip away at the ice and practicing how to create a receptacle beneath the cup so her magic didn't spill.

"It sounds like she's working hard together with Miss Alice," I said.

"Yep. Maybe she's been doing a lot of prep work, but Alice praised her, saying she's got a lot of talent for a magic novice. Where she couldn't hear, of course."

"Why? She should've just told her directly."

"It's complicated, you know. She isn't Kurosawa's owner but her teacher now."

"I see... I guess? Is that right...?"

I supposed it made sense when I thought of Alice as one of those Spartan sports team coaches.

However, the no-nonsense philosophy was only good for students who got a big head and slacked off when they were complimented. I felt like it might have a negative effect on Kurosawa... But it wasn't my place to say that...

"You're muttering to yourself again," Haneda teased.

Ack... My face must've given me away again. How embarrassing.

I didn't want to make this about me and my problems. *It should be okay to tell Haneda at least, right?*

"...I think Kurosawa's the type to grow with praise," I said.

"Really? Great, thanks for the advice! I'll tell Alice."

"How long have you known Miss Alice?"

"How long, indeed. Since before I found this place. Back when Rome was on the up-and-up! Alice was so cute and innocent in those days."

Rome's heyday was between the first century BC and third century AD...!

The sheer absurdity of it all was mind-boggling...

"The human world is always changing. It's fascinating. Take your buildings, for example; they've evolved from wood to stone. Now there's even skyscrapers."

"It must've passed in the blink of an eye for you..."

"Hmm, is that how it felt? Maybe."

It was amazing that she remembered it all. My memories of college had already become full of holes, and I barely remembered anything from ten years ago.

"Random question, but what happened to the nobleman who Sakura was in love with? The one you told me about a while before," I asked.

She had told me the story when we had gone camping, and I had been low-key curious ever since.

"Oh, right. He continued his life as a human, got caught up in an inheritance dispute, and died...or, at least, that's the future that Shirou saw for him, which is why we ended up sheltering him in the shrine, thereby saving him from the dispute he never wanted to be involved in anyway. He said he would do anything in his power to repay us. Such a good kid."

Disputes over power had been common in that time period, so that kind of fate wasn't impossible to imagine...

"It was perfect timing, since I wanted to know more about humans. So I gave him eternal life while he was at this school—or to be more precise, I stopped time for him," Haneda added.

"Um? That's terrifying!"

"He said he'd do anything, so why not?"

He tossed those words around too carelessly...

"He was born to nobles, wasn't he? And he was fine with that?" I asked her.

"I can't speak to how he truly felt, but he did agree to it."

"I see... And what happened to him after that?"

"He taught here for a while as a human. Teaching licenses didn't exist at the time—I guess he was unlicensed?"

"He sounds like a protagonist in a manga. That's awesome..."

"Rather than a cliff with an ocean view, we have a forest with a mountain view, though," she said.

That nobleman had lived under Sakura's protection within the barrier.

I disliked the idea of him falling into misery since Sakura hadn't been able to become human, but it looked like they had a happy ending. Thank goodness.

Hmm? He "taught"? Then he isn't here anymore, I suppose.

"What is he doing now?" I asked.

"He returned to human society. He forgot everything that happened and is living as a normal human. His clock has been restarted, and he's aging like every other human."

"Oh? He's still alive?"

"Yeah, it all happened pretty recently. With the world at peace, he said it was about time."

He lost his memory but is still alive. Don't tell me—

"Am I that nobleman?" I asked.

"Don't be ridiculous." She shot my hopes down immediately, her gaze cold and half-mocking.

"Nooo... I wanted to be one of those special-from-birth heroes you see in manga and light novels. My dreams, dashed...!"

"Ah-ha-ha. You're an average Joe born into a somewhat well-off household. Too bad, so sad. Show some appreciation for your parents, okay?"

Working at this school, I found the abnormal had thoroughly permeated the normal, so I'd begun to think that maybe I had something special, too.

I guess I was wrong... I'm just an average Joe...

Along with the faint disappointment, relief sprouted inside me knowing that I was truly my parents' child—my parents, who have been supporting me ever since I was born.

There weren't many opportunities to say so, but I actually was grateful. On that subject, I'd never had what you could call a serious rebellious phase, either.

"If you want to live as a normal human, it's best to forget about this school," Haneda said. "The ring on your pinkie isn't all-powerful, to tell you the truth. Once you leave the barrier, after a while, it deactivates and your memories are replaced with dummy ones."

"How long...is a while?"

"Who knows. Until I think the timing is right, I guess."

"That's too vague..."

The silver ring on my left pinkie glinted. I had assumed I would remember this school as long as I had it… Would the day come when I, too, would forget the days I spent here?

"It's crueler if you know exactly when it's coming."

At that moment, I saw a trace of forlornness in Haneda.

* * *

"*Squeeeak!* I haven't been studying for entrance exams at all…!!" Nezu whined.

"Seriously…? Nezu…," I said.

"It's already November," Usami warned. "Second semester's half over."

I frequently made announcements to the advanced class about entrance exams during homeroom. It went without saying that the exam schedule differed depending on the school. The students who were planning to sit the general exam wouldn't be taking it until the next year, but Ohgami (the usual one), who had applied for early admission, and Ohgami (the full-moon one), who was looking to go to a technical college, already knew their results. Of course, they had both passed.

"You don't fool me, Machi," Ryuzaki said. "When push comes to shove, you can get things done, can't you?"

"You're right! I suddenly feel like it'll be okay!" Nezu said.

"Are you suuure?" Haneda said.

"Positive! I'm even willing to bet you Ryouko's special, extra crispy croquettes we're getting for dinner! They're made with the potatoes her family grows!"

"Nezu's putting food on the line…?!" I exclaimed.

That must mean she's super confident!

"If you're worried, Machi, you should ask Mr. Hitoma for advice…," suggested Ohgami, the voice of reason.

"True. I would prefer that, too," I added.

It would definitely help me out if Nezu talked to me.

That being said, while there were a few bumps and dips in her grades, they weren't bad at all. In math and science, she was number three in the class after Haneda and Usami. Her grades in the other subjects were plenty high for the department she was aiming for. However, that was no reason to get sloppy.

Life after graduation…

Mr. Hoshino technically oversaw the students' future academic and career trajectories, but starting this year, I had become his secondary, since it was a subject related to my homeroom class.

"Hmm, maybe I'll get in on that action," Haneda drawled.

"Eh?" I said.

Haneda? Smells like a scheme…

"*Squeak?!* Then me too!" Nezu cried.

"Be my guest," Haneda said.

"That's not how the script goes! No one else is interested?! Wait! Don't tell me you were waiting for me to volunteer…?!"

Haneda gave her a thumbs-up and winked jauntily. "Well, what are you gonna do?"

How far had she calculated?

"*Squeak!!* That rubs me the wrong way! You better follow through, Haneda!!" Nezu demanded.

"Sure," Haneda agreed easily.

"Oh."

Just like that, it was decided that I would be talking to Nezu and Haneda about their post-graduation plans.

* * *

The tropical heat of the director's office was perfect for the winter. It felt like being holed up in a kotatsu.

The day after I had talked with Nezu about her future aspirations, I followed up with Haneda as a courtesy, and ended up being dragged into her office. According to her, "My power is unstable during this time of the year, so better to talk somewhere I can return to my director form."

Come to think of it, last year around the same time, she had left classes to go to the nurse's office. Ms. Karasuma, the school nurse, had also said that Haneda always fell ill around the winter. The more powerful you were, the more suspect you were to fluctuations in your power, too, I suppose.

The moment we stepped inside the director's office, orange flames engulfed Haneda, and she reappeared as the director.

"…Those flames never fail to shock me no matter how many times I see them," I said.

"I figured. That's why I try not to transform around you," the director replied. "Humans are scared of fire, or so I've heard. But it's easier for me to be in this form, so give me a break today. Now, let's talk. Sit." She gestured to one of the couches.

I sat as I was told. She sat down across from me.

"Um… So, Haneda…" I faltered. "…Or do I call you Director?"

"Haneda's fine. My current form notwithstanding, we *are* talking about Tobari Haneda."

"Oh, right. Okay."

I was never sure how to address her in her director form. I lightly cleared my throat to switch gears.

"What do you want to do after becoming human?" I asked her.

"Play music."

"…Really?"

"Yeah. I'm fifty percent serious."

She propped her chin on her hands and smirked mischievously. She must have read what I was thinking.

Haneda had said she was interested in music during her introduction in front of the class. However, I didn't know how much of that was to maintain her pretense as a student and how much was real.

"What about the other fifty percent?" I asked.

"I want to live like you do."

"Um?"

What a worthless answer.

"Are you making fun of me?"

"Nope. I'm being extremely sincere," she insisted.

…Her intentions were becoming even murkier.

"When you say you want to live like me...what exactly do you mean by that?"

"It's what it sounds like."

"I don't understand. There's nothing good about the way I live."

"You think? You're a passionate guy, yeah? You're looking forward to tonight, aren't you?"

"Yes, but can't you phrase it in a better way?!"

Ignore the misleading statement! I'm just going to be gaming tonight!

Haneda grinned impishly, but seeing that I was peeved, she stood and plopped down next to me. The sofa shook when she sat.

"...I want to live a life where I can make the things I love, like you do," she said. "There may be rough times, but they only make me kinder. Like you!"

"I'm not kind."

Bitterness welled up in my chest.

"You are. Only kind people have regrets. That's what came to mind when you told me about your past. 'How human he is,' I thought."

Is she mocking me? No, I'm being overly distrustful. She has no such intentions.

"What does 'human' mean?" I asked.

"Flawed."

"Other animals are flawed, too."

"And that way of thinking is also very human."

It sounded to me like an argument for argument's sake.

"There are other lives I want to try living. Like Seiko's—Usami's owner—or Roost Rep Ryouko's... Other than that, hmm..."

Haneda told me about all sorts of ways of living, all mundane stories you could find anywhere. Nevertheless, they were lives engraved with the history of the ones who lived them.

She spoke of them with envy.

"You have quite a backlog," I noted.

"I've seen a lot."

In her infinite years, how many lives had she borne witness to?

How had she lived before becoming the Haneda we knew?

"I like humans," Haneda remarked.

A weight settled against my left shoulder. It was Haneda's weight as she leaned against me. She crossed her legs and folded her hands over her knees. Her hair, sleek and shiny, cascaded down over my suit.

"I've been meaning to tell you…," I said. "Your neckline is too low."

From this angle, I had an amazing view. I awkwardly averted my gaze.

"I knew you were a closet pervert," she teased.

"I'll have you written up for sexual harassment."

"Sorry, sorry," she said, but I doubted she was going to ameliorate her behavior.

In any case, who would I even complain to?

Anyway, I didn't find it unpleasant, but not everyone was like me. If Haneda were to become human and find herself targeted by a creep, just the thought made me—

"Not all humans are kind," I told her. "There are ones who get off on hurting others, too. Even so, can you still say you like humans?"

Haneda glanced at me thoughtfully before dropping her gaze to her feet. "That, too, is human. I like it," she said in the same tone as before.

I didn't want to accept such twisted emotions as human.

"Aren't those just empty words?" I asked. I knew I should've kept my mouth shut, but I wasn't able to. "If a tragedy were to occur, one that left you unable to forgive either yourself or someone else, I doubt you'd be able to say that you like humans. Becoming human might be all it takes for you to start loathing life. Your love will fade. You're fond of humans because you aren't one. Your strength is immeasurably greater—"

The moment I said the word *strength*, Ryuzaki's face popped into my head.

She had been isolated because of her strength. She wanted to become human in order to be loved.

Could it be that Haneda—?

"Hmm, maybe you're right. In that case, if I were to despise humans, would that make me closer to being one?" she said blithely.

Despite the horrible things I had said, she was grinning.

"…You don't have to purposefully try to despise humans," I replied.

"Yeah? And what do you *really* think?"

Why was she pushing me?

I was trying to be a good adult and suppress these shameful feelings so they wouldn't show. I wished she wouldn't deliberately drag them out into the light. She didn't understand how it felt to bury my own emotions!

"Tell me. I won't be angry," Haneda said.

"That's exactly what someone who's going to blow their top would say," I retorted.

"You think? Mm, that's tough... But you know, Mr. Hitoma, I want to listen to your stories. Teach me to be human."

Stop.

I didn't want to speak. These feelings of mine were a tangled mess. There was no logic behind them. I knew that if I was to open my mouth, only an emotional deluge would come pouring out.

But contrary to my intentions, the words spilled from my mouth.

"...Humans form expectations of others without realizing. They want to be treated kindly; they get angry when they are wronged; they come to hate others. But I think that's the result of desiring to meet the other person on equal terms... Granted, opinions like that are often dismissed these days. Nonetheless, everyone feels that desire to some extent, even if they don't show it... You're a phoenix. That's why you can take things as they come, no matter what they are... You say you like humans; I want to be able to say that, too. I'm sorry that I can't. I'm thoroughly prejudiced. I know what I'm saying is unreasonable. But when I hear you claim you like all humans, I can't help but feel that you're repudiating my feelings of hatred toward them. So—"

"So dislike them. I don't think there's anything wrong with that."

"I don't need you to tell me that!" I shouted despite myself.

Silence filled the room.

"...Sorry. I said too much," she admitted. She was still being so friendly with me even after I had yelled at her.

I felt like even more of an idiot seeing how calm she was.

I'd never matured into a proper adult, always stuck in this half-assed state.

I really hate myself...

"Why are you apologizing?" I asked. "...I'm the one who should apologize to you... I'm sorry. I shouldn't have blamed you. I was being unreasonable. You should've gotten mad at me. I *want* you to get mad... No, *please* get mad..."

"Wooow. In all my years, no one's ever begged me to get angry before."

"Have you ever lost your temper?" I asked.

"What? Um... Nothing comes to mind."

"Anything you hate?"

"Not in particular."

I bet. That was what I had come to realize after listening to her stories.

"Anything good?" I asked.

"I guess when the students who become human succeed."

"What about when they're met with misfortune?"

"That's a part of life, too."

"Have you ever been sad?"

"No idea." Haneda smiled wryly.

She and I were completely different. You could say I had the kind of personality that made living difficult. People like Haneda, who went along with the flow, would never have a hard day in their lives. That was the direction the world was moving in. I knew that very well. But I wanted to be able to expect things from others. I wanted the world to be a kinder place. For tragedies to happen less often. Haneda, on the other hand, thought like an adult.

Was it selfish of me to hate humans? Was I just sulking because things hadn't gone my way?

Ugh, I'm such a kid. Pathetic.

When had I stopped maturing? I'd always been stuck in the same place. The more I thought about this, the more it pained me.

I hung my head, my thoughts going around in circles.

"...Sorry," Haneda said gently. "This might only make you angry again, but I still think you're more human than anyone else."

"What?"

What did it mean to be "human"?

"Have you ever been angry, Mr. Hitoma?"

"...Yes."

"Anything you hate?"

"...Plenty."

I'm right in the middle of hating myself, in fact.

Haneda nodded. "Okay, okay." Next, she asked, "Anything good ever happened to you?"

"...Plenty of that, too."

"Painful things?"

"Truckloads."

"Ever given up on anything?"

"Every single day."

"Ever been sad?"

"I lost count."

"Ever felt happy?"

"...Lost count of those, too."

She asked me question after question of the same kind I had thrown at her. But they were filled with compassion. Rather than sizing up my life, it felt as if she were taking everything I had experienced into her embrace.

"I see. Your life is painted with a rich variety of emotions. They're what made you who you are," Haneda said.

Not all of my experiences had been sad. However, they hadn't all been happy, either. That was my life.

A life in which I had always been helplessly envious of others no matter how much time had passed.

"You have much that I don't, Mr. Hitoma."

"I could say the same for you."

"Really?"

"Your perspective, for one. If I thought the way you do, my life would be easier."

"Hmm." It didn't look like she understood. "I said it earlier, but I wanna try living the way you do… A life filled with both happiness and sadness… How nice. A proper life…," she lamented. "I've always been empty. You said your life would be easier if you thought like me, but is an easy life a fun one? Would it not feel hollow? Oh, I'm not saying one has to experience sorrow… But I think a life is better lived the more often one's heart is stirred, no matter by what emotion.

"That's why you're fine the way you are. More human than anyone else— I'm jealous. Whether you're happy or sad, you're fine the way you are—besides, you would never make another person sad in order to satisfy yourself."

"…I vented my anger on you just a minute ago."

"You apologized, and you're reflecting. You deeply regret it, don't you?"

She was right on the money, but it felt wrong to admit it myself, so I stayed silent.

"Ah-ha-ha! Your face! The way you're scrunching it! You're killing me. Ahhh… You're so human."

"Haneda…"

We both wanted what we didn't have.

Looking with envy at the green grass on the other side, ignorant of what we already had.

What *did* I have?

"Tell me: If you had the opportunity to confront your regrets, would you give it your all?" Haneda asked.

"What kind of question is that?" I replied, troubled by her abrupt and strangely specific query.

"Just wanted to ask," she said blithely.

"…Don't tell me you can *actually* rewind time."

"Didn't I say during the special training that there are no time travelers? I can't manipulate time," she replied. "Oh, did you already forget? Should we redo it?"

"Right! I remember now! Don't worry. I haven't forgotten… I think…"

Since I'd started working here, there had been so many episodes that defied common sense it was hard to remember them all! The diligent me back in college would have memorized everything, though…!

"So? Your answer?" Haneda urged.

"I don't know…"

For starters, the question itself was too vague. I had no idea what to say.

What did it mean to confront my regrets? Was she talking about the incident at my previous school? In that case, she was talking about the past… But not about returning to the past… *Hmm, it would be easier if I had an example.*

"…If it was a chance at a redo, I would like to try, I guess," I said.

The present me understood very well what the past me lacked.

By spending time with the students here, I'd learned several things, like relying on people around me, having an actual dialogue with other people, respecting their intentions—obvious things that I had nevertheless failed at.

"Heh-heh, you've gotten stronger," Haneda told me.

"…I hope you're right."

Actually, there were many fronts in which I still lacked confidence.

The audience was everything when it came to communication. I hoped I would be able to properly say what I wanted to without creating any misunderstandings going forward as well.

On the tail of that thought came a second thought: *I want to continue my life here, in this place.*

The Misanthrope and the Heart's Truest Desire

A MISANTHROPE TEACHES A CLASS FOR DEMI-HUMANS

I stirred at the sound of my phone alarm. As I woke up, my immediate thought was, *It might snow today.*

Unlike other days, the air was a biting and brisk kind of cold. I turned off the alarm, picked up my phone, and huddled under the covers, making sure I was covered from head to toe. The clock on my screen told me it was six in the morning. I reflexively tapped the passcode—the license plate number of my college moped—into my phone to unlock it, and then I opened the weather app lazily.

"Damn... Are you serious?" I muttered.

The temperature was negative two degrees Celsius, and it was already snowing.

Today was the start of the third semester.

* * *

"Here, Mr. Hitoma," Mr. Hoshino said, handing me a cup.

"Ah, thank you."

The warmth of the cup spread through my palms, and the numbness from the cold dissipated instantly.

So warm...

I caught a whiff of sweetness mixed in with the bitter scent wafting from the cup. The drink of the day was—

"Since it's so cold out, I figured I would brew some coffee for the teachers. Something easy to drink was best, so I picked café au lait," Mr. Hoshino explained.

"You're too kind," I said.

The coffee filled the cup with its soft beige color. I looked at it as I slowly brought the cup to my mouth. The sweet and mellow flavor had me sighing in satisfaction. The steam warmed the tip of my nose. What an indescribable feeling of security.

I hadn't had a taste of Mr. Hoshino's superb coffee since Christmas last year.

"It was still slightly warm yesterday, so the sudden snow was a bit of a shock," Mr. Hoshino said to me.

"Yeah, agreed."

I had thought we weren't due snow for a while. I suppose the weather was more temperamental here, since we were close to the mountains.

"Hello, Ms. Yuki. Would you like a cup?" Mr. Hoshino asked Ms. Saotome, who had just walked into the teachers' office.

"Yay! Thank you! I would love one!" she replied.

Ms. Karasuma had come in behind her and added, "One for me, too." It was rare to see her in the teachers' office.

"Here, Ms. Haruka," Mr. Hoshino said, handing her a cup.

The two of them joined our coffee circle.

"Bwah-choo!"

"That was a powerful sneeze, Haruka," Ms. Saotome said.

"It's got nothing on yours, Yuki," Ms. Karasuma retorted.

"I don't sneeze like that!"

They got along like birds of a feather. I felt like I was watching a conversation between two students. It warmed my heart. I suppose women are playful with each other no matter their age. It was so sweet.

Setting that aside.

"...Mr. Hoshino," I began. "What's the truth?"

"Um... No comment," he said.

"What?! You're horrible! Not to brag, but I'm tough against the cold!" Ms. Saotome bragged, puffing out her chest.

Mr. Hoshino scrunched up his face. "...Tell me, how much did you drink yesterday?"

"Um, let's see… Two liters, maybe?"

"You should fix your bad habit of warming yourself up with alcohol."

"But, ugh… Fine."

Ms. Saotome was a little childish when she was with Mr. Hoshino.

At the moment, she was clearly pouting.

"Stop. Don't flirt in the workplace," Ms. Karasuma warned.

"Whoops. Sorry, Ms. Haruka," Mr. Hoshino said.

"No probs. I'm willing to overlook it in moderation."

"*Pff!* Ha!" I laughed despite myself.

Mr. Hoshino was clearly the more experienced between the two of us, considering his work history. My laugh sounded extremely condescending. Nonetheless, something about Ms. Karasuma—her charm, perhaps—made me feel like I wouldn't be strung up for my transgression. Must've been the chill vibe in the room.

"What are you laughing at, Mr. Hitoma?" Ms. Karasuma asked.

"Ha-ha, my bad."

"Let's cut the chitchat. Time to get to work," Mr. Hoshino said.

"You're right! Third semester starts today! The snow is a good omen! I'll do my best!" Ms. Saotome exclaimed.

"Right, I came here to restock some supplies," Ms. Karasuma said. "Thanks for the coffee, Satoru. See you later."

"Of course. You're welcome," he replied.

She calls him by his first name…

Ms. Haruka Karasuma was an odd one. She was the principal's daughter…but they didn't look a bit alike. However, maybe she had special abilities just like the principal…

Oh, darn… I forgot to wish them a happy New Year.

The snow and coffee had taken up all my attention, but it was indeed the new year. The older I got, the less I noticed the passing of the seasons. I felt ancient.

Wait, but I'm still only thirty…for now…

I climbed the stairs to the advanced classroom on the third floor.

The climb wasn't so bad yet, but eventually it would become strenuous. That was the kind of useless worry that occupied my mind as I approached the classroom door and opened it.

"Happy New Year, Mr. Hitoma," Haneda said as I walked in.

"Happy New Year," I replied.

"Hey, Mr. Rei! It's a new year, but my love for you hasn't changed! Cheers!"

"Th-thanks, Ryuzaki," I answered awkwardly.

"The year's barely started, and you're already ogling her," Usami said. "Pathetic."

"I'm not!" I retorted.

"I'm looking forward to another great year, Mr. Hitoma!" Ohgami said.

"Same here."

"Meester Hitoma!" Nezu chirped. "Happy New Year! I'll take goods instead of cash for my New Year's present!"

"I'm not giving you either!" I paused. "...No, wait."

"Really?! You have something?! *Squeak!* Times like these, you gotta shoot your shot!"

There was something I needed to pass out to the students, although I didn't have it on me at that moment.

"I have news about your final graduation assignments, which will be announced next week," I said.

"*Squeak!* Don't use such important information as a punch line!!"

* * *

Yes, the season of the students' final assignments was upon us.

Like last year, they were given out individually when the students met with the principal.

The meetings were scheduled for a week after the initial announcement—in other words, first period today.

The students had been going to the principal's office one by one, and the period was nearly over.

In the waiting room that was the classroom, the students were self-studying, napping, or doing whatever floated their boat. Nezu was in the middle of her meeting. Ryuzaki was next and would close off this year's round of talks.

A lively voice broke through the silence in the classroom.

"*Squeeeeaaak!* The mood is sooo heavy!"

A strange tension filled the room.

"Machi…," Usami said.

"Eep! Sorry, Uchami. I just blurted it out!"

Usami had been on edge ever since the third semester started. Since she'd suddenly pivoted her post-graduation plans, she just barely met the academic requirements. On top of that, with the large point deduction she'd received last year, graduating would be difficult unless she got full marks on her assignment. She was backed into a corner. At the moment, she was using the self-study time to prep for exams. I watched her from the lectern.

Usami glared at Nezu with irritation, but with a deep sigh, she said dully, "…Whatever. Sit down already." She returned to her own work.

Nezu looked like she had something to add, but she walked slowly back to her seat, having perhaps decided that it was better not to speak to Usami just then. She sat and dropped the large paper envelope she was holding onto her desk. It landed with a heavy *thud*. Was something in it? Was that her assignment?

Ryuzaki switched with Nezu and left for the principal's office. I watched her go. Our eyes met when she stepped to the door, and she smiled. Then she winked and blew me a kiss, before rushing out the door.

Sheesh… Let's pretend I didn't see anything.

* * *

"What are your assignments?" Nezu asked. "Why am I the only one who got this huge envelope?"

"That's my line," said Usami. "What *is* that?"

"A *kintsugi* kit," Nezu answered.

"*Kintsugi*…? Really?" Ohgami said.

"First time I've heard of it. What is it for?" Ryuzaki asked.

"It's a technique where you repair cracked or chipped pottery with gold," Nezu explained. "My assignment is hands-on *kintsugi*! There's a broken teacup inside, too!"

"Wow, that's fair game for an assignment?" I mused.

I hadn't heard of it, either. If your plateware broke, you bought a replacement right after, and that was that.

"It's my first time learning about it, too," Nezu said. "What's yours, Uchami?"

"Writing letters to everyone in the advanced class."

"What?! No fair! You'll finish that in a flash! Cheater!!" Nezu protested.

"Who do you think I am? I won't get good grades if I just scribble whatever comes to mind."

"True, true!"

"Ugh, you drive me crazy…," Usami grumbled. "Isaki, what about you?"

Ohgami scrambled to answer the sudden question. "Um…! M-mine is to write ten reports on novels, manga, essay collections, and the like…!"

Manga is fair game, too, huh?

"Is there a reading list?" I asked.

"Y-yes. I received one. It includes… *The Tale of Genji*, Kafka's *Metamorphosis*, Harry P*tter, and even *Batm*n*. The selection is very broad."

"No kidding," I said. "From classic literature to American comics."

I was a fairly avid reader myself, but my tastes weren't quite that broad. I'd only ever read the classics as a student for class.

"Oh, there's a light novel on the list, too—a romantic comedy," Ohgami added. "It sounds like something you would enjoy, Mr. Hitoma."

"Is *that* what you all think of me?!"

I do read them, but that's not important!

"What kind of rom-coms do you like, Mr. Rei…?!" Ryuzaki asked me.

"What? Errr… I like stories about the dazzling days of youth, with plenty of gags for flavoring. They're fun to read."

"I see… That's good to know," she said.

Then I asked her a question: "What's your project about?"

"Starting the day after tomorrow, I'm to take up Roost Rep Ryouko's responsibilities for ten days."

Haneda walked up to Ryuzaki and commented, "Seriously? Sounds tough."

I wondered what Ryouko's day-to-day responsibilities were.

"Hmm, so you'll be making meals at the dorm…I guess?" I said.

"That's not all Ryouko has to do," Haneda interjected. "She looks after the beginner class, cleans, does laundry, and handles any emergencies."

"Emergencies?"

"Like when there's no hot water for baths or when someone loses their belongings, annoying chores like that."

"Must be exhausting…," I said.

She has to do all that every day… Now I see just how crucial Ryouko is to the school…

Ryuzaki seemed disheartened by Haneda's explanation of Ryouko's job. Her curled-up tail showed her uncertainty. "Am I qualified for this…?"

"I believe in you, Karin. Don't give up."

"Tobari… Thanks! I got it. I'll think of it as practice for when Mr. Rei and I get married!"

"Are you the type to want your wife to do all the housework, Hitoma?" Usami drawled.

"No, not particularly…"

I'd had next to zero chances to talk about the topic, so I had never really thought about it in the first place…

"Oh yes? But I like challenging myself, so I'll do my utmost, Mr. Rei!"

"G-great…," I mumbled.

Setting aside Ryuzaki's reasoning, it was good to see her motivated. I decided not to dig any further.

"And what do you have to do, Tobari?" Ryuzaki asked.

"Make an instrument by hand."

"What kind of instrument?" said Usami.

"Good question," Haneda replied.

Then Nezu asked, "You're going to brainstorm?"

"Guess I have to."

"It sounds difficult…," commented Ohgami.

"Yeah, but…I can't wait to start."

The atmosphere in the room softened after Haneda's proclamation. The students were uneasy about whether they would be able to complete their assignments properly, but Haneda's words had given them the flexibility of mind to enjoy the projects, too.

That was beyond my ability.

She was able to be the mood maker because she was Tobari Haneda, a student.

Thus, final assignment season began for this year's advanced class.

* * *

This time of year, there were few normal classes. The students spent most of their days on their projects. It was day one. Haneda was sawing away at a large, thick plank of wood.

"What are you making?" I asked her.

She looked like a DIYer, and an enthusiast at that.

"A guitar," she answered. "I'm thinking of making an electric Les Paul. Already ordered the transmission cables and the sound check amp."

"Oh, wow." I didn't understand a word of the instrument-related jargon. "Guitars seem hard to make."

"Maybe. But I still wanted to try making one. It seems fun."

I suspected Haneda was half picking—no, 100 percent picking her projects based on her own hobbies. She whistled as she moved the saw back and forth.

Meanwhile, Nezu was working with *urushi* lacquer off to the side, grumbling, "*Squeak-squeeeeak!* Talk about a real pain in the neck!" She was wearing gloves and a long-sleeved apron to cover any exposed skin. Touching the lacquer with bare skin could result in a chemical burn. Apparently, she was annoyed with the protective gear.

"Machi! Shut up!!" Usami spat.

"*Squeak?!* Isn't Tobari making more of a racket sawing through the wood?!" Nezu protested.

"That's part of her assignment, so it's fine."

"That's favoritism! You're biased!" Nezu turned to me. "What say you, Meester Hitoma?"

"You're asking me...? More importantly, what is your assignment like?"

"I got a traditional *kintsugi* repair kit, but I'll be working with lacquer from start to finish," she explained. "I've just finished applying raw lacquer to the cross section of the teacup. It has to be stored in a drying room, and the temperature and humidity have to be strictly controlled! TBH, it's a giant pain!"

"Hmm, it's like you're raising microbes," I remarked.

An acquaintance of mine from college who had a different major had done similar work. He was a STEM major, and he staked his livelihood on maintaining the temperature and humidity of his machines in order to grow his colonies. In the lab, the microbes had higher standing than the people. STEM folks were serious business.

"You have a point...," Nezu mumbled. "Microbes... Hmm."

Then she took a cardboard box and silently began building a simple drying room. Her focus mode had been switched on. She seemed like she would be fine.

Usami, who had been bickering with Nezu a minute ago, was battling it out with a math problem set. The college entrance exam period and final assignment season overlapped, so she had asked Mr. Hoshino, the entrance exam expert, to draft a schedule. Her days were divided into assignment days and exam-prep days. That day was the latter, apparently.

As for Ohgami, she had been quietly reading a book that had colorful sticky notes spouting from between the pages. I wondered if the colors stood for different categories.

Ryuzaki was looking at her notes, her face scrunched in concentration. From what I had heard, Ryouko was away for the ten-day period, and while Ryuzaki was at school, the female teachers had divided up the work, with Ms. Karasuma acting as the point person.

All the students were working hard and facing their challenges head-on.

The director and principal were really something to think up such assignments time after time.

* * *

One week passed after the assignments were revealed. That day, fifth and sixth period after lunch were dedicated to working on the final assignments.

Haneda had finished cutting out the parts of the guitar from the wood she had procured, and she had filed everything down. At the moment, she was drilling holes into the largest of the flat wooden pieces. It was amazing watching a guitar emerge from what had started as a regular plank of wood. Observing the creation process, I realized that all the things around me that I thought nothing of had been made by someone, and it gave me a deeper appreciation. When I watched Haneda, on the inside, I felt like I was getting to experience the excitement of a behind-the-scenes factory tour.

I was relaxing, absorbed in Haneda's work, when Nezu shattered my peace and quiet:

"Meester Hitomaaa!! Listen, listen!! Karin's being mean!! Lay down the law!!"

"Wait a sec! Machi! Don't go crying to Mr. Rei! That's cheap!" Ryuzaki protested.

"Huh?! What exactly is going on?!?" I asked. Was there a problem with one of their assignments?

"We won't be allowed to have seconds at dinner!" Nezu exclaimed.

"...Come again?" *What is she talking about?*

"There's a budget! I have no choice! Those are the rules!" Ryuzaki said.

"Managing the funds is your job! Rule this, rule that... You're no better than a corrupt solicitor! The magistrate is pissed, and at this rate, my belly is gonna be destroyed like the Tower of Babel!"

"That time period and that slang don't mix!" I said.

That goes to show how cornered Nezu must feel...

"Listen to the voices of the unfortunates! You dictator!!!" screamed Nezu.

"Wh—?! What are you talking about?! I—," Ryuzaki started to say.

"SHUT UP!!!"

The loud *thud* of a book slamming against a desk followed that scream. The classroom fell completely silent.

Usami, the one who had just screamed, was panting. Her face was turned down.

"Usami…," I said.

She snapped alert, and her steely expression fell apart. "Ah, I-I'm sorry."

"No, I—I was being too noisy. I'm sorry, too," said Nezu.

"Me too," Ryuzaki added. "Wait—Isaki?!"

At the other end of Ryuzaki's gaze, tucked into a corner of the room, was Ohgami, clutching a book and sobbing. "*Hic…* N-no, it's not… I—I was just s-surprised…," she stuttered, rushing to wipe away her tears.

The blood drained from Usami's face. "It's my fault," she mumbled, the words tumbling from her mouth in a frenzy. Her expression contorted, and her brows furrowed. For a moment, I thought she had gotten a hold of herself, but then she flew out of the classroom.

"Usami!" I yelled after her. Then I told the other students, "Sorry! Finish up class without me!"

I thought I heard Haneda say "'Kay" from one corner of the room.

"How is Usami this fast?!" I cried.

She was running down the stairs. I gave chase.

Come to think of it, the other classes were still in session. I was about to shout after Usami, but I didn't want to accidentally sentence her to a public execution by making the wrong move nor reveal to the other classes that something was amiss… I had already called her name once, but I chose to believe I'd be able to explain my way out of that one somehow!

I scrambled down to the ground floor, but I had lost sight of Usami. I scanned my surroundings, but there was no sign that she had gone outside. Just in case, I checked the shoe cubbies, and Usami's outdoor shoes hadn't been touched.

"You've gotta be kidding me…," I muttered. I hung my head, wondering what to do.

Just then, I heard my name.

"Mr. Hitoma."

"Ack!" I yelped. "…Ms. Karasuma."

Standing behind me was Ms. Haruka Karasuma.

"Have you seen Usami?" I asked her.

"She's in the nurse's office. In fact, I came here after getting Usami's go-ahead. I figured you'd be worried and asked if I could bring you to see her."

"Th-thank you…"

Unflappable as always, I thought. Thanks to that, I had regained a bit of my cool.

Ms. Karasuma led me to the nurse's office, and I went inside. I hadn't been there since the previous year to see Haneda. It was my second time.

Usami was sitting on a bed, hugging her knees, with a blanket thrown over her head.

"Usami…," I said softly.

Her ears twitched. "…I'm the worst," she mumbled, her voice lifeless. "I have no patience. I lose my temper right away. I made Isaki cry…"

Her words, which contained no trace of her usual strength, put me at a loss.

"Usami," Ms. Karasuma began. "Which would you like? Lemonade or green tea?"

"…Green tea," Usami whispered.

"You got it. What about you, Mr. Hitoma?"

"I'll have the same."

"'Kay."

Ms. Karasuma ambled over to the window and started boiling a pot of water in the electric kettle.

The air between me and Usami was thick with tension.

The first to break the silence was Usami.

"…I'm sorry for running out in the middle of class."

It was an apology.

"I was the one who disturbed class the most."

"It's fine," I told her.

She met my noncommittal reply with an accusatory gaze. "What is?"

"...Everyone has times when they find it hard to get along with others. I understand," I said.

"He's right," Ms. Karasuma chimed in. She was holding a tray with three teacups, and she handed me and Usami each a cup of green tea. "Be careful. It's hot."

"Th-thank you," I stammered.

"Thanks...," Usami said.

"A hot drink will calm you down," Ms. Karasuma told us. "I'm just echoing what Satoru said, though."

It did sound like something Mr. Hoshino would say.

"Are you close with Ms. Saotome and Mr. Hoshino?" I asked Ms. Karasuma.

"No closer than normal," she replied.

Normal, she claimed... Considering the way they called one another by name and their familiarity, I had thought they were good friends—but Ms. Karasuma was the principal's daughter. Maybe she had known the teachers at the school ever since she was little.

"It's delicious," Usami said.

"Great," Ms. Karasuma replied.

"...I'll apologize to everyone when I go back," Usami promised.

"Okay," I said. "I'm sorry I didn't warn them about the noise earlier."

"Hmph. Yeah, you should have."

"All right, it looks like you've calmed down," Ms. Karasuma commented.

The false bravado in Usami's words hadn't escaped my notice. However, if she wanted to show that she was fine, I wanted to honor her wish.

"Usami," Ms. Karasuma said from her desk, where she was sitting and sipping her tea. "I don't have the full picture, but thanks for coming to me. I'll be here, so stop by at any time."

"Thanks, Kara—Ms. Karasuma," Usami said.

"Call me Haruka."

"Thanks, Haruka."

"There you go."

"Why did you want to become a nurse, Haruka?" Usami asked.

Ms. Karasuma thought about her question and turned to look out the window with a nostalgic expression on her face. "I wanted to create a space where anyone could run away to."

"What do you mean?"

"I've been at this school since long before. Occasionally, you get a student who's a little *too* hardworking, *too* hard on themselves."

I glanced at Usami despite myself.

She glared back and said, "Don't look at me."

As she watched us, Ms. Karasuma's expression softened. "It's never a bad thing to have more places to rest your feet," she said. "And you're free to come by, too, Mr. Hitoma."

"Wh—? Um, thanks…?"

At the same time, the bell rang. Class was over.

"I'm going back to the classroom," Usami announced.

Ms. Karasuma smiled warmly and waved. "Sounds good. Take care."

A curious character as always.

With fifth period over, the hallways were filled with students and teachers coming and going, thanks to which Usami and I were able to return to the advanced classroom without drawing attention.

The door had been left open, and I could see into the room.

My eyes met Haneda's. *Ah. Whoops.*

"Welcome back," Haneda said.

"W-we're back," Usami responded.

In contrast to Haneda's easy attitude, Usami was stiff and awkward.

"Sorry to leave you in charge of the class, Haneda," I said. "Thanks."

"I'm sorry, too," Usami added.

"Hmm? No worries." Haneda grinned and flashed a thumbs-up.

That put me at ease.

Man, it might have been an emergency, but I relied too much on Haneda this time...

"Uchami!" Nezu cried. Having noticed we were back, she ran over and bowed her head low. "Sorry about earlier, *squeak!*"

"Machi...," Usami said. "I'm the one who's sorry." She bowed.

"Me and Karin talked! Seconds are a-okay!" Nezu told her.

"Yep. In exchange, Machi will help with cleaning the dining hall," Ryuzaki added. "Sorry about earlier, Sui."

"It's all right, Karin. I'm sorry, too," Usami said.

An atmosphere of harmony filled the room. It looked like they were able to reconcile.

"By the way... That's all good and all, but...what were you doing alone with Mr. Rei this whole time?" Ryuzaki asked while darting glances at me. She was trying to act nonchalant, but it was obvious that she was dying to know.

"Ah, what a pain," grumbled Usami. "Your turn, Hitoma."

"Excuse me?!" I yelped.

"Mr. Rei!" Ryuzaki exclaimed, switching targets immediately.

That jerk. Just when I thought she was being sweet...

Tsk...! Fine, I'll overlook it for today...

While I was being bombarded by Ryuzaki with questions, Usami went to talk with Ohgami to apologize for alarming her by yelling, for being quick to anger, and for scaring her in general.

Ohgami listened compassionately to Usami the whole time. At the end, she apparently said, "Thank you for that. I was just a little surprised. I still love you, Usami."

* * *

Perhaps owing to Usami's explosion, everyone was especially focused and well-behaved during the rest of the allotted assignment time that day. There was a sense of frenzied energy in the room as they worked, in a good way.

Haneda had her hands full with a tangle of mysterious cables, the... mechanical workings...of the electric guitar, I supposed. I had no clue about instruments. I'd done something similar when I had built my PC, but a gamer friend who was knowledgeable about machinery had walked me through the process over the Web. I myself only had a layman's understanding of electronics.

In any case, she's seriously skilled with her hands...

As usual, Ohgami was quietly reading a book. The sticky notes in her pile of books were steadily multiplying. Was she planning on finishing all the books before writing her reports in one go? It seemed like a stressful approach. I found myself worried for a moment, but I realized I was sticking my nose where it didn't belong again. I decided to observe from the sidelines for the moment.

Usami was working on her assignment that day.

We locked eyes accidentally.

"...What? Don't stare at me," she snapped.

"How's everything going?" I asked.

"This assignment isn't my strong suit... Letters should be written by writers like Isaki..."

"Wasn't it assigned to you precisely so you could overcome your preoccupation with your weaknesses?"

"Stop responding so seriously to my grumbling. I'm not looking for advice. I know that without you telling me," she replied sharply.

Says the one who is usually equipped with no-nonsense retorts, I thought, but I was relieved that she was back to her normal, prickly self. Was this what Haneda meant by "humanlike"? I felt like the pieces were falling into place. If I was right, then Usami was quite humanlike herself...

Usami was writing and erasing and rewriting and re-erasing her letter with a scowl on her face as usual.

Nezu was waiting for the lacquer to dry and had her hands free. She had brought the *kintsugi* kit back to the dorm so she could store it in a temperature- and humidity-controlled environment. She was self-studying instead.

The other day, I had bumped into Chiyu by coincidence and asked her casually about Nezu's progress. "Machi dotes on that teacup," she'd revealed to me. "She even says good-bye to it before going to school."

Apparently, she was treating it as if it were a cute pet.

Ryuzaki was working hard in the dorms with the support of the other teachers. Guys were forbidden from entering the dorms, so I couldn't check for myself, but I heard about her efforts from the other students, particularly the ones in the beginner class.

They said things like, "I was scared of the dragon lady at first, but she sleeps with us at night" and "Her cooking is just as yummy as Ryouko's."

At that moment, Ryuzaki was sewing. It seemed that she was repairing clothes that were ripped as a result of a student's unhuman-like behavior.

It must have been no easy feat, but she was tackling the challenge in her own way.

* * *

The weekend came and went, and it was Monday again.

It was the final day of Ryuzaki's assignment.

The assignment had seemed tough, but she was reluctant to part with it.

Haneda was working on the finishing touches of her own assignment, tinkering around with the guitar's surface. She had made a simple wooden guitar. To be honest, it looked pretty awesome.

She completed her adjustments—"Cool. Great, I think I'm done"—and hooked up the instrument to the amp excitedly.

"I can't believe you actually built a guitar!" Nezu said.

"Wow, it's amazing!" Ohgami exclaimed.

"The wood grain looks cool," Usami noted.

"It's my first time seeing a real electric guitar!" Ryuzaki chimed in.

The other advanced students had Haneda surrounded in the blink of an eye.

"I'll start by tuning it," Haneda said.

She plucked at each string individually, twisting the screwlike knobs to adjust the sound. I could tell that the pitch was getting higher and lower, but not which knob was doing what.

"That just about does it."

Once Haneda finished the tuning, the others burst into applause.

"Sing something for us, Tobari!" Nezu urged.

"Making it is one thing, but do you know how to play?" Usami asked.

"A little," Haneda replied. "We're still in the middle of class, so I'll play a quiet song. Better leave the amp out."

She unplugged the cable from the guitar. The soft, unfiltered *twang* of the electric guitar was a novel sound.

It was a soft but gentle tune. The somewhat cheap sound of the guitar supported the warmth infused into the song.

Haneda really is a good singer.

With a single refrain, the atmosphere in the room had completely changed.

"Yeah, it feels good," Haneda remarked afterward. "Thanks, guys."

"Your singing and playing are really incredible," I told her.

"Really? Heh-heh, thanks, Mr. Hitoma! Do you play guitar? Give it a try." She held the guitar toward me.

"I've never played any instruments!"

"It's fine. Just fiddle with it a bit. It might be more fun than you think."

Seriously...

But I couldn't deny that watching Haneda had piqued my interest. I reluctantly took the guitar.

The guitar is Haneda's final assignment. No matter what, I must not break it.

The instrument was heavier than I had expected, perhaps because it was constructed from solid wood. I plucked a string at random.

Bwaaan.

"Whoa...," I found myself whispering, touched by the sound.

Amazing. This is what it's like to play a guitar.

My musical experience was limited to playing around with electronic music as a hobby, so I had hardly ever held a real instrument before. The only instrument I'd ever played was the recorder back in grade school.

"Haneda... You're incredible...," I said.

"Hmm?"

"You made an instrument from nothing. That's astounding." I handed the guitar back to her for fear of breaking it.

"Heh-heh, thanks! I'll go turn this in to the principal," she declared before heading to the principal's office.

Once again, Haneda was the first one to turn in her final assignment. *More importantly...*

"Being able to play instruments is so cool...," I mumbled.

"Do you like girls who are good at instruments, Mr. Rei?" Ryuzaki had come up to me at some point.

"Hmm... I really respect people who are multitalented, I'd say."

"I see... Good to know! Thanks, Mr. Rei! Love you!"

"...! Errr, thanks."

She threw these straight-ball confessions at me on occasion, and that one had been coming right at me, but I dodged it by a hair.

I couldn't escape Usami's ire, however...

"You guys have no manners," she grumbled under her breath in annoyance.

Even though she was throwing out these complaints here and there, she was making progress on her letters in between her studies. On her desk was a stack of envelopes with letters she had finished.

"You're working hard, Usami," I said to her.

"...I do what I'm told. Isaki must be a masochist, writing every day."

"What?! That's not true...!" Ohgami protested.

"Ohgami isn't like that," I said in her defense, in case she had taken Usami seriously.

"Suffering looks different for everyone," Nezu added.

"How is your assignment going?" Usami asked Nezu.

"I'm glad you asked, *squeak!* Bowledoodle, under my loving care, is heading into the last stage of the process!"

"Huh? Bowla-what...? What're you talking about?"

"Bowledoodle. It's the name of the rice bowl I'm taking care of."

"First time I've heard of someone naming a bowl...," I mused.

"But, Mr. Rei, humans often name inanimate objects, too," Ryuzaki said.

"Oh yeah?"

"Yes. To use an old example, there used to be princes who named their own weapons."

"Yep! Same thing, pretty much!" Nezu said.

It's a little different..., I thought, but I was reluctant to run my mouth, so I kept my opinion to myself.

"Hmm, it's admirable how you treat your things with care," Usami commented. "It's a weird name, but I'm sure Bowledoodle is happy."

"*Squeak!* Exactly! I can't wait to eat rice out of Bowledoodle!" Nezu said. "Look! My lock screen's background is Chiyu with Bowledoodle."

On the screen, in what looked to be a dorm room, was Chiyu making a peace sign next to a rice bowl.

Nezu was head over heels. She was so excited about the work waiting for her that she could barely sit still.

By the end of the day, her assignment would be all but done.

Unlike the previous year, it seemed as though everyone would finish around the same time.

However, Ohgami was still locked in a fierce battle with her assignment.

For every work she'd read, she had to write a review of two thousand characters or less, and apparently, she was having trouble summarizing her thoughts.

Unable to fit what she wanted to say within the word limit, she was writing nearly double the requirement. According to Ohgami, every example was a little different, and if she was going to put in example A, she wanted to add example B, too... And the result of all her vacillation was the current state of affairs. She had drafted her thoughts and was in the process of rereading her reviews over and over again, deepening her understanding of the original work in the meantime, in order to figure out what to cut out. In short, she was currently in the middle of revisions.

The end-of-period bell rang; the in-class time to work on their assignments was over for the day. Around the same time, there came a *knock-knock-knock* at the door to the advanced classroom.

They're here.

The students were wondering what was up.

I turned to the door. "Come in," I said, sliding it open.

On the other side were several beginner students.

"E-excuse us," said a student who seemed to be the representative. She bowed slightly, then entered the room, the other students streaming in after her.

The students instantly made a beeline for Ryuzaki.

"Oh? What are you all...?" Ryuzaki began.

The rep held out the small package in her hands. She took a deep breath before saying, "Thank you for the last ten days, Karin!"

The others chimed in afterward. "Thank you very much!"

Ryuzaki looked flustered, but she took the package. "Th-thanks?" she said, bewildered by the sudden turn of events.

Seeing her take the present, the beginner students exchanged words of relief with accomplishment written on their faces.

"We did it."

"Hooray!"

Then they flooded the classroom.

It was like a scene from Valentine's Day at an all-girls school, where the younger students lined up to give chocolates to an adored upperclassman.

"What was that...?" Ryuzaki wondered aloud.

"What did you get, Karin?" Nezu asked. "It smells sweet, *squeak...!*"

Ryuzaki opened the small package she had been given. There was a smaller box inside. She opened it slowly to reveal:

"Ah, wow—"

Inside was a cookie with a likeness of Ryuzaki drawn in icing.

"Awesome! So cute!" Nezu exclaimed. "I couldn't possibly ask you to share..."

Actually, on Friday, the beginner-class students had asked me if they could stop by for a moment after school on the last day of Ryuzaki's duties as dorm mother—in other words, Monday. They'd said they wanted to thank her. Of course, I had instantly given them the green light.

"I... They came to me asking me to teach them how to make icing. I had been wondering what for..." Ryuzaki held the box tenderly and whispered, "...And now I know."

I hadn't been able to watch over her, but I was sure she must have done a wonderful job as the dorm mother.

The cookie in her hands was like a medal, the best one in the world.

* * *

The day after that, Haneda and Ryuzaki, done with their assignments, were self-studying at their own pace.

For Usami, it was an exam-prep day, not an assignment day, and she was tearing through practice questions. Maybe it was because exam day was close, but she was working more furiously than usual.

Exam season began that week, starting with the standardized Common Test. Usami's top choice was the medical program of a highly selective public university. On test day, she was to sit the exam alone in the AV room in the annex building. She was able to take the exam at the school thanks to the director and the cooperation of an influential person stationed in human society who had ties to the school.

Other than the time she set aside for her final assignment, she was always working on some problem set or other. She spent her time after school in the math prep room, working rigorously with a top-of-the-class alumnus of an American university, Mr. Hoshino, in what was pretty much private tutoring. The prep room was my sanctuary, but having found that out, I'd started restricting my social calls.

There was the abrupt change she'd made in her career aspirations last year to consider as well. Usami was giving her all.

All I could do was watch over her. I hoped her hard work would bear fruit…

Nezu was self-studying as well. Was she done with her assignment? Given her personality, I would've thought she would have paraded the finished product in front of us before turning it in to the principal…

"How is your assignment, Nezu?" I asked.

But her response was only a truncated "*Squeak.*"

…That "I'm 100 percent doomed" expression of hers almost makes me want to laugh.

"Ah, um—I'll hand it in at some point," she said.

"You're done? You did say you were at the last step..."

"Tsk. Why'd you have to remember that...?"

"Don't click your tongue at me."

Why is she being so evasive? No way—

"Did you mess up?!"

"Rude! I finished repairing Bowledoodle properly!" she snapped.

"Then why haven't you turned it in?" I asked.

"Squeak...!"

Can there be any other living being to whom the gnashing-teeth sound effect is more suitable?

Sweat beaded on Nezu's forehead. It was the dead of winter.

"But if I turn it in... If I...! Bowledoodle will never come back to me!" she sobbed.

"Nezu...!" I exclaimed, her tears tugging at my heartstrings.

I didn't realize she cared so deeply...

"That's why...I'm going to display Bowledoodle in my room until the very last moment! That way we can be together until the last day—"

"What? Isn't it gonna be returned to you?" drawled Haneda.

"Really?!" Nezu cried.

"Five years ago a student was given a similar assignment. After the principal checked the submission, he gave it back to her."

"Seriously? ...Hoh-hoh-hoh! If there's a precedent, it'll be easy to get my way, no matter what they tell me... Thanks, Tobari!" Nezu said, her face instantly lighting up. "Sounds like a plan! Geez! I was worried for nothing! I'll bring Bowledoodle to the principal tomorrow!"

What happened to her tears from a second ago?

With a bright smile and an upbeat mood, Nezu returned to her self-studies.

I didn't know whether there had been a similar assignment before, but regardless, judging from what Haneda said, Nezu would be reunited with her work by the power of the director.

Good for you, Nezu. You'll be able to eat rice from Bowledoodle.

Ohgami had finished condensing her reviews and was in the middle of polishing her writing and pinning down the right turns of phrase. The following day was the next full moon.

I wondered what Ohgami's flamboyant alter ego thought of her assignment.

* * *

"Wa-ha-ha! That's sooo interesting! Isaki is the queen of summaries!" Full-Moon Ohgami said, cackling. "Tell me! Was *The Tale of Genji* always so nasty?! It's like a daytime soap, LMAO! But it's pretty deep, too! I think I like the Safflower Princess! Maybe 'cause she knows what she wants?"

"How do you know about daytime soaps...?" I asked skeptically.

"This model I follow is in one, so I looked it up!"

"Gotcha."

Casting played a critical role in attracting a wide audience.

"Wow! *Batm*n* and Harry P*tter are on the list, too! She read Western works, too?! I've been curious about them!" she said. "Hold up—isn't my other half legit amazing?! She wrote all these reports herself?! Talk about straight and narrow!"

She's not wrong...

Ohgami had faded into the background while working on her assignment, but there, she had been devotedly plugging away at her tasks. The collection of reports was the result of her labor.

I had taken a quick look at her request. She had definitely leveled up her ability to convey herself through writing.

"She's literally a genius! Oh, I like this part. I'm going to leave a note for her here!" Full-Moon Ohgami declared, adding a gaudy sticky note to the report.

That's the part she was having trouble articulating yesterday.

"Isn't this insanely well-written?! All her best qualities shine through. I hope she gets to graduate... If she does, I want to watch the film version of this book in theaters! Usually, we can only watch the Blu-rays the school owns or catch reruns on TV..." Ohgami turned to Usami. "Hey! Do you watch movies?"

"What...? No."

That day, Usami was working on her letters. Unlike when she was doing practice problems, she seemed to have her head in the clouds. In fact, she was more enervated than usual. Maybe she was burned-out from studying...

"Okay... Wait a sec, aren't you a little dead today?! What happened?!" Ohgami asked worriedly, grabbing Usami's shoulder.

Way to dive right in, Ohgami. She's a tough cookie...!

"Isaki...," Usami said.

She looked woozy, like a stuffed animal just out of the wash. Then, her eyes snapped wide open like she'd just remembered something. She took out an envelope from her bag.

"I need you for my assignment, Isaki," she said.

"What?! Me? Not the other Isaki?"

"Yeah. My assignment is to write letters for everyone in the advanced class."

"...Am I included in 'everyone'?"

"...? Obviously."

Usami had an air of *What are you going on about?* Ohgami seemed to be processing their conversation.

Ohgami wagged her tail, and her ears drooped. "Usamiii!" she cried, wrapping her arms around Usami and rubbing their cheeks together.

"Wh-what the heck?! Get offa me!" Usami yelled.

It was a heartwarming scene. The atmosphere in the room turned soft and fuzzy.

"Isaki, sit!" ordered Usami.

"*Ruff!*" Ohgami barked. Smiling, she sat down on her knees obediently with her hands on her lap.

"Way to play along!" I said.

Usami looked at Ohgami and huffed in satisfaction. Then she held out the envelope. "I'm not as good as Isaki at writing, so cut me some slack."

"Nah, letters aren't about how good or bad your writing skills are! Awww! I'm so happy! Hooray!! Can I read it now? I don't wanna wait!"

"Uh, um, I guess… I mean, I gave it to you. You're free to do what you want with it."

"Amazing! Thanks!!"

Ohgami's carefree smile and joy seemed to melt Usami's tension.

Ohgami opened the envelope and took out the letter with care. There were four pages. She ran her eyes down the letters, taking her time.

Usami watched restlessly. The other advanced students were curious about her writing as well. Nezu wasn't content with sneaking a furtive glance or two—she was staring outright.

The last page of the letter. Ohgami's reading pace noticeably slowed; she seemed reluctant to finish. There was a hint of tears in her eyes. She shut her eyes slowly and reopened them before stretching her arms out to Usami.

"Usamiiiii! Thank you! Everything you wrote makes me sooo happy! Like how you said I'm usually smiling cheerfully, but I worry about people when push comes to shove, or that I'm chill and have no mean bone in my body. I'm touched! I didn't know you thought so highly of me!" Ohgami exclaimed. "Ah, oh no! I was trying hard to hold back, but I'm at my limit! I think I'm gonna cry. Geez!! I can't tell you how happy I am, Usami…!"

"Gah! I told you not to cling to me!!" Usami said.

"I looove you, Usami! We don't get to meet very often, but you still look out for me, and you remembered to include me in your letter-writing assignment. I'm so, so happy! Thank you, thank you, thank you!"

"Hmph! It's hard to forget someone so noisy!"

"Yeah!! In that case, I'm never gonna shut up!!"

Usami didn't seem altogether displeased with Ohgami's sappiness.

"Cool. Can't wait for mine!" Haneda said.

"Way to raise the bar, Tobari…," Usami grumbled.

"It was really touching! Usamiii!" Ohgami cried.

The only ones who hadn't finished their assignments were Ohgami and Usami, but considering the way things were, they would likely be done by the deadline.

* * *

The last of the entrance exams for advanced students were over—with Usami bringing up the rear—and the deadline for the assignments was approaching.

Usami and Mr. Hoshino predicted that she had cleared the bar for the Common Test, but she was on the cusp of the cutoff for the early admission exam for her target university.

"Hitoma," Usami said, surprising me by showing up right when I was thinking about her.

"Hey, Usami, what's up?" I replied.

"I wrote all the letters. I handed them out, too... This is the last one." She held out a single envelope. "It's for you."

"Me?"

"'Everyone in the advanced class' means you, too, duh. I won't fall for such an obvious trick. Also... Here." She took out one more envelope. "This one is for Neneko. I wasn't sure if I should write to her, but she... she was our classmate this year, too..."

There was a tiny cat sticker on the envelope. I wondered if Usami had picked it herself.

"Thanks, Usami. I'll take care of it."

"Good. You better."

Am I allowed to give Kurosawa Usami's letter? I'll ask the director later.

I looked at the two letters in my hands. One envelope had a black cat sticker. The other was undecorated.

I hadn't expected to receive a letter from Usami.

Had it really been a trap? I had my doubts, but if Usami's interpretation was right and I had received the same assignment, I might have fallen for it. There were very few instances where the teacher was included in "everyone in the class." The students' lives at school were mostly spent around other students... Actually, that was what was healthy and appropriate.

The other students had all reacted with delight.

Ryuzaki, after Usami gave her the letter, said in surprise, "It's my first time getting a letter. What a remarkable gift. It feels like you're here in the paper, Sui!"

Ohgami was delighted. "Your writing isn't flowery. Your feelings come straight through. It's a gracious and warm letter. I love it!" she had commented.

Haneda smiled and said to Usami, "You've been looking at both me and yourself closely, I can tell. I like the way you hate to lose."

Nezu laughed. "*Squeak*. Heh-heh. Uchamiii! I didn't know that's how you see me! Shucks! You really love me, don't you?! Kee-kee-kee!" But just when I thought she was only going to tease Usami, suddenly she went quiet and started crying, large tears dripping down her face.

"Machi! What are you crying for all of a sudden?" Usami exclaimed.

"D-don't cry!" Ohgami said. "If you cry, I…I'm going to start crying, too…!"

"Huh? Don't you start, too, Isaki. Not when I'm trying so hard to stay strong…!" Ryuzaki chimed in.

"What?! You too, Karin?! Tobari, Hitoma, emergency! Help!" cried Usami.

Seeing Usami all shook up next to the bawling Nezu, Ohgami, and Ryuzaki was a novelty.

"Wooow, you made them cry!!" Haneda said.

"Excuse you! That's slander!" Usami protested.

"But it's true! You're the one at fault, Usami!"

"*Et tu*, Isaki?!"

"I can't help it! You're usually so strict, but your letter was so kind!"

"Yeah, that's right! It was so mushy! What's up with that?" Nezu added. "And ease up on finding everyone's good spots! Behind that harsh front of yours is a pure maiden at heart! Take off those rose-tinted glasses! You're too trusting! It's almost like…you like me more than I like myself!"

"Are you crying or are you pissed?! Pick one!" Usami demanded.

"Then I'm pissed!!" Nezu shouted.

"*That's* what you went with?!"

Nezu leaped at Usami and hugged her tightly. Usami made a valiant effort to peel the smaller girl off her, but it didn't go well. Ohgami and Ryuzaki were sobbing the entire time.

Sheesh, what a mess. But maybe moments like these were what you called happiness. In one corner of my heart, I wished for the shenanigans to never end.

"Mr. Hitoma, did you read Usami's letter?" Haneda asked, having come to me during the chaos.

"No, not yet."

"Aren't you going to?"

"When I get home."

"Whaaat? Just read it already."

"Don't wanna. I might cry."

"Ha-ha, fair point!"

I couldn't fathom what Usami had written, but even so, I knew: I would end up in tears.

A letter from any student would already have pushed me to the edge, and this was from *Usami*, of all people. Not to mention, judging from the state of the other letters' recipients, she'd looked for all our strengths. Yep, I was definitely gonna be weeping.

"Oh, right. There's a letter for Kurosawa, too," I said.

"Wow. Go, Usami. You'll have to give it to her later, then," Haneda replied.

At the other end of her gaze was Usami, who was still having it out with Nezu.

The two of them fought like an old married couple. They made a good pair.

Next to them, Ryuzaki and Ohgami had stopped crying at some point and were now talking.

"You're almost done with your assignment, then, right, Isaki?" Ryuzaki asked to confirm.

"Yes. I'm worried about whether I properly described the appeal of each work, but the other me complimented my reports profusely, so I feel a little more confident…," Ohgami replied. "There were parts I was unsure of, but I was able to have faith in my own judgment thanks to her advice."

"How wonderful!"

I see. Ohgami is nearly done.

I peeked over at Ohgami's desk. On top was a giant stack of books and her notes.

I can't believe she read all those books in such a short time… On top of that, she wrote a two-thousand-word review for each one…

In the beginning, I hadn't really grasped the scale of her assignment. I had thought vaguely that it seemed difficult, but nothing more. However, looking at the books and sheets upon sheets of notes, I finally registered that most people wouldn't have stood a chance.

Anyone who only saw Ohgami for her meek demeanor might think her accomplishment implausible, but actually, she had a laser focus and grit. She was the type who could fully immerse themselves in their own world and ignore everything around them.

Just then, Ohgami was saying to Usami, "Because of your letter, I think I can try even harder. Thank you again."

"Hmph. Hurry up and finish your assignment already. It should be a snap for you. You're an excellent writer. I can vouch for it."

"I will!" Ohgami said with a smile, motivated by Usami's pep talk. She returned to her seat and got back to work.

Her expression said that she had already dived back into her own world. Her pen was flying across the page once more.

"I'm finished!" Ohgami declared, collapsing onto her desk.

It was five minutes before the period was over. She had just stapled the final pages of her assignment together.

"Congratulations, Isaki! Good work!" Ryuzaki said.

"Th-thanks, Karin…!"

"Congrats," Haneda said.

"Good for you," added Usami.

"You're amazing, *squeak*!" Nezu exclaimed.

"Y-you guys... Thank you..."

Gone was Ohgami's demon-like concentration from a minute ago. She drooped limply, as if she had been switched off.

It was seriously impressive that she had managed to plow through all her work.

"Good job, Ohgami," I told her. "You've worked hard."

"Mr. Hitoma..." Her smile was dopey, relieved as she was to have finished her assignment. "Heh-heh-heh, thank you very much."

"I expected nothing less. Not everyone could digest so much information. You should be proud of yourself. All that's left is to turn it in to the principal."

"Oh no! That's right! I was so focused on the fact that I was done writing...!"

"Calm down. You finished well before the deadline, so there's no need to rush."

"Agh... I-I'll head to the principal's office now."

She picked up her last report and took out the ones she had previously written from her bag.

"You're all good, Isaki?" Ryuzaki asked. "You didn't forget anything?"

"Ummm... One, two, three... I—I have everything."

"Great!" Nezu said.

"The principal's probably in his office, I think, so you oughtta get going," Haneda told Ohgami.

"Thanks, Tobari."

With the sheaf of papers in her arms, she said, "I'm off," and left for the principal's office.

"She worked her butt off," Usami said. "I hope she'll get a good grade."

"Yeah," I agreed.

Not just Ohgami; I hoped everyone would do well.

A few minutes after Ohgami left, the end-of-class bell rang.

At the same time, the door to the classroom slammed open, and a yellow ball of something barreled into the room.

It was the principal. Behind him was Ohgami.

"Hello, advanced class!! Congratulations, everyone!!!"

The surprisingly thunderous voice pierced my ears. Ohgami, who was closest to him, let out a quiet, "Eep!"

His appearance must have meant that—

"Now then, we have verified the completion of all your assignments! And after a long and arduous evaluation process, we have decided which of you have met the graduation requirements."

What does he mean by "long and arduous"? Usami and Ohgami literally just turned in their assignments. Did he even get a chance to check what Usami wrote in her letters?!

Then I remembered the principal was a precog and clairvoyant. Maybe he was using his powers to determine who graduated… That was how I had been hired anyway…

"This year, the number of graduates is—"

The principal thrust his index finger into the air.

One… Like Minazuki last year, there was only going to be one student graduating this year.

That spoke to how difficult it was to graduate from this school.

Everyone in the classroom waited for the principal's next words.

"This student is unfailingly earnest, considerate, and passionate about her interests. Through the ups and downs, the worries and struggles, she has walked this far hand in hand as *one half of a pair*. She is bright and kind and has learned to love herself. In addition, over the course of her assignment, through the writings and words from all over the world and time immemorial, she has learned the power of expression, which is to say, she has learned how to properly communicate her thoughts and emotions."

All eyes fell on one person.

"The student with the aforementioned traits eligible for graduation is you, Ohgami Isaki and Isaki."

The Misanthrope and the Comet's Pilgrimage

A MISANTHROPE TEACHES A CLASS FOR DEMI-HUMANS

The advanced class's final assignments and exams had been completed without a hitch, and the end of the school year was in sight.

The students were allowed to come to school as they wished, and attendance was sparse. Ohgami, in particular, was busy preparing for her new life, and had her hands full with packing and other such tasks.

The other day, Ryuzaki had given me a letter. It wasn't especially out of the ordinary for her per se, but maybe she had been inspired by Usami. It was a love letter so sickeningly sweet I couldn't read it without spreading it out over several days. The contents made me prickle with embarrassment…but I couldn't deny I was pleased, too.

I had read the letter from Usami after I got home the day I received it. Her writing was brusque, but woven in it was her kindness, her enjoyment of her school life, her happiness at having a wider circle of people she cared for, her apology for dragging me into her runaway attempt the previous year, and her gratitude for helping her meet Seiko at the risk to myself.

Ever since the day the principal had announced the results of the final exams, Usami had been looking glum.

That was understandable. She'd struggled to recover from last year's suspension and the ensuing point deduction, leaving her unable to graduate. On top of that, she'd been just a few points away from passing her entrance exams.

It had come as a shock to Usami. That day, she hadn't spoken a single word.

At the moment, she was staring vacantly out the classroom window.

Outside, thin clouds were drifting across the blue sky.

* * *

"Hitoma, be my mailman," Usami said to me one day.

"Come again?"

It was the first time we'd spoken in a while. What was this about a mailman...?

"I wrote a letter to Seiko along with the ones for my assignment. I want you to deliver it to her for me." She held out an envelope with a cosmos flower sticker. "I wanted to go myself, but I won't be graduating. So—I want you to go instead." She smiled weakly. "To visit her grave." Her tone was a mix of forlorn and sentimental.

"Usami..."

I wanted to help, but whether that was possible wasn't my decision to make.

This school was special. For example, students were allowed to browse social media, but they weren't allowed to post.

"...First, let me check with the principal whether I can deliver the letter," I said. "Can I take the letter for now?"

"Got it. Honestly, I'm not expecting anything. If you can't, I'll accept it... I have no other choice. Thanks, Hitoma."

Afterward, I consulted with the principal. In this case, I could deliver the letter as long as the contents were approved by the principal. I had him check over the letter and received his permission. In the meantime, I also asked where Seiko was buried. I would have to cross three prefectures, but the trip was doable in a single day if I had the day off.

I told Usami as much, and she smiled in relief and murmured, "Thanks."

* * *

It was a sunny day. I left the barrier for the first time in ages.

I figured dressing formally was the safer option in this case, so even though it was my day off, I was wearing a suit.

When was the last time I crossed the barrier...? When I went home during the New Year?

Since my dad had retired last year and I'd moved out of the house, my parents were now able to spend more quality time together. Apparently, my mom had been dragging my dad along on trips all over the place. In the time I was away, the number of mysterious souvenirs decorating the entryway and hall never failed to multiply. My dad was a man of few words, so it was hard to tell whether he enjoyed traveling, but in the photos my mom showed me, he looked as though he wasn't entirely hating the experience, surprisingly.

Those were the kinds of thoughts I was thinking as I bought my ticket for the bullet train.

It was nostalgic being back at this station. I'd rarely come to the bullet-train platform, but this station was the closest one to the high school I had previously worked at. It had been four years since then. I wondered how those students were doing. Assuming they had graduated as expected from college, they might have already entered the workforce. The ones who had gone to technical schools would no longer be fledgling employees but standing on their own.

Time is the great equalizer. I looked at Usami's letter. Unlike the letters she had given me and the other students, there was no name on the envelope and the envelope was securely glued shut. The unassuming cosmos sticker was the only memorable identifier.

Ms. Kizaki had been born in the north, it seemed. However, she had moved to the Kanto region after she had married. I was currently heading toward the station near her hometown. Afterward, I would take a twenty-minute ride on a shaky bus to my destination.

Nothing lasts forever—not happiness nor sadness.

Not the time I spent at my last school, nor the time Usami spent with Seiko. Not this moment.

I took the bullet train and got off at the first stop. Next came the bus.

I checked the map in the station and headed toward the bus stop. It wasn't very far, just a brief stroll.

On my way, a woman in business attire stopped me: "Hi, excuse me!"

"Hmm?"

The woman exuded confidence and cheer. She looked to be around Mr. Hoshino's age.

"Are you from this area?" she asked. "Actually, I'm a little lost…"

"Oh…"

I'm not a local, either, but she seems to need help, so I might as well hear her out…

"Where are you looking to go?" I said.

"Um, this is the place," she replied, showing me a map on a tablet.

What? Hold on—

"My mom passed away last January, and I'm on my way to visit her grave," she explained. "But I lived abroad, so the only time I've been here was for the funeral, and my dad and relatives showed me the way. I have zero sense of direction, and I don't know where to go…"

What a coincidence. The location shown on the tablet was the same cemetery I was going to.

* * *

"Wow, so you're a teacher? I see. And you're going to visit the grave of one of your student's caretakers, you said?" the woman asked me.

"Yeah, that's right," I replied.

"I'm sure that student wanted to come here herself. It must be stressful nearly failing every class, not to mention having to spend her entire spring break in a supplementary boot camp."

That was the story I had gone with. *Sorry, Usami.*

"It's already spring break, huh?" the woman mused.

That had been a lie, too. I felt guilty, but the excuse had just slipped out when I'd tried to explain why Usami hadn't been able to come.

The woman and I ended up riding the same bus since we shared a destination, and for some reason, we were sitting together, too.

The woman continued speaking. "It's wonderful that she wanted to give her caretaker a letter no matter what. I'm sure she's a very conscientious person. By the way, please call me Sae."

"Ah, um, Ms. Sae?" I parroted.

Is that a nickname? Maybe it's short for the family name Saeki? Or is Sae her first name?

Maybe it was because she lived overseas, but her friendly and familiar attitude threw me for a loop.

"My mom chose my name," she explained. "I like it a lot. The kanji are beautiful, too. 'Sa' written as 'silk,' and 'e' is the first character in the word for 'comet.'"

"Sae" must be her first name, then. You don't see a name like that too often. The first character in comet... *Isn't that also pronounced "sui"? Nah, what are the chances?*

"You're right. It's a wonderful name," I said.

"Yeah... When my mom was alive, all we used to do was fight, but when I reminisce about those times, I only remember the happy things." She stared out the window at the increasingly green landscape.

* * *

"This cemetery is larger than I anticipated... Will I be able to find it...?" I wondered aloud.

"That'll be tough, considering it's your first time here and you're looking for the grave of a stranger," Sae said.

"Yeah. I did ask for the general whereabouts, but..."

Thanks to the principal, I knew roughly where Ms. Kizaki's grave was located but not its exact location.

In that case, my only option was to check each headstone in the area one by one.

"Um, if it's all right with you, can I help you find the grave as thanks for helping me at the station?" she suggested.

"Really? Are you sure? But—"

"Besides, my mom would be angry if I didn't help someone in need." She smiled brightly.

How could I refuse?

"Sorry to impose... I'll take you up on your offer, then," I said. "Um, if I remember correctly, Ms. Kizaki's grave is in zone B1..."

"What?" She looked at me in surprise. "Kizaki...? Don't tell me your student's caretaker was Kenichi Kizaki."

"No, it was Seiko Kizaki."

"That's my mom's name, the person I've been telling you about."

"No way!"

The name had rung a bell when she had introduced herself earlier, but I hadn't imagined such a coincidence was possible... Sae turned out to be Seiko Kizaki's daughter after all...

"How...?" she muttered, before changing her mind. "The world sure is a small place. I'll show you to our family graves. I remember where to go from here."

She took the lead in a reversal of our roles from the station.

The Kizaki family plot was bigger and grander than any of the others in the section.

In front of the graves, Sae said her greetings. "Hi, Mom and Dad. It's good to see you."

Next to her, I bowed deeply.

I had asked her to guide me, but I wondered if it was really all right for me to be here.

At a private moment like this, the right thing to do is excuse myself...

"Excuse me, Ms. Sae," I said. "Thank you for showing me the way. I'll take a breather at the rest area over there and come back. I apologize for disturbing you."

"You're not disturbing me at all! But thank you for your consideration. I hope you'll tell me more about your student later."

We bowed to each other, and I showed myself to the rest building.

There was a smoking area next to it. Inside was a simple space with several sizable couches, and three vending machines for drinks.

The moment I sat down on a couch, the exhaustion of speaking to a stranger for the first time in a long while hit me.

Man... I was really wound tight...

I wasn't great at dealing with people I didn't know. Not to mention, I wasn't even sure what my own position was under the circumstances. I'd acquiesced to Usami's request, but visiting a grave as a representative of a student was unusual, to say the least. It wasn't anything for me to feel guilty about, although I was worried that Seiko's family would think I was a weirdo.

Haaah... Might as well try to relax while I'm here...

I bought a small can of coffee from the vending machine. In the last two years, whenever anything happened, I always went to Mr. Hoshino for a cup of coffee and a friendly ear. It had become a habit to drink coffee to calm down when I was anxious.

I popped the tab, musing on how long it had been since I last bought a can of coffee. Even canned coffee was delicious these days, though it couldn't hold a candle to Mr. Hoshino's brew, of course. I could feel my nerves starting to unwind as I immersed myself in the taste and smell.

Oh, I should bring Ms. Sae a drink while I'm at it... No, wait, it's unnerving to be handed a drink by someone you just met. I certainly wouldn't take it. Yeah, scratch that idea.

I returned to the couch, sipping on the coffee.

I wondered what Usami had written in her letter. The principal had been the one to review the contents, so I had no idea what she'd written.

While I was lost in my idle thoughts, the door to the building slowly opened, and Sae stepped in.

"Sorry for the wait, Mr. Hitoma," she said.

"No problem. I'm the outsider here, so I should be apologizing."

"Should I stay here while you pay your respects?"

"E-either way."

"Okay, then I'll stay here."

She bought a bottle of sparkling water from the vending machine and a pack of cigarettes.

I didn't realize she's a smoker.

Then I switched places with Sae and went to visit Seiko Kizaki's grave.

* * *

The Kizaki family plot was cleaner than it had looked earlier. The grave-stone had been polished, flowers and small cups of water had been placed, and incense had been lit. I experienced a momentary regret that I hadn't stayed to help with the cleaning, but then I figured that would have been overstepping. In any case, what was done was done, so there was no use thinking about it.

"...It's a pleasure to meet you, Ms. Kizaki. I'm Usami's homeroom teacher, Rei Hitoma." I bowed my head low. "I came in Usami's stead today to tell you what she wants to say to you," I went on. "Usami is work-ing hard on her studies every day with the help and support of her class-mates. As her homeroom teacher, I can tell she is studious and considerate of others. I brought with me a letter she wrote."

I took out the letter from my bag.

The unlabeled envelope with only a sticker of a cosmos flower on it.

Should I open it and read it out loud? I hesitated for a moment, but then I placed the letter on the grave next to the flowers and water.

It was better for me not to read it.

The contents were for Usami's and Seiko's eyes only.

* * *

When I returned to the rest building, I found Sae smoking outside.

"Thank you for waiting, Ms. Sae," I told her.

"Were you able to talk to Mom?"

"Ah yes. Thanks for your help... By the way, do you know what the rules are around the offerings at this graveyard?"

"Offerings? Ohhh, you mean the letter you were talking about on the bus? Hmm, usually you're supposed to just bring it home with you, but I have a suggestion, if you're okay with it."

She stubbed her cigarette out on an ashtray and walked off in the direction of the Kizaki plot.

Suggestion, she said? I wonder what it could be.

I trailed after her.

"This letter?" Sae asked me when we arrived at the grave.

"Yes, that's right."

"A cosmos flower..." She picked up the letter and looked as if she were going to cry. "Your student really knew my mom well. Cosmos was her favorite flower. She was born in the fall, and cosmos flowers are a similar color to the stuffed rabbit she treasured ever since she was a child... But that toy went missing a couple of years ago. My mom was heartbroken..."

She was talking about Usami. Seiko wasn't the only one; Usami existed in Sae's heart as well.

"Mr. Hitoma, this might not be the best thing to do, but how about we burn the letter?"

"Really?"

"Yes. I'm sure this letter is filled with your student's memories and thoughts of Mom. Let's deliver it to Mom in heaven."

Send it into the sky by way of the smoke, huh?

"I wonder...," I mused out loud.

What would Usami want? I doubted she would want me to bring the letter back. Making sure it reached Seiko would be her first priority.

"I think we should burn it, Mr. Hitoma."

That would be such a shame, though. And yet—

"All right," I agreed.

Best to listen to the family in this case.

Once I gave the okay, Sae took out her lighter she'd used earlier. Then she lit the letter.

The papers crackled as they were quickly swallowed up by the flames, and the smoke drifted into the heavens.

The scent of smoke filled the air.

Usami's letter turned into ash, and the smoke melted into the sky.

* * *

On the bus ride back, Sae and I talked about a variety of topics.

She had a daughter who was turning fourteen. Her father's family was well-known and wealthy in the local region, thanks to which she was about to work abroad as an accountant. She'd been able to come back due to her job. Her mother had owned a plush rabbit that she'd cherished more than any jewel, but they hadn't been able to find it. Even now, Sae still regretted not being able to put that stuffed animal into her mother's coffin.

I couldn't tell her about Usami; even if I could, she wouldn't believe me. Nonetheless, I wanted to resolve the misunderstanding. But how…?

The bus arrived at the station. Sae was staying overnight at a hotel nearby and was returning overseas the next day. It was approaching the hour of the last train I could take. Now was my only opportunity to set her straight!

"Hold on!" I said, stopping her before we could part ways once we got off the bus.

She looked at me in puzzlement.

"About that stuffed animal… Ms. Kizaki gave it to my student," I told her. "In the fall last year—no, two years ago, my student went to visit her in the hospital and received it then… So…so don't worry. That stuffed animal is doing really well."

Sae looked surprised. Then her expression turned hopeful. "Is that… true…?"

"Yes."

The stuffed rabbit was living as Usami to that very day.

"Thank goodness…!" she cried.

She covered her face with her hands and crouched down. It was as if a dam had broken, and she was hiding the emotions—or something else—that had poured out of her.

"I was so afraid I'd thrown it out by accident… Thank goodness… Seriously…!"

Perhaps the guilt had been tormenting her all this time.

She slowly rose to her feet again. "...Sorry I lost my composure...," she told me. "The stuffed rabbit's Usami aka Bunny. Your student might already know this, but Bunny is a chatterbox. I hope your student talks with it a lot. *Sigh...* So that's what happened... Thanks."

It was painfully clear how important Usami was to Sae. The time she'd spent with Usami—no, with Bunny—had surely been invaluable.

"I'm glad I met you today, Mr. Hitoma. I'm glad I know where Bunny went. Please give my regards to your student. Oh, and if it's not a bother—" She took out a small container—a business-card case—from her bag and handed me one of her cards.

"Um...?" I mumbled.

Crap. I didn't bring any of my business cards.

But Sae didn't seem to care about that.

"Please give my contact information to that student," she urged. "If there's anything I can do for her, I'll be happy to. At the very least, I would love to talk with her someday...! Thank you for today, Mr. Hitoma." She bowed to me several times.

Sae was bold and brash in some ways, but she was courteous and humble at her core.

I'll have to tell Usami I met her.

"Bunny" was doing her best at school every day for Seiko's sake.

I was glad I could clear up Sae's confusion.

* * *

It was the Monday after my day off. My feet were sore from my long journey. Ever since I'd moved to the staff dormitory, my commute had become shorter, and I felt like my body was steadily growing weaker.

I'll be in trouble at this rate. What am I gonna do if I can't climb these stairs up to the advanced classroom anymore?

As I neared the top of the stairs, I saw Usami up ahead.

"Ah, Usami," I said.

"Hmm? Hitoma."

She seemed to be on her way from the library to the classroom.

I finished my climb as Usami walked toward me.

"Did you deliver my letter to Seiko?" she asked point-blank. She must have been curious.

"Yeah, I did. Also…coincidentally, I bumped into Ms. Sae."

"You met Sae?!" she exclaimed. "Was she still a cheeky brat?"

"Just how do you remember her?"

"As a rebellious little punk."

When I'd spoken to Sae, she was every inch the modest career woman. I guess she'd gone through a rebellious teen phase herself…

"What did you talk about?" Usami asked.

I relayed Sae's current situation and my impression of her. When I told Usami about Sae's suggestion to burn her letter, she smiled and said, "Outrageous as always, that one. But she was thinking about Seiko in her own way. I'm glad."

"You're right. Also, I got her contact information."

"Really? Can you share it with me…?" Usami asked hesitantly.

"I discussed it with the principal, and he'll hang on to that information until you graduate."

"I…I see…"

I wondered if she wanted to meet with Sae.

"Fine. I'll just have to work harder," Usami declared. "Then, after I graduate, I'll go meet with the grown-up Sae! Now I have another new goal! Hitoma, thanks for chatting with Sae."

She turned away and started heading toward the advanced classroom.

I called out to her as she left. "Speaking of chats, she told me 'Bunny is a chatterbox, so talk with her a lot.'"

Usami spun on her heel and said, "…Sae and Seiko are the real chatterboxes."

That's true. Ms. Sae did like to talk.

"I hope I get to talk with Sae someday, too," Usami mumbled to herself.

However, her quiet whisper didn't escape my ears.

Usami was only a step away from graduating.
She knew that very well herself, so she was likely the most antsy of all.
Her back looked more diminutive than usual.
How heavy were the expectations and grief she had to carry on those tiny shoulders?

Graduation day was near.
I wished that one day Usami would graduate and be able to chat with Sae to her heart's content.
And in a comet, I stored away that tiny wish of mine.

A Misanthrope
Teaches a Class for
Demi-Humans ②
Mr. Hitoma, Won't You Show Us the Light of Hope...?

The Misanthrope and the Heartfelt Graduation Ceremony

A MISANTHROPE TEACHES A CLASS FOR DEMI-HUMANS

Haneda was the first one to bring up the subject.

"I wonder if a single graduation ceremony's really enough for Isaki," she mused out loud.

It was early March, nearing the night of the full moon. Isaki Ohgami's graduation was set in stone. That day, busy with the preparations, she was absent from class.

"True," Usami said. "I heard from Isaki that after graduation, they become two separate people."

It was exactly as Usami had said. Ohgami was to become two humans once she graduated—a different body for each personality.

"In that case, let's have two ceremonies, then," Haneda proposed.

"Wow! How wonderful!" Ryuzaki exclaimed. "When is the next full moon again?"

"In four days, *squeak*! Graduation is in a week," Nezu answered.

"What d'you think, Mr. Hitoma?" Haneda asked.

Of course, I was in total agreement. But four days was tight.

"I'm with you. I think it's a great idea, but…what about the arrangements for the venue and such?" I asked.

"The ceremony in a week will be the official one held by the school. The one in four days will be planned by us and held here, in the classroom," Haneda replied. "What do you think?"

"Great! That's amazing! It's like a wedding! The kind where you have a private ceremony for family only, and a second one for friends and everyone else. It's marvelous!" Ryuzaki said enthusiastically. "What kind of wedding do you want, Mr. Rei?"

"I don't have that many friends, so if I had to pick, I'd say a small ceremony with family— Wait, we're talking about the graduation ceremony right now!"

"Heh-heh. I'll file that away for the future."

"You're a shrewd one, Karin...!" Nezu said.

"Knock it off. Stay on topic," Usami warned. "Figure out what to do about Isaki's graduation first!"

"A surprise would be the best!" Ryuzaki said.

"Yeah, I think so, too," Haneda agreed. "A surprise, hmm..."

"We'll spoil the surprise if we do it here," Nezu said.

"Then how about the vacant classroom? You know, like the one next to the library," I suggested.

It was the room Full-Moon Ohgami had dragged me into once. It had used to be the computer lab, apparently, but during renovations, the lab had been moved into the annex building, so the room was unused except as a storage space for extra desks.

"Not a bad idea," Haneda said. "Let's go with that."

"Isaki might find out when she goes to the library," Usami noted.

"Has she been going to the library recently?" Ryuzaki asked.

"She might have things to research!" Nezu said.

"Hmm, then what about the conference room? The one next to the stairs on the second floor," I offered instead.

"That could work," Usami replied. "But it's close to the teachers' office, so we have to mind the other teachers... We won't be able to go all out!"

"Where should we hold it, then?" Haneda asked.

We all thought over the problem.

Suddenly, Ryuzaki seemed to have been struck by an idea. "How about the new AV room?"

"Oh! Good thinking! The room has some soundproofing, and we can use the projector, too!" Nezu exclaimed.

"I agree," Usami said.

"Nice, nice. Good plan," Haneda added. "I think the AV room would be the best, too. What about you, Mr. Hitoma?"

"Same—it's not bad at all. First let me check if we can use the room that day before we commit, all right?"

"Of course! Thanks."

"*Squee*-hee-hee! Now what do we do about the ceremony?" Nezu asked.

"If we're gonna do it, we have to make it a party!" Ryuzaki said.

"Graduation is a critical junction! A serious ceremony better suits the levity of occasion! We should do it properly!" Usami protested.

"Both have merits," Haneda said.

The conversation around the ceremony grew fiery among the students. The ceremony had a do-it-yourself feel to it, which was heartwarming.

I had to check on the AV room's availability as soon as possible. As far as I knew, it wasn't reserved for any other occasion, so we should be able to use it.

I looked forward to seeing how the ceremony would turn out.

* * *

"I don't know why, but everyone's been standoffish lately," Ohgami said to me the day before the full moon.

The preparations for the graduation ceremony were in its last stages, so all the students besides Ohgami had been going straight to the AV room after school day after day. Finding it suspicious, Ohgami had come to me for advice.

"They've been disappearing somewhere right after class," she said. "I mean, I've been busy getting ready to graduate, so I haven't been spending much time with everyone... Ngh... But still. They seem different from usual... Like they're avoiding me... Waaah..."

Her ears and tail were drooping dejectedly. It hurt my heart to see.

You've got it all wrong, Ohgami...! They're just setting up for Full-Moon Ohgami's graduation, and asking you to help would ruin the surprise...! They're absolutely not trying to exclude you...!

I was shouting that in my head, but obviously Ohgami didn't hear it. What was I to do?

It might have been for Full-Moon Ohgami's sake, but if the plan ended up hurting the other Ohgami, then we were getting our priorities backward.

Even if we were to hold the ceremony, Full-Moon Ohgami would probably not be able to enjoy herself.

"Can I tell the others what you just told me?" I asked Ohgami.

"Um, that's a bit… If they really are avoiding me… *Hic*… I don't think I'll ever recover…"

"There's no way they're avoiding you," I reassured her.

"Really…?" She was teary-eyed and visibly worried.

But this much I could promise her. Not a chance.

"…Then, ngh…you can tell them," she said.

"Thank you," I replied. "Sorry, wait here a minute. I'll be right back."

"*Sniff*… Okay…"

She still seemed doubtful, but it looked like she at least half believed me.

I left Ohgami in the advanced classroom and headed to the AV room. Everyone was most likely there.

I'll explain everything and get their okay to raise the curtains a little ahead of time.

* * *

"The…AV room?" Ohgami asked.

"Yeah, everything will be answered there," I promised.

"Sure… All right…"

After explaining the situation to the students in the AV room, I returned to the classroom where Ohgami was waiting, so we could go to the AV room together. She seemed somewhat dubious, but she followed me obediently nevertheless.

"I haven't been there since last year's New Year's Eve countdown party," she said to me.

"Ah, I see. It's not used much for classes, I suppose."

The only time I'd been here was for the director's special training lecture.

It was well-equipped, so I figured it was convenient in various ways, but it wasn't really necessary for everyday school life. Events were a different story, though.

"We're here," I announced.

"The curtains are drawn," Ohgami pointed out.

Because the room was for projector-use, there were blackout curtains hung on the wall next to the corridor as well. Thus, we couldn't see inside the room.

"Um... Is it okay to go in?" she asked.

"Yeah."

Ohgami slowly opened the door. The room's interior was still hidden by the curtains.

Then she nervously peeled open the curtains.

"ICHAKI!!! Congrats on graduating!!!" Nezu yelled, leaping through the curtains onto Ohgami.

"Ee-yaaaaah!!!" Ohgami screamed.

Nezu swept her up in a tight hug. "Sorry to make you worry, Ichaki!"

"M-Machi...? What...?" Ohgami stammered. Blindsided by Nezu's fervor, she had yet to make sense of the situation.

She had likely only caught a glimpse of the room when Nezu had come flying out...

The other students came streaming out of the room.

"We're sorry, Isaki," Haneda said. "Tomorrow's the full moon, right? So we wanted to have another ceremony for the other Isaki."

"Yeah, we wanted it to be a surprise," Ryuzaki added. "But we discussed it earlier and concluded that if our plans ended up making you anxious, then we were doing something wrong."

"That's right. We want to congratulate you. Both of you," Usami said.

The curtains parted.

"Wow...!" Ohgami gasped.

The room was decked out like the gym had been during last year's graduation. Paper flowers and garlands chained from paper links decorated the room.

It was far more lavish than what I had seen earlier. They must have added more ornaments when I had gone to fetch Ohgami.

"It's amazing! You prepared all this?" Ohgami exclaimed.

"Eh-heh! You betcha!" Nezu told her.

"We did our best to make it cute!" Ryuzaki said.

"I don't know about our *best*," Usami drawled.

"So she says, but she was pretty gung ho herself, saying, 'I hope Isaki likes it,'" Haneda commented.

"Tobari! Butt out!" Usami snapped.

"Ha-ha-ha! Sorry, sorry."

"You guys…" Ohgami looked around the AV room with teary eyes. "Thank goodness… I was afraid you didn't want anything to do with me anymore…"

"Ohgami…," I said. "We're all here to celebrate you. Don't worry. Everyone here loves you."

"…Yes! Thank you!" she replied.

"Anyway, all we're doing is holding a graduation ceremony tomorrow!" Haneda added.

"That's plenty…," Ohgami said. "I also thought it would be nice for the other me to have a proper graduation. So…so I'm happy she's precious to you all, too!"

"Hmph. Don't get it twisted," Usami groused. "Tomorrow's Isaki is important, but the current you is important, too."

"Exactly!" Nezu said. "Remember that!"

"Usami… Machi…," Ohgami mumbled.

"You know, I was actually envious of the two of you," Ryuzaki told Ohgami. "You're irreplaceable to each other. You care so much for each other… I respect that! I hope you'll both find your path to brilliant futures!"

"Karin… Thank you!"

The advanced student's DIY graduation ceremony.

What face will tomorrow's Ohgami make when she sees all that everyone prepared?

Next to me, Ohgami and the other students were weeping and laughing joyfully at the same time.

* * *

The next day, we had gotten permission to use the AV room starting in the morning.

Full-Moon Ohgami stood in front of the door to the room, more subdued than usual. She had little to say, and the mood around her was a complex mix of nervous tension and happiness.

The day before, I had given Ohgami the day's schedule.

I was by her side at the room's entrance, watching over her.

"Enter, graduates," came the announcement from inside the room.

Ryuzaki was facilitating the ceremony. With her resounding and clear voice, she was perfect for the role, in my opinion.

Ohgami's ears perked up. She muttered a quiet, "Oh snap," and padded slowly into the AV room.

"Oh, should I sit?" she whispered to me, standing at the door, to confirm.

"Go ahead," I answered.

She took a seat in the only chair in the middle of the room.

"We will now confer the degrees," Ryuzaki began. "Isaki Ohgami."

"Present," Ohgami said.

She stood up with confidence and walked to the front.

Haneda was playing the role of the principal, and quite frankly, there could be no better substitute. "Isaki, congrats on your graduation," she said.

"Thanks, Tobari!"

"I have faith that you'll thrive as a human even after leaving this school. I swear it," Haneda continued. "Please live a wonderful life without any regrets."

"I will! Hearing you say that puts me at ease!" Ohgami said. "One day, let's eat some delish desserts together as humans!"

Haneda's eyes grew round. She smiled softly, her gaze full of affection and focused on some point far in the future. "Yeah, one day."

Haneda handed Ohgami the diploma. Ohgami's grin was brimming with confidence. Everyone in the room knew she deserved it.

The rest of the mini ceremony was a festive affair, with Nezu and Usami's stand-up comedy routine, Ryuzaki's magic show, and Haneda's singing. It might have been a homespun affair, but the program was packed with a vibrant motley of events.

* * *

March 10. The day of the Shiranui High School graduation for the year.

The gym was as cold as always, so several kerosene stoves had been placed around the room.

Ohgami was standing next to the principal. Stiff with nerves, she wasn't moving so much as a muscle.

I was somewhat worried. Would she be okay...?

Thus, the ceremony began—

"We will now confer the degrees," announced Ms. Saotome, the facilitator again this year.

Her voice was lovely as always.

"Isaki Ohgami," she called.

"P-present...!" Ohgami answered, her voice trembling.

All the students in the school were watching her.

She climbed up to the stage with stiff movements.

"Ms. Isaki Ohgami," the principal said. "Congratulations, my dear."

"Principal Karasuma..."

"You being able to graduate is the fruit of your efforts. That is the unshakable truth. I will always be proud that there are outstanding students like you."

"Thank you very much, Principal Karasuma...!"

He handed her the diploma.

Ohgami glowed in the soft light of the spring sun, as if the sun itself was showering her with its blessings.

* * *

"BWAAAAHHH!!! I'll be so lonely after you graduate, Ichakiiiii!!" Nezu sobbed.

"Machi! Keep it down!!" Usami yelled.

"I can't help it!! Boo-hoo-hoo!!"

"D-don't cry... *Hic...* Machi...," Ohgami said tearfully.

After the ceremony, I returned to the classroom first with the other advanced students and talked to them about the next school year. Just when everything was settling down, Ohgami came back to the room— that was when Nezu burst out crying.

Then, triggered by Nezu's tears, Ohgami started sobbing, too.

"Great. Now she's crying, too!" Usami groaned.

"Now, now, today's a special occasion," Haneda told her.

"That's right," Ryuzaki said, backing Haneda up. "Aren't you sad, too, Sui?"

"What?! I... Well, the class won't feel quite right," Usami relented.

"Usamiii! I'll miss seeing your prickly side, too!" Ohgami said.

"*That's* what you'll miss about me?!"

As I watched the students shriek and shout like they were at a festival, a wave of sentimentality washed over me.

I'll never again see these exchanges between them...

I was about to slip out of the room when I heard someone cry, "Mr. Hitoma!"

Ohgami had stopped me. "Thank you for these two years...!" she said. "The Isaki inside me had always been my light. She's amazing... Beautiful... I looked up to her. That's why I'm so grateful that you helped us understand each other, that you uncovered the two of us in this world...!"

"Ohgami..." I felt tears welling in my eyes, but I managed to control myself. "Thank you, too. Your actions and these outcomes were all chosen by you. They're the result of your own strength. I know that the two of you will be fine. Believe in yourself. I hope that you will live a happy life."

"Mr. Hitoma... Thank you so much...!"

"I'm gonna try my best, too!" Nezu chimed in.

"Me too!" added Ryuzaki.

"Heh-heh! Thanks, everyone!" Ohgami said brightly.

I was sure they still had lots to say to one another. I took one last look at the students chatting away as I left the classroom.

* * *

Staff drinks were an annual tradition after the graduation ceremony.

With alcohol flowing through me, I was in a maudlin mood.

Last year it was Minazuki. Now Ohgami's graduated, too...

Graduating and becoming human were the students' goals, so of course the bigger part of me was happy for the graduates. Nonetheless, it was depressing not being able to see them again. We teachers were here for good, but that wasn't the case for the students. They mature and evolve, graduate, and set off on their own path.

"What's this?" said a voice. "Your glass is empty, human. Big Sis here will pour you a drink. Eeny, meeny, miney, mo."

I roused from my thoughts. "Oh, thank— Wait, what?! Wh-why?" I did a double take.

"Remember me?" she said.

Remember? I couldn't forget even if you ordered me to.

"Why're you here, Miss Alice?!" I demanded.

Beside me, Alice the witch was filling my cup. She hadn't changed a bit since I had last seen her. Alice was Kurosawa's owner. Ever since Kurosawa had withdrawn from the school, the two of them had been living together and researching magic in the shrine at the center of the school's barrier.

Seriously, what's she doing here...?

"I figured I'd crash the party. Seemed like a lark," she said.

"C-can you do that…?"

"It's fine, it's fine! Right now, I'm using magic to conceal myself from anyone who I've never met before."

That was when Mr. Hoshino asked me, "…Who's that, Mr. Hitoma? Your friend?"

"Huh?" I mumbled.

She's totally visible!

Maybe her magic had failed. Maybe it was less effective because she had been drinking. Either way, Mr. Hoshino was eyeing her with mild suspicion.

"Hold on. I know you," Alice said.

"Me?" Mr. Hoshino said.

She stepped right into his personal space.

"Wait, you shouldn't get so close to a married man!" I cried.

"Oh yeah? He's married?" was Alice's response.

"Seriously, Mr. Hitoma. Who is this woman?" Mr. Hoshino asked me again.

Oh man, oh man… Where am I supposed to start…?

That was when my savior appeared.

"Alice! Why have you shown your face here?!"

Principal Karasuma!!!

Have I ever been more grateful for his existence? Nope, never!

"Ugh, damn," Alice spat.

At the same time, she disappeared from my sight, too.

The principal went into a corner of the room, grabbed a fistful of air, and started speaking in a language that was neither Japanese nor English, so I had no idea what he was saying.

"Ohhh… She knows the principal? Is that right?" Mr. Hoshino asked.

Having been abandoned to his own devices, he seemed to have drawn his own conclusions from the principal's reaction.

"Um… Yeah… Something like that." I gave an ambiguous reply, not knowing how much I was allowed to say.

"I see. That's how it is," Mr. Hoshino mumbled to himself as he digested my nonanswer.

Ms. Karasuma ambled up to us. "Satoru, Mr. Hitoma, is something wrong?"

"Um... Hello, Ms. Karasuma. Errr..." I hesitated. I wasn't sure how to explain.

Mr. Hoshino answered in my stead. "Well, it looks like Principal Karasuma's friend came to visit..."

"Okay... Great," she said.

She glanced over at the principal. That split second was enough for her to grasp the general situation. "That punk might have a foul mouth, but she's harmless. It should be fine," she said. "More importantly, Satoru, Yuki's already emptied six bottles. She might be a liiittle tipsy."

"What?! Thanks for letting me know!" Mr. Hoshino exclaimed, and rushed off in Ms. Saotome's direction. She was clinging to a bottle of sake with a blissful expression.

"...Alice is here?" Ms. Karasuma asked me.

"..."

She was right, but was I allowed to confirm as much...? What if she was fishing for answers?

"...Heh. You're a good kid, Mr. Hitoma. Your deer-in-the-headlights expression is a riot." She chuckled softly. "Sorry to make things difficult for you. I know Alice has been living at our place. It's fine."

"Y-your place...?"

"The shrine. We don't live there anymore, though. The staff dorm is much more convenient, seeing as it gets electricity and water."

The utilities I considered a given were to her a "convenience"... But she was right... They certainly were convenient...

Hold on! What century are we talking about here?! Modern shrines are for sure hooked up to the power grid and waterlines!

Ms. Karasuma seemed levelheaded, so it was funny to see her drop the ball. She was the principal's daughter, after all. She must have been alive long before such infrastructure was built...

The principal returned. "...*Sigh*. Sorry about the fuss, my boy."

"No, not a problem..."

I wondered what he had done with Alice.

"Did Alice have business here?" Ms. Karasuma asked the principal.

"She came to pocket some delicacies to feed her cat."

"Wow, what a Good Samaritan...," I said.

Her mischief reminded me a little bit of Nezu.

"Alice can produce cakes and cookies with magic, but not sushi and meat like the ones we have here," the principal explained.

"I didn't realize magic had such limits..."

It was amazing to me either way, but I supposed magic wasn't all-powerful.

"She should have just asked. She's cute when she plays coy, though," Ms. Karasuma added. "She's a total snack."

I know that one. Kids these days call good-looking people "snacks"...!

"Slay, queen," Ms. Karasuma said as she made a finger-heart in the direction Alice had disappeared.

In any case, it seemed like Alice was showering Kurosawa with affection, which gave me peace of mind.

"Alice tried to shoot her shot with Satoru a second ago," Ms. Karasuma told the principal. "Thought you should know."

"...I see."

Whoa. His mood just shifted.

"Another thing I'll need to lecture her about," he muttered darkly.

Poor Alice... The principal's scary when he's angry. One of these days, if I get a chance, I'll go bring some sushi and meat to Alice and Kurosawa. I wonder if they'd like that.

I'll ask the director.

This year's advanced class had started with six students. With Kurosawa's withdrawal and Ohgami's graduation, the number was down to four.

It was lonesome, but such were the paths the students themselves had chosen.

We live on, repeating this cycle of encounters and good-byes.

What awaits us in the next year?

Will new students from the intermediate class be joining again?

No matter what happens, as a teacher, I will be here to walk alongside the students.

Nonetheless, if I were to find along the way a spark of hope leading to the future—

Would I continue down my path, facing this life of mine head-on?

A Misanthrope
Teaches a Class for
Demi-Humans ②

Mr. Hitoma, Won't You Show Us the Light of Hope...?

Epilogue

Cherry blossom season was here again.
How many times had I seen these flowers bloom?
I looked up at the tree.

I had the slightest doubts.
But I chose to believe that Mr. Hitoma would show me the way.
To the future leading beyond that spark of hope.

* * *

Ughhhhh. My head hurts…
After the ruckus Alice had made during the post-graduation staff celebration, Ms. Saotome had introduced me to a selection of her recommended drinks, and I'd ended up indulging more than I usually did.

Her recommendations had been spot-on, and all of them had been delicious, but idiot that I was, I drank with complete disregard of the next-day consequences. I was like a college newb who had just discovered alcohol… I wanted to lecture my past self at the top of my lungs on the importance of finding one's own limits after reaching the legal drinking age.

To make things worse, I was due to meet with the director that day, an end-of-the-year conference on how the year had gone.
Haaah. Will it go all right? I hope I don't stink of booze…
Just in case, I popped a mint-flavored candy into my mouth and sprayed

myself with a deodorizer… If nothing else, that gave me a temporary peace of mind…

I knocked on the door to the director's office. It was my first time here since the winter when I had talked with Haneda about her future aspirations.

"Come in," the director called from inside.

I opened the door. The room was sweltering as usual.

"Long time no see," I said to her.

"Yeah? We saw each other yesterday."

Sure, when you were Tobari Haneda.

"Let's get right down to business, shall we?" she began, moving from her desk to one of the sofas stationed in the center of the room. "Sit, Mr. Hitoma. What're you standing around for?"

"There's this little thing called courtesy."

"Ha-ha, I suppose, but where's the fun in that?"

"There isn't any."

"See? No need for all that pomp with me."

"But courtesy is about showing respect for the other person, about choosing to jump through the hoops even if it is a bore."

"…You and Usami are kind of similar."

"You think?"

"Yeah. Like the way you can be surprisingly old-fashioned at times, or how you can be considerate to a fault."

"…Sounds to me like the Barnum effect."

"Whoops, you got me."

"Come on."

After a bit of bantering, Haneda broached the main topic of the meeting. "Tell me. How do you feel about Isaki graduating?"

"I'm sorry to see her go, but she deserves it," I answered. "Her actions may not be showy, but she has been accruing points more studiously than anyone else. It's the result of her consistent effort and persistence."

Actually, she had just fallen short of the cutoff last year. She'd missed her chance to graduate because her test scores had been a tad low and she had been docked some points for unhuman-like behavior. However, this year, she had scored above the average, she had no infractions on her record, and her final assignment had received top marks from the principal.

She had slowly but steadily collected her points. Her graduation was the product of her toil.

"Uh-huh, yep," the director said, agreeing with my assessment. "On top of that, the preparations for her post-graduate life—lives—turned out to be quite challenging, too."

"Right…"

Ohgami had chosen to become two separate people. Full-Moon Ohgami had been human from the start, but since this *was* a high school, she still sat for tests in the limited time she was around.

Luckily, the two Ohgamis shared memories of everything they saw, so I didn't have to plan test retakes or teach the same material twice. Nonetheless, the subjects they were strong and weak in were different.

The usual Ohgami's specialty was humanities, whereas her counterpart's was the sciences. It was difficult to score well on subjects one was weak at without focused studying. The two of them had really put in the work on that front.

"When will they become human?" I asked the director.

"The day after tomorrow."

"They'll live as twins in the human world, right?"

"You got it. The identical twins Isaki, written in kanji, and Isaki, in hiragana. That's how their names'll be written in the family register. There doesn't seem to be any issue on the official government side of things, so I agreed to it."

"I see."

Starting in the spring, the normal Isaki would be attending the private liberal arts school she'd been aiming for. She had applied for early admission on recommendation, so her enrollment had already been decided back in the fall. Full-Moon Ohgami was going to a cosmetology specialty school. They would be taking their first steps on their respective paths.

"How exciting," I said. "I hope they'll make the most of it."

"Yeah. They'll be living their own lives from now on, but still, it'd be nice if they help each other along the way as they always have."

Considering that the two Ohgamis had grown up together, it wouldn't be unusual to call them sisters, especially if they were going to be living as twins.

Perhaps in the future, one of life's shake-ups would split them apart, but even then, they would lend the other a hand in times of trouble. That was how I pictured their relationship evolving, at least, although that might have been my own biased opinion as an only child.

Next, the director asked me placidly, "How was your year?"

A lot had happened. Ryuzaki had professed her love for me, I'd gone on a hunt for the missing Chiyu with Nezu and witnessed the principal's powers, and we'd gone camping as a class. Kurosawa had returned to live with Alice; I had found out about the school's past and had grown to know the director a little more, I thought; Usami had given me a letter; and Ohgami had graduated.

"…I learned a lot this year, too," I told her. "I learned that there are times when it's necessary to be weak and let others help you. I learned that the shooting stars in the summer are beautiful and to be true to myself. And I learned that when you have something on your mind and you have the chance to say it, you should."

Also, I have found a trove of my own emotions—is what popped into my head briefly, but I didn't say it out loud.

"Oh-ho, great." The director chuckled. "One last thing—"

She slowly closed her eyes.

Then she opened them just as slowly and stared straight at me.

"So, Mr. Hitoma, do you like humans?"

It was the same question she had asked me last year.

I had responded, "*I still hate humans, but that feels fine the way it is for now*," if I remembered correctly.

What about now?

The director waited for my answer with an unreadable smile.

"I hate humans," I replied.

That was right. I still couldn't like them.

However—

"However, I think there's more I can forgive compared to last year."

Both in regard to myself and others.

Same as the previous year, once again, the director seemed pleased by my answer.

* * *

"Will there be any intermediate students joining the advanced class next year?" I asked.

"Yep," the director said. "There's a new teacher coming, too."

"Really?!"

There hadn't been any new hires this year, so that was exciting news.

I wondered how they'd react when they found out about the school's background for the first time. Would they be incredulous like I'd been? But slowly come to the understanding that this was reality as they took in everything, all while warring with their common sense? Yeah, I'd been there. If they'd been hired here, did that mean they enjoyed fantasy? Would I be able to chat about video games with them?

Or maybe they'd be an alum like Ms. Saotome. In that case, I wanted to ask them about their school days and about their reason for enrolling and such.

"I wonder what they're like…," I mused.

"Hmm? Wanna look at her profile?" the director asked.

"Can I?!" I exclaimed, louder than I had meant to. Guess I was more excited than I realized.

"Eager, ain'tcha?" she drawled.

I felt a bit embarrassed.

The director summoned a flame in midair and, from it, withdrew a single sheet of paper.

"Remind me why paper doesn't burn up in your fire again…," I said.

"Why indeed. Because that's just how it works?" she replied glibly.

Maybe the director's fire wasn't fire at all. While I was distracted by such dilemmas I had no business worrying about at this late juncture, the director held out the paper, hot out of the oven. When I tried to take it, she refused to let it go.

"...? Is it confidential information after all?" I said in confusion.

"Nah. But I think you should brace yourself, at least a little."

"Why?"

"The plan is for her to serve as the advanced class's assistant home-room teacher."

I get it. I'll be working with her often. I suppose that's the reason for all this gloom and doom.

"Ready?" the director asked me.

"Yeah."

Ready for what? Is it that big of a deal?

I was unsure whether I was truly prepared, but I was genuinely glad to have another teacher to work alongside. I was fortunate to have reliable veteran teachers around me to lean on when anything went wrong.

I'll be okay next year, too. I'm sure of it.

"Are you? Then here you go." The director let go of the paper.

It was a résumé.

The name was familiar.

Memories came flooding back—the memories of the days before I had come to this school.

Hers was a name I could never forget.

On the résumé was a photo of a face that was slightly more mature than the one I remembered.

The last time I'd seen her, she had been crying and her face had been screwed up with hatred.

I remembered the handwriting on the résumé, too.

Yes, this familiar handwriting with its peculiar *ka* characters.

The note I had been handed.

The navy blazer of the stylish uniform suited for the big city.
The plaid skirt.
The high school whose name was written on the résumé.
The classroom that one winter day.

All of it came back to me in an instant.

Why is she…?

Is this retribution for enjoying myself after coming to this school?
Is this punishment for laughing so carefreely?

Mirai Haruna.

The new teacher was the student who had quit school because of me four years ago.

Afterword

Hellooo! I'm the author, Kurusu Natsume.

Rei! Sorry to put such a sad expression on your face!

…The story will continue in Volume 3! Yippee! The continuation is all thanks to everyone who has enjoyed and supported the series. Thank you so much!!

How was Volume 2? I hope you liked it. Actually, the manuscript ended up being longer than the first volume, so this afterword will only be one page.

The artist in charge of this volume's illustrations and character designs was, once again, Sai Izumi. Drumroll, please, for the three new characters and Lady Shiranui! Da-dum! Look! Mind-blowing! The gorgeous, classy, and adorable Karin; the energetic Machi with her rich expressions; the mysterious Neneko, who is hiding a passion stronger than anyone else; and Lady Shiranui with her adult allure but whose looks contain a trace of Tobari as well…!

All the characters are bursting with life, and with their art, Izumi has enriched the world of the story even further.

Once again, I am indebted to the illustrators who worked on the special in-store displays!

To Fumi, for the illustration of Machi and Neneko in maid uniforms and the color palettes that match the characters to a T. To Yoka, for the heartwarming illustration of a soft and mellow Tobari and Neneko. To Sakura Shiori, for the illustration of the cute and cheeky Machi and Usami, which is full of life and fills me with energy. To Nana Kagura, for the illustration of an adorable and feminine Karin and Isaki. And once more to Izumi, for the wistful and nostalgia-filled illustration of Usami and Isaki in yukata, which makes the heart ache! Thank you all very much!

In this volume, I once again included the audience-suggested prompts in sections of the book, so I hope you'll enjoy those, too!

Thanks for reading! See you again!

Kurusu Natsume

Karin Ryuzaki

"Mr. Rei! Have you started to want to marry me yet?"

Sai Izumi's Character Design

▼ Kurusu Natsume's Vision

"Wherever there's food...
there's me, Machi!"

Neneko Kurosawa

"...I don't like colors... They... deviate...from what's normal."

▼ Kurusu Natsume's Vision

Sai Izumi's Character Design

The Director
(Lady Shiranui)

▼ Kurusu Natsume's Vision

"Sorry to surprise you! I take Tobari Haneda's form so I can observe the students up close."

Sai Izumi's Character Design

N

River

Student
Dormitory

Hot
Springs

Bus
Stop

Cherry
Blossom
Tree

Campus Map

Gymnasium

Annex

Main Building

Field

Barrier

Staff
Dormitory

Main Building Floor Plan

Annex Music Room • Art Room • School Store • Computer Lab • AV Room • Home Ec • Science Room

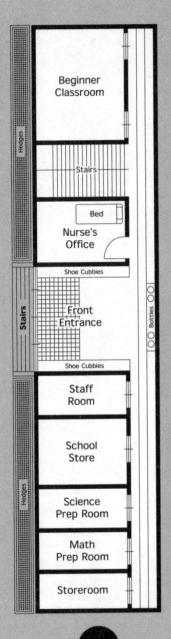

Hedges

Beginner Classroom

Stairs

Stairs

Bed

Nurse's Office

Shoe Cubbies

Front Entrance

Bottles

Shoe Cubbies

Staff Room

School Store

Science Prep Room

Math Prep Room

Storeroom

Hedges

1F

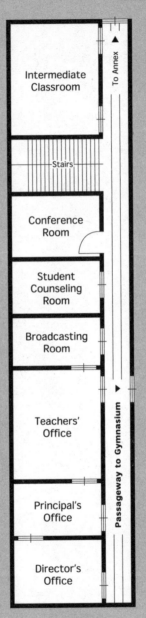

Intermediate Classroom

To Annex

Stairs

Conference Room

Student Counseling Room

Broadcasting Room

Teachers' Office

Passageway to Gymnasium

Principal's Office

Director's Office

2F

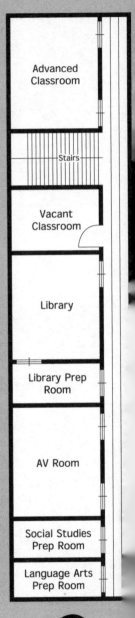

Advanced Classroom

Stairs

Vacant Classroom

Library

Library Prep Room

AV Room

Social Studies Prep Room

Language Arts Prep Room

3F

A Misanthrope Teaches a Class for Demi-Humans

Mr. Hitoma, Won't You Show Us the Light of Hope...?

②

Author
Kurusu Natsume

Illustrator
Sai Izumi

Editor
Suguru Ohtake

....

Special Thanks

Chapter Prompts Contributors

Prologue

Sukoya Kana
(cherry blossom, cat, train)

The Misanthrope and the Love Fortune of the Barren Flower

Leos Vincent
(cryptid, poisonous smoke, 10,000 microbes)

The Misanthrope and the Gluttonous Hero

Elu
(revolver, packing tape, hero)

The Misanthrope and the Summer Vacation in the Forest

Shiina Yuika
(bath, sauna, food)

The Misanthrope and the Magic for Peace and Quiet

Shellin Burgundy
(alien, superhero time slot, cake)

The Misanthrope and the Tobari from Days Gone By

Inui Toko
(potato, manga, skyscraper)

The Misanthrope and the Heart's Truest Desire

Hanabatake Chaika
(*kintsugi*, *Batm⁺n*, solicitor)

A **Misanthrope** Teaches a Class for **Demi-Humans** ②

Mr. Hitoma, Won't You Show Us the Light of Hope...?